2037 was a really bad year.

Lexi Brennan's best friend was killed in a plane crash. Two weeks later, an intergalactic crisis threatened the fate of humanity. Authorities responded by launching a genocide.

Lexi opposed this vicious attack. Then again, what could she do? An eccentric flight attendant drawn to glamorous trysts, she felt powerless to incite change.

Until tragedy struck close to home. Suddenly, Lexi was forced to acknowledge the widespread atrocities. She uncovered a network of lies along with an opportunity to restore basic human rights. To protect others, Lexi would have to launch a movement that could destroy everything important to her, including her promising new romance.

Mid-Flight

ISBN: 978-1-4874-3650-6
Cover art by Martine Jardin

Published by eXtasy Books Inc

Look for us online at:
www.eXtasybooks.com

Mid-Flight

By

Lisa Wilkes

Dedication

To the romantics who view love and justice as inextricable forces. To the optimists who envision better days, then fight like hell to attain them.

You are a catalyst for change in this aching world. Lexi's story is also yours.

Prologue: August 27, 2037

The moment the sky exploded, Lexi Brennan was trying to remember how her companion looked naked. It had only been a week since their previous encounter, but the details felt hazy.

Lexi and the man were nestled into a corner booth at a bar near Santa Fe Regional Airport. They were both fully clothed with the mutual expectation of ending the night otherwise.

Was it big? Lexi wondered, equal parts intrigue and boredom. *Probably average.*

Nothing memorable, at any rate.

A clap of thunder shook the building. Self-generating diode lights flickered overhead. There was a brief pause before a second thunderous roar erupted in the distance.

Lexi dug her nails into her legs. She exhaled slowly. An indentation on her left thigh oozed one dot of blood. Staring at the red bubble, she shook her head. She'd pressed too hard this time. The hemoglobin fountain bursting from her skin was a rare mistake. Lexi rubbed the spot with the hem of her shorts. She pressed the fabric against her leg until the well ran dry.

Across the booth, deep brown eyes and a scruffy beard observed her curiously. The man's t-shirt was one size too small, presumably to show off his hard-earned biceps. Lexi simultaneously loathed and loved his generic style. The guy was a walking cliché.

Lexi knew she was one, too.

"Everything okay?" the man asked.

Lexi nodded, swallowing her embarrassment. She hated her visceral response to loud noises. It had started at age sixteen, when the crack of a fallen chair ripped through her home. That sound signaled the end of Lexi's adolescence and the beginning of her inescapable journey into hell.

"Let's order some food," her companion suggested. It seemed like a feeble attempt to carry on as normal.

Lexi found the gesture endearing.

While she pulled up the digital menu in the center of the table, a chorus of buzzes erupted from EarLinks throughout the bar. Lexi sighed, assuming it was another media stunt from the nation's unhinged president. That crazy asshole had been on a tirade recently.

Tucking a strand of hair behind her ear, Lexi leaned forward. She angled her body just right, with the top of her camisole plunging down her neck.

"I can't stop thinking about last time," she lied. She swirled her vodka cranberry before taking a swig. "Amazing. Next-level shit."

The man opened his mouth to speak, then promptly closed it. Frowning, he tapped a finger to his ear.

Lexi sighed, trying to squash her growing frustration. *This is why the silence function exists. VirtuAlarms go off ten times a day. The President's newest rant can wait. Ugh. Why didn't I go see that woman from last week's flight to New York?*

Lexi bit her lip. Maybe she should be tangled up with that chick, Sierra something-or-other, instead of lying about this guy's impressive bedroom skills, which were little more than a vodka-induced blur.

She'd had her reasons, though. New Mexico was an easier trip. One flight here, two flights back tomorrow. Nineteen hours to spend in the arms of this stranger. What was that, two rounds' worth? Possibly three, Lexi had figured. Assuming the man didn't get too drunk. Whiskey dick had ruined plenty of nights in her three years' worth of flying. It was one of the many perks to being with women.

Lexi exhaled slowly as she skimmed the menu. Her gaze landed on the hatch green chile queso. Jorge had introduced her to the joys of spicy New Mexico cuisine a few years back. Since that magical moment, Lexi had never been disappointed. Not once.

In a flourish, she resolved to hang out with Jorge the following week. She'd drive to his apartment with a bottle of prosecco. The one with the translucent peachy-pink label. His favorite.

It was the least Lexi could do after hosing her best friend. She'd left him in the dust again. Jorge had tried to mask his disappointment, but it was obvious.

Lexi and Jorge had promised to buddy bid the whole summer. Their goal was to endure the busy season together, busting their asses on full flights with screaming babies and disheveled parents. They'd planned to suffer through the madness one trans-continental flight at a time. And then laugh about it on their overnights, presumably while drunk.

But Lexi couldn't keep a promise to save her life.

She silently apologized to her best friend. He was jetting up the East Coast, somewhere between Charleston and Philly. On a work trip Lexi had agreed to cover with him. Until her cravings had gotten the best of her.

This was the fourth trip Lexi had backed out of, ditching her absolute favorite human at SkyLine Airways in pursuit of another cheap hookup. Four swapped trips over the course of two months. Lexi's buddy-bidding track record was less than stellar.

Priorities. Lexi exhaled slowly, aware of how twisted hers were.

Her focus dropped below her companion's waist as she contemplated whether this dude, this strapping nobody she'd met on a flight last week, was worth ditching her best friend.

She sure hoped so.

Lexi placed a hand on the man's arm.

"Um, Alexis," he stammered, his expression inscrutable.

Lexi frowned. "Nobody calls me that." Thoughts of delicious queso evaporated. She was no longer hungry, just eager to do the deed. Her patience was waning.

She slid her drink toward the center of the table, wishing she'd set up ThumbPay like Colin had urged on countless occasions. If she'd heeded her brother's advice, she could press a finger to the scanner embedded in the table's wooden surface and leave. She could avoid additional dialogue and get down to business.

But Lexi had boycotted the two-second ThumbPay setup. It quickly became a running joke in the Brennan family, and she decided to keep it that way, just to hear Colin laugh. Didn't matter that it was at her expense.

So instead of swiping her hand across the scanner like every other human being on the planet, Lexi had to wait for an invoice to pop up on her phone and authorize it with ocular swipes. Like a freaking dinosaur.

"Sorry. I meant Lexi," the man corrected himself.

By this point, Lexi had forgotten he'd even gotten her name wrong. She faked a smile.

"Something's happening," the guy said breathlessly. "Are you seeing this?"

"Another absurd press conference?"

He shook his head. "This is different. It's bad. The predictions were wrong."

"The meteor shower, you mean?" Lexi pulled her phone from her pocket. A single ocular swipe turned on AutoScan, and a thousand notifications came flooding in. She blinked as the messages scrawled across her cornea, one after the next. There were too many. She couldn't keep up.

Her first concern was her brother's safety.

AutoScan – Colin Brennan, she screamed internally, summoning the faint electrodes that routinely scanned her scalp for impulses. *Where are you? Are you safe?*

Lexi sent the message with a double blink. The Virtu-Alarms had mentioned Baltimore, Seattle, and a few other cities, but Lexi hadn't seen anything about San Francisco or Sacramento. She bit her lip, waiting for a response from her brother.

AutoScan – Colin Brennan, I'm worried, kid. Call me.

No answer.

Wordlessly, Lexi grabbed her purse and darted for the exit. She needed to see it. She had to know for sure.

The midnight sky was pierced by jagged red veins. A thousand burgundy fingers tore through the stratosphere like lightning etched in the wrong color. Puffs of smoke dotted the horizon, mushroom clouds rising toward the ominous red ether. From the descriptions and images in Lexi's Virtu-Alarms, it appeared Santa Fe had gotten off easy. Other cities looked like they'd been struck by an atomic bomb.

The world was blazing. The sky was breaking apart in pieces.

AutoScan – Jorge Rodrigues, I didn't see your texts 'til just now. They're grounding all planes immediately? Scary stuff. Wish I was there with you. Where's your plane landing?

With a rapid-fire double blink, Lexi sent the message.

Jorge's response flitted across Lexi's cornea. His words felt frantic. *Can't get down. Capitol Hill is burning. Dense population, nowhere to land. 80 miles from Dulles Airport. I don't think we'll make it.*

Lexi read the last sentence and crumbled. She fell to her knees on the hot New Mexico concrete, sirens blaring in the distance and meteors crashing to the ground with a fiery scarlet vengeance.

"No," she begged the universe. "Please, no."

Her vision blurred. Lexi ached to rip her skin off her body, inch by inch, melting into a heap of exposed veins. It was so enticing. It was what she deserved, truly.

She should've been on that airplane with Jorge. Self-reproval spun through her mind on an endless loop. *Should have, should have, should have, you piece of shit.*

She gasped for air.

AutoScan – Colin Brennan, dial right now, she instructed, calling her brother via electrical impulses connected to her cranium. Five beeps sounded in her ear, then the line went dead.

Tears rolled down Lexi's cheeks as she mentally composed another note to her best friend at SkyLine.

AutoScan – Jorge Rodrigues, don't talk that way. You will land safely. Reagan International probably has space for diverted aircraft. You'll be fine. I promise.

As she waited for Jorge's reply, she dug her nails into her leg, reopening the wound on her thigh. She picked at it, forcing the gash to widen. It was the size of a dime, then a quarter. She kept pulling, peeling, exposing her insides. She wanted her entire soul to leak out.

"Don't leave me, Jorge," she whispered. "Don't you dare leave me."

Colin tried to leave all the time. Lexi couldn't handle another loss. She needed Jorge. He was her partner in crime, her other half. He was the best thing about being a flight attendant.

Words appeared in front of Lexi's eyeball. Her chest tightened.

I don't think we – Jorge began.

"What?" Lexi murmured aloud. Her hands fell to her sides, limp. "What is it, J.R.?"

Lexi craned her neck toward the red-streaked sky. She shouted, pleaded, implored her buddy bidder to write back. She wanted to hear details about his safe landing, after the pilots found an open runway someplace in Maryland or perhaps Delaware.

Arms clasped around Lexi's waist, dragging her back into the restaurant. She kicked and screamed, fighting to stay outside. She wanted the sky to collapse on her and drag her into the deep black unknown. She didn't deserve the safety of four solid walls and a roof. She didn't deserve to be in a city that had received minimal damage from the celestial hellfire.

Lexi began to chuckle as she was forced back inside the restaurant. She could barely breathe from laughing so hard. Through narrowed eyelids, Lexi saw customers and staff staring at her in disbelief. She continued flailing her limbs. She laughed with all her might, a deep guttural guffaw that echoed through the bar.

When a VirtuAlarm informed Lexi that two planes in the Northeast had been struck down, she was convinced she'd dreamt the whole thing. The aircraft she was supposed to be on that night had not burst into flames. No way, no how. Jorge was not dead. Lexi would wake up soon, she knew. She would call him. They'd talk about her silly nightmare, her tendency to imagine the worst possible scenario, her bizarre fear of erupting into laughter during a moment of crisis.

Lexi would wake up and chat with Jorge for hours. And she would not swap out of their next scheduled airline trip.

Jason Bresline was finishing a soggy cheesesteak when his armband lit up with an urgent alert.

Employee 89348, Repairs needed for SK949. Landing in one minute. Fourteen-inch hole in fuselage above forward galley. Smoke reported.

"What the—" Jason stumbled backward, nearly knocking his chair into the makeshift kitchen counter. There were no SkyLine flights scheduled to arrive in Nashville for half an hour.

The letters on his arm shifted, displaying additional

information about the mystery aircraft.

SK949 follow-up report – structural damage severe. Hole in galley floor. Pilots believe object is lodged in cargo compartment. No known injuries. Additional repairs needed on six planes landing before 22:30. More information to follow.

A splash of color flooded his peripheral vision. Jason turned to the west side of the break room as neon letters materialized on the wall. A nanoscreen had sprung to life, illuminating the chipped paint with its ominous crimson warning.

Emergency procedures activated. SkyLine Airways unplanned landings in Nashville – SKY9119, tail no. 949 – one minute, SKY2654, tail no. 7117 – three minutes, SKY573, tail no. 332 – four minutes, SKY466, tail no. 5525 – seven minutes.

Jason's armband synced with the countdown on the wall, tracking the arrival of Flight 9119. He stared at the numbers, assuming there had been a system-wide malfunction. Had a nanoscreen at Headquarters imploded? Maybe the system had been hacked? Everyone at corporate swore up and down that SkyLine's tech systems were untouchable. They'd hired the best and brightest minds in the world to ensure there would be no meltdowns, no fatal mishaps.

But just a few years ago, DefenderTech had hacked its way into top-secret documents belonging to the world's most ruthless despot. So anything was possible, really. Hackers held all the cards. No person or business was ever bulletproof.

59 seconds from touchdown. 58. 57. 56.

The nanoscreen switched to an alert issued by the Department of Transportation. All public transport had been halted, effective immediately. People were advised to take shelter until further notice.

Jason couldn't make sense of these directives. What had changed since he'd ordered a sandwich at the food court? Twenty-five minutes ago, everything had been routine. Calm. Predictable.

He yanked his phone from his pocket so hard that he nearly dropped it. With a flick of his eye, he activated AutoScan. SkyLine executives could trace his activity if they chose to do so. They'd see Jason had turned on the restricted function during his shift. Right now, that didn't matter. He needed to know what the hell was happening.

Once AutoScan was activated, messages rolled in at an impossible speed. Horrific descriptions sped across Jason's cornea. The meteors had veered off course. Astrophysicists claimed it was an anomaly, some type of gravitational glitch that defied science.

Jason shook his head. *How is this even possible? How does gravity just fail?*

The meteors, which were not supposed to penetrate the Earth's atmosphere, had done exactly that. Even worse, they'd split apart in the process. Oversized space bullets, threatening enough in their original form, had become deadly cosmic buckshot. Thousands of sharp fragments had pummeled major cities. And the hits kept coming. Splintered meteors continued to decimate everything in their path. The world was smoldering.

A grim voice echoed through the break room, startling Jason. "Essential staff report to base leaders. Do not leave the airport unless advised. Lockdown initiated. Hazardous conditions outside. Stand by for updates."

Jason glanced down at his arm band. The letters rearranged themselves, issuing new instructions. *Flight 9119 has landed without incident. Report to management before proceeding to SK949.*

Jason called Talia during his quick jog to the mechanics' meeting room.

"C'mon, pick up," he murmured as her phone rang. Five beeps sounded in his ear, then nothing. Maybe she'd gone to work early, Jason reasoned. Talia's Emergency Room shift didn't start until eleven o'clock, but they probably needed extra help. After all, the night had taken a shitty turn. Fast.

But he was puzzled by the fact that Talia hadn't texted him. The world was on fire. Where was his fiancée?

A message floated past his cornea.

Can't talk. Vella's home safe. She's in the master bathroom. ER's full, all-hands-on-deck. See you tomorrow.

Jason breathed a sigh of relief at Talia's update. She was okay. Busy saving lives, as usual. Thankfully, she'd placed Vella in the safest room in the apartment. Still, Jason ached at the thought of his dog all alone, scared and whimpering on the checkered bathroom tile. He silently promised his pup he'd be home soon.

Inhaling sharply, Jason composed one more text, this time to his parents in Denver. He wasn't worried about their safety. They'd stay vigilant. They would protect themselves, he knew. His mom, a retired AirBird engineer, was nothing if not level-headed and thorough.

She'd know exactly what to do in a crisis. Debra Bresline wouldn't take any chances.

With a double blink, Jason sent the message. Then he deactivated AutoScan, sucked in a deep breath of air, and entered the conference room. He was the youngest mechanic there by about a decade. He was also the least rattled, which surprised him. A few guys in the corner spoke in hushed voices, their heads tilted down. One was sweating profusely, dark rings soaking through his gray jumpsuit.

Shelly, the most senior female mechanic in Nashville, was staring blankly ahead. Even from across the room, Jason could see tears pooling in her eyes.

Rick, who had been with SkyLine for nearly twenty years, lifted a coffee cup to his lips with trembling fingers. Rick was a man of few words. He completed his work at break-neck speed. He always remained calm and collected. No matter what general fuckery was occurring all around him, his repairs were flawless. The guy worked well under pressure.

And he'd never emitted so much as a hint of insecurity, not that Jason had seen.

Until that moment.

While Jason watched, Rick lowered his coffee cup. His hand shook uncontrollably. A wave of black liquid cascaded over the cardboard rim. Rick grabbed a napkin to wipe at the spot and knocked over the whole damn cup. Expletives slipped from his mouth as he cleaned the soggy mess.

The shift leader, Kyle, marched to the front of the room and cleared his throat. Everyone turned toward him.

With his head slightly lowered, Kyle ran through the newest information he'd received from Headquarters. He distributed tasks among the mechanics present and explained that those at home would be called in shortly. By the following morning, SkyLine would have approximately ten damaged aircraft parked in Nashville. Perhaps more. Time would tell.

Commercial airliners could be grounded indefinitely, depending on the government's directives. There was no way to predict that yet, Kyle warned, so SkyLine wanted the planes in working order. As many of them as possible. Even the ones with significant damage from meteoric activity.

Kyle promised to upload supplementary materials to everyone's armbands within the next fifteen minutes. He advised all employees to don protective equipment when venturing outdoors in case there were lingering cosmic incidents. The meteors appeared to be finished pummeling the planet, he reflected. Then again, nobody had expected their arrival in the first place.

So, in sum, all bets were off.

Jason listened as best he could. Kyle's speech was punctuated by a rattle overhead as plane after plane touched down on Nashville's runways. The noise had become part of Jason's soul in recent years. He had learned to distinguish SkyLine's AirBirds from aircraft bearing other insignia. Each plane model had a unique rumble, an echo all its own.

Kyle paused, scanning his tablet for updates.

He informed the group several aircraft wouldn't make it to Nashville. Instead, they were landing in Knoxville, Memphis, Huntsville, Chattanooga, and other nearby cities. SkyLine might need assistance at outstations. If so, they'd ferry mechanics to those locations or use ground transportation.

With a heavy sigh, Kyle petitioned his employees for patience. The days and weeks ahead would be a challenge, he admitted. The situation was dynamic. The extent of the meteor damage had yet to be seen.

Jason swallowed. There had been no lesson on meteor repairs during his training sessions. This was uncharted territory. He was also the least experienced mechanic in the room.

Still, he'd busted his ass to get there.

He'd been the only Black mechanic in his SkyLine initial training class three years ago. He'd surpassed everyone's expectations, including his own, by transitioning to a major carrier at age thirty-two.

Captain Colleen Johnson's glowing recommendation had helped, he knew. Her words carried a lot of weight at SkyLine. Ultimately, though, Jason had stood on his own merit. There had been hundreds of sleepless nights and painful sacrifices along the way. He'd scrambled to pay rent for years while earning a wildly inadequate wage at a regional airline. And he had accumulated a dozen awards in the process. Jason had even been featured in a national publication before signing on at SkyLine.

He could fix these damaged planes, he reminded himself. He'd figure it out. Like he'd done a thousand times before.

In the past, Jason had devised some incredible solutions to wacky problems. He could do it again. SK949 was probably in the hangar by now, or close to it. He'd head over there and dive into the task at hand. He would fix whatever was broken.

He'd find a way.

Kyle ended the meeting, dispersing everyone to the unknown issues awaiting them in various hangars.

Jason had almost reached the door to the tarmac when his armband lit up with an alert. *Employee 89348 – Sensitive information. Do not disclose.*

Jason pressed his thumb to the side of the device, confirming he understood the clandestine nature of the message.

Meteor struck SK8474, Flight 2434, over Annapolis, MD. Right engine exploded on impact. No survivors.

Jason stopped in his tracks. The screen displayed five crew members' names. None of them sounded familiar, but that didn't matter. This was his airline. These were his people.

Someone placed a hand on Jason's shoulder. He turned around to face Shelly, who was in worse shape than he'd ever seen her. The tears were no longer a discreet glint in the corner of her eye. Now they tumbled down her face steadily. Her eyes were bloodshot, two red ovals framing brilliant blue irises. Mascara coated her cheeks like a roadmap drawn in charcoal.

"I'm sorry," she mouthed, her words barely audible over the deafening roar of Jason's own heartbeat.

He frowned. *That we lost a crew? Me, too.* Maybe Shelly had known one of the flight attendants or pilots. Maybe they'd been friends.

"She's the best, Jason," Shelly continued. "One of a kind. A real legend."

Jason blinked, unsure which crew member Shelly was referring to. His arm buzzed once more, and he stared at the screen in disbelief. Another SkyLine plane had been obliterated. Flight 4339. This time over Olympia, Washington. Six employees had been killed.

Colleen Johnson's name illuminated his screen, but Jason knew it was a mistake. That woman was invincible. She was a force to be reckoned with. He'd just passed her in the airport a couple weeks back. After a quick hug, Colleen had shared that she'd been awarded the Denver base. She planned to move out there with her wife and youngest son. Her fiftieth birthday was coming up, and she hoped to settle into her Colorado home before the big day.

Colorado. That was where Jason and Colleen had met, years ago, climbing the ranks at a commuter airline. Fate had brought them to Nashville a decade later with a different emblem on their uniforms.

And fate would not rip her away like this, Jason knew. It wasn't possible.

He couldn't fathom a world vicious enough to slaughter the best damn captain at SkyLine Airways. Not under these circumstances. Not on the eve of her fiftieth birthday, with so much to look forward to.

Colleen was a hero, a leader, and a trailblazer. Jason refused to accept that she was gone.

Chapter One: October 4, 2038

"Should I get a little, um, creative?" Lexi whispered to Tamika.

Across the room, a tall man in his thirties stood in front of his seat. His New York accent echoed off the walls as he introduced himself. The guy informed everyone he was based at JFK International Airport, as though his accent wasn't a dead ringer. He proceeded to tell the class he used to own a candle shop in Manhattan, he'd been flying for nine years, and he was married to a fellow SkyLine Airways flight attendant.

As the man wrapped up his monologue, Tamika turned to Lexi. A grin spread across her burgundy lips. "Honey, lie your ass off."

Lexi nodded. "I was hoping you'd say that."

"Forty flight attendants from all twelve hard bases and eight satellite bases," Tamika mused, her voice smooth and melodic. "You think a single person has told the truth? Anyone?"

Lexi tilted her head to the side. A beautiful flight attendant stood up, commanding the room. She articulated each word with a type of precision Lexi found equally compelling and suspicious. Zero hesitation between words. Eloquent in a rehearsed way, as though she'd drafted and memorized her introduction the night before. Her hair was curled with impossible consistency, all strands twisted into identical spirals.

To complete the woman's aura of perfection, her clothing fit impeccably. A sleek red pencil skirt hugged her hips. The woman looked like a sophisticated avatar of a human being. She had no flaws. None.

Lowering her gaze, Lexi noticed a pair of sky-high heels. Conference Room 116's overhead lights, an eco-friendly concoction designed to keep students awake, reflected off the chic black stilettos.

Lexi sighed, estimating the flight attendant's shoes to be more expensive than her car. Admittedly, Lexi had an outdated vehicle, a relic from the old days. Her sedan lacked self-driving capability and predated the HoloRoute era, which Lexi viewed as a vintage quirk, like evading ThumbPay even though it made life infinitely easier. Lexi's entire existence was retro, and she loved it that way. It kept things interesting.

The next person to stand up was a short guy with massive brown eyes. He opened with a joke about the nomadic lifestyle. A peal of laughter ensued. The man seemed likable despite his nerdiness, or perhaps because of it. He was eager to embrace his dorky side. There was something endearing about that.

Instantly, Lexi's mind flashed back to Marco. She had loved his corny riddles. She appreciated how Marco had slid into her world so easily, becoming a Brennan in a few short months. For a while, it had been difficult to imagine the family before his loud, happy arrival.

Lexi had loved that dynamic. Colin lit up every time Marco reached for his hand. There was no shortage of booze or laughter when Marco was seated at Shawn and Erin's kitchen table.

Those were the days before the sky collapsed. Lexi would give anything to travel back in time, but the chrono-technicians had not achieved that feat. Not yet, anyway.

Lexi missed the hell out of Marco. She missed the way he made her family feel whole. The guy had represented a changing tide. He was supposed to fix the Brennans' collective problems. Instead, he gave up. Quit mid-stream, a few months before the catastrophic meteor shower.

Not that Lexi could blame him.

She released a sigh, struck by the urge to text Colin. She needed to remind him there was a big world out there. Other Marcos. Better ones, maybe. A million ways to find joy, especially now that it was safe to socialize again. Well, mostly safe. For ninety percent of the population, give or take.

AutoScan – Colin Brennan, you'd love SkyLine Headquarters. Handsome dudes everywhere. Energetic vibe. Wish you were here, kid.

She waited for the reassuring high-pitched ding to indicate that her message had been delivered. Instead, a dull thud sounded in her ear, reminding Lexi that she'd turned off AutoScan this morning. Disabling AutoScan during training was a strict requirement, one of the conditions Lexi agreed to when she accepted her position as a flight attendant instructor. She was not a fan of the rule, but she didn't have a say in the matter. So she'd signed on the dotted line and turned off all notifications for the day.

Lexi glanced up. The flight attendant concluded his introduction by flashing a winning smile. The woman seated next to him, a petite brunette wearing a cute floral sundress, launched into her monologue. She blinked a lot. Her tone was hushed, nearly inaudible. Lexi observed the woman for a moment. She was attractive, with billowy hair and delicate facial features. But the chick seemed painfully straight-edge, which didn't appeal to Lexi. She found it uninspiring. A little boring, in fact.

Using ocular swipes, Lexi wrote a note on her company-issued tablet. She used broad strokes to ensure the lettering was big enough for Tamika to see. Then she highlighted the text with a flick of her eye and changed the color to neon blue.

This lady sounds honest to a fault. I think she's telling the truth.

Meh. Even more reason to shake things up, Tamika responded with a swipe of her eye. *Get creative. You can be anyone you want, Lexi Brennan.*

The statement gutted Lexi. She'd been attempting to do that for more than half her life. Eighteen years, to be exact.

Lexi responded with an oversized heart emoji. Then she closed the notes section.

As the home screen materialized, she spotted the PersonableSpin insignia in the top right corner. Lexi marveled at the tiny icon. She summoned her electrodes to snap a photo for her brother. *AutoScan – Send screenshot to Colin Brennan.*

Lexi waited for a clicking sound, then blinked in frustration when she realized she'd made the same exact mistake a minute earlier. AutoScan was still disabled, of course. There would be no electric currents traversing her scalp until after class had ended for the day.

"Idiot," she whispered to nobody.

In one swift motion, Lexi used ocular swipes to highlight the PersonableSpin icon. She tucked the image in a new folder and set a reminder to send the file to her brother on Friday. Colin would have a ton of questions, Lexi knew, accompanied by an equal number of long-term predictions. Lexi hoped that by the end of the week, she'd have something meaningful to contribute to the conversation.

Out of nowhere, Tamika jabbed her elbow into Lexi's side. Hard.

"Sorry. My turn?" Lexi cleared her throat. She hopped to her feet. "Hi, friends and fellow instructors. I'm Alexis Brennan, but everyone calls me Lexi or Lex. I've been at SkyLine for eight years."

Tamika nodded in approval at the bald-faced lie.

"I'm based in San Francisco. Used to live in Bakersfield, then Vegas, San Jose, and Los Angeles after that," Lexi fibbed, surprised by the cities she'd rattled off with ease. "But Sacramento is my hometown. I moved back a couple years ago."

"*Ball-sack town!*" someone hollered from across the room.

Lexi offered a curt nod. "Yep. Born and raised in The Sac. Let's see . . . favorite layover is Port of Spain, Trinidad. I also love ziplining in Costa Rica, so that's at the top of the list, too. Favorite thing about being a sky waitress? Probably the people I've met along the way. Before becoming a flight attendant, I mostly hung out with California folks. Now I work with flight attendants from all over. It's cool to hear their perspective on things."

Tamika pretended to vomit.

"Cheesy but true," Lexi affirmed, raising her right hand in mock solemnity. "I've lived in California most of my life."

Correction – all my life. Thirty-four years and counting. She swallowed before continuing. "My airline friends have lived everywhere. They've got the most amazing backgrounds. They're from other cities, even other countries."

Lexi paused, the blood draining from her face. Jorge had been born in Mexico City. He'd moved to America as a teenager and lived in El Paso for a decade before relocating to California.

Jorge was one of seven flight attendants and four pilots who vanished during the meteor shower. In a nanosecond, Jorge and ten other SkyLine crew members dissolved into tiny fragments of nothingness. Ashes to ashes. Dust to cosmic dust.

Lexi swallowed, fiercely hoping Jorge was part of the atmosphere now. She wanted to believe that was how it worked. Maybe Jorge was powering the few remaining bright spots in the world. Maybe he'd become a ray of sunshine or a flicker of hope deep within some lost soul. It was even possible Jorge had been the guiding force that prevented Colin from hurting himself over the past twelve months. There had been plenty of opportunities, but Colin had remained stable. It felt like a miracle. One Jorge would have orchestrated. He was always so kind to Colin. To everyone, actually.

Sometimes Lexi felt Jorge's presence. It took up space in the room, an overwhelming force as real as anything Lexi had ever experienced. Other times, J.R. felt gone forever, completely and irreversibly out of reach. On a different plane of existence that Lexi couldn't access, no matter how hard she tried.

Tamika cleared her throat, drawing Lexi's attention back to the moment.

Lexi jutted her chin at her buddy. "For instance, Tamika grew up in New Orleans. I'd never even visited that city before this job."

"Smooth transition, Lex. Guess it's my turn to take the floor," Tamika said with a smile. She explained to her classmates that she was also based in San Francisco. She claimed to have been flying for fifteen years, which was not only false but logistically impossible, since SkyLine's minimum age for flight attendants was twenty-one.

Tamika was thirty-four. Same age as Lexi. But only two people in Conference Room 116 knew that. Lexi leaned back in her chair, nodding at her friend's shameless fabrication.

"Favorite layover is Toronto, and my favorite thing about being a flight attendant is FAA audits," Tamika deadpanned. "Along with emergency outbreak procedures. ContaCan has enhanced my appearance big time. You wouldn't believe how good I look in a medical-grade face mask, containment hood, and Hazmat suit."

The room fell silent. Lexi broke the ice by chuckling.

"Just kidding. Tough crowd. Look, it's been the worst year on record, and humor's my coping mechanism. Without laughter, I'd have a full-on nervous breakdown," Tamika explained with a shrug. "Okay, let's see, my favorite aspect of the job is that we can relocate to new bases whenever we want."

"But you've been in San Francisco most of your career,"

Lexi blurted, thankful for Tamika's presence in that base.

"True. I've enjoyed living in The Bay, but I'm moving to Seattle soon. It will be nice to start over."

Lexi leaned toward Tamika as the next flight attendant, a soft-spoken girl named Lynn, introduced herself to the class.

"You're not leaving SF, right?" Lexi hissed. "That part was made-up?"

Tamika shook her head. "No, it's true."

"What? Why?"

"I lost too many friends in SF. When I walk through Union Square, I get depressed. It will be good to start over somewhere else. Seattle's always been on my radar."

Beneath the table, Lexi stabbed her nails into her legs. She applied enough pressure to awaken her nerve endings without puncturing the skin. She hated Tamika's plan. Washington was so far. She'd never see Tamika if she switched to the Seattle base.

Despite her personal objections, Lexi had to admit Tamika's logic made sense.

Everyone had lost friends, neighbors, peers, and relatives. ContaCan took out a fifth of the world's population. While that percentage was smaller in America, it was large enough that everyone felt a significant loss. Nobody had emerged from the last twelve months unaffected.

You'll stay based at San Francisco through the end of this project, right? Lexi scrawled across her tablet with rapid ocular swipes.

Of course, Tamika responded immediately. *We finish in January. I'll move to Seattle in March or April. The market's hot right now. There's never been a better time to buy.*

"Noted," Lexi murmured aloud. Real Estate VirtuAlarms sounded every hour, advertising brand-new homes available for less than one year's salary. Each block in America had multiple houses for sale. Bafflingly low prices. Holoscreens built into floating shelves. Dedicated PersonableSpin rooms collecting dust because nobody ever got the chance to use them. Automated kitchen appliances that used algorithms to predict and cook what a person was craving that day.

There were tons of impressive vacant homes, and they were move-in ready.

Nobody had seen this shit coming. Astrophysicists had botched the biggest cosmic event in human history, assuming the meteors wouldn't hit the planet. That evening had been excruciating. A night of terror and devastation caused by giant spheres of intergalactic dust.

But what came next was even worse. The meteors had transported a foreign bug to Earth. An unrecognizable carbon-based pathogen tore through humanity. Some people assumed it was alien warfare, but nobody knew for sure. They couldn't pinpoint the source of the vicious pathogen, they could only watch it decimate the human race. Those who were infected stood a fifty-fifty chance of survival. Once the pathogen began to evolve, the odds of survival decreased.

The meteorites had been child's play, an insignificant blip on the radar, compared to ContaCan's fast-paced destruction of humanity.

"You're still renting, right?" Tamika whispered. Her eyes flicked to the right side of the room, where a Denver-based flight attendant was introducing herself.

Lexi nodded. "Yeah. Same apartment on J Street. I considered buying my own place when real estate prices took a nosedive."

"What stopped you?"

"Couldn't make up my mind. Plus, it would be a hard transition for Cleopatra. She's already had to adjust to living with me."

Tamika tilted her head. Lexi pretended not to notice the doubt scrawled across her friend's face.

"There were other reasons," Lexi conceded.

"No kidding. Your cat would've been fine." Tamika's voice was gentle.

Lexi sighed. *Jorge's cat, actually.* Lexi had inherited the tiny feline upon her best friend's untimely death. She'd grown to love Cleopatra, of course. But Lexi viewed herself as a substitute caregiver. A devoted assistant for life.

She swallowed. "Are you planning to buy a house in Seattle? Townhome?"

"Condo. Less work, more reward," Tamika explained. "I never thought I could afford my own place in that city. I can even pay in cash . . . that's how cheap real estate is. I've done some research. Hoping to snag a condo in Beacon Hill. Ballard seems nice, too."

Lexi paused, musing at the tenacity of this flight attendant she considered her good friend. A sting of envy pierced her core.

From the front of the classroom, Reggie Hortens, the Inflight Educational Director for Skyline Airways, tapped a finger on the podium. "Tamika and Lexi, anything you'd like to share with the class?"

Lexi bit her lip, scrambling to conjure an excuse.

Tamika jumped in without missing a beat. "Lex just reminded me to turn off AutoScan. She felt the vibration."

"Sorry, Reggie," Lexi chirped.

"I thought I disabled it earlier today," Tamika continued with an apologetic frown. "Won't happen again. Promise."

"That's a good point. We've all grown dependent on AutoScan over the past year, but please remember the agreement you signed when you were offered this position. Take a moment to double-check the app has been temporarily disabled," Reggie implored the class. "We need to focus. This project is a big opportunity for the whole airline. It's a step in the right direction. VirtuAlarms can wait until after class."

With a quick nod, Lexi adjusted her company-issued tablet,

which was propped up on the table.

Flight attendants continued to introduce themselves as she swiped through the training materials preemptively uploaded onto the device. There was a plethora of instructions for teaching SkyLine's newest flight attendant course.

Intricate diagrams outlined new service methods and crew member responsibilities, along with CDC standards for everything under the sun.

Lexi scrolled through a chapter on SkyLine's enhanced technological tools, smiling when she reached the page with instructions for PersonableSpin. She highlighted the step-by-step instructions and saved them to the file she'd created for Colin. He would appreciate this stuff, Lexi knew. He'd nerd out, discussing it for hours. And Lexi would feign interest, like she always did, because her brother's excitement and enthusiasm made it all worthwhile.

CHAPTER TWO

"What's your favorite section of the class?" Brandon asked. He held his martini like a prized possession, the stem clasped between two fingers.

"Safety-conscious dispute resolution," Lexi quipped, unable to hide her smirk.

Tamika rolled her eyes. She accepted a glass of chardonnay from the bartender, then lifted her thumb to the shimmering holographic payment scanner. "Ugh. The worst part of every SkyLine class, right? When I taught recurrent, I sped past that portion."

"You taught recurrent?" Brandon inquired, leaning against the bar. "Annual training must be totally different from this new class."

"I taught for six months in Salt Lake City," Tamika said. "Recurrent is tedious and stale by design. It's stuff everyone already knows. But we have to drill it into flight attendants' heads to meet the federal requirements."

"Makes sense," Brandon mused. "Recurrent is recycled old info. But the class we'll be teaching includes procedures nobody's ever seen before. It's a breakthrough course. First of its kind."

"And much-needed, considering the shit-show this year turned out to be," Lexi added.

The trio advanced toward a long, rectangular table where the rest of their group was seated. The restaurant was busy tonight. Nearly every seat was occupied.

With each step, Lexi's drink sloshed dangerously close to

the rim. The bartender had given her a generous pour. Lexi figured he'd spotted the sobriety in her eyes. He must've known she'd fare better without it. Lexi agreed wholeheartedly.

Tamika cleared her throat. "This new class provides a lot of critical info. But I'm worried there might be pushback. A couple flight attendants will give us hell for trying to move forward and keep everyone safe. It's inevitable."

"True. Some people will throw a tantrum. This airline has a few certifiable wackos." Brandon sighed. "It's maddening, right? Do they have eyes and ears? Were they living under a rock when the sky exploded? I'll never understand the angry folks who deny, deny, deny. Or the ones who invent spiteful theories."

"Unproven theories," Tamika added as she grabbed a seat at the table. She gestured toward the remaining open chairs, beckoning Lexi and Brandon to sit down. "Just another outlet for hate and fear. Damn, what happened to compassion? We should take care of each other and offer support. ContaCan nearly destroyed SkyLine. We could've folded like every other major carrier."

"ContaCan threatened more than just our airline," Lexi reflected. "Two billion deaths. A fifth of the world's population."

Brandon nodded solemnly. "But some flight attendants still spew their nonsense about how it's justified. Some kind of Biblical plague."

"Heartless," Tamika said.

"Those fools have lectured me about how ContaCan is an End-of-Days blessing. Apparently, the sinners were weeded out by righteous aliens." Brandon shook his head in dismay. "It's an insult to my roommate and everyone else who died from ContaCan."

Lexi sighed. "Ouch. Sorry to hear that. I didn't know about

your roommate."

"I lost him in April, just a couple weeks before the antidote was released."

Tamika grimaced. "That's rough. Wish I could've kicked those flight attendants' asses for you, Brandon."

"Thanks. Me, too."

"It kills me when people can't look beyond their own selfish bubble," Tamika continued. "Instead of trying to learn and grow, they go on a pious rant about the wrath of God. Do they have a soul? ContaCan caused immense suffering. And the AR situation is so sad."

Brandon shook his head. "Not to mention the seven flight attendants we lost to the meteor shower. And four pilots. I've met a few folks who insist the whole thing was an intergalactic terrorist attack. Apparently, aliens targeted weak and damaged employees. These conspiracy theorists claim the FAA is covering it up."

"Where do people come up with this shit?" Lexi muttered. Rage stirred in her core. If she'd heard anyone say Jorge's death was part of an alien-led moral retribution scheme, or that he had earned that type of gruesome demise, she would've lost it.

"There's a podcaster in Texas, some angry dude who never finished high school." Brandon sighed. "You know, typical self-declared expert. The kind who rants that the government is too controlling while endorsing sexist and anti-LGBTQ legislature."

"Those podcasts are infuriating. The hypocrisy frustrates me to no end." Tamika groaned, staring at the half-empty glass in her hand. "Ten bucks says that guy lives in his parents' basement and conducts all his research while taking a dump."

"Yep. With a soul that rotten, I bet he can't get laid," Lexi quipped. "Unless it's with a sex bot."

"Hey, don't insult sex bots. I packed my favorite one for training week," Brandon reflected with a sly grin.

Lexi chuckled, thankful for the burst of levity. "Oh, I have nothing against boner bots. They got me through the lock-down phase of ContaCan. I'm just saying there are lame-ass folks who *only* have that option. Forever. Because they are cruel, selfish, and socially inept."

"Did you bring yours?" Brandon asked, running a finger along the rim of his glass.

"To training? Unfortunately, Tonya broke from overuse. Rest in peace, Tonya the Tigress," Lexi noted wistfully. "I have another one, a dude, but he's a little, um, bulky. He takes up a quarter of my suitcase even when he's compressed." Lexi's attempts to fit Mr. Dickey in her roller-bag had been futile.

"You two are funny. We've all got priorities, right?" Tamika laughed. "My suitcase has a yoga mat and twenty minis."

"Tipsy yoga. Nothing better." Brandon smiled.

"I should do more yoga," Lexi noted, downing half her glass.

"It saved my life this year," Tamika said. "Yoga helped me find my zen. I needed optimism and balance. Badly."

Lexi understood her friend's craving for normalcy amid chaos. She'd been on the hunt for endorphins since her sophomore year of high school, and things had gotten especially bad over the past twelve months.

"To the things that restore hope, even just a little tiny bit." Lexi raised her mostly empty glass to Tamika and Brandon. "Cheers."

While Tamika shared a story about her cousin's miraculous recovery from ContaCan in March, Lexi chewed the inside of her cheek. Jorge's face had lingered in the recesses of her mind since Brandon's comment about SkyLine's conspiracy theorists. Lexi wondered how long her best friend's memory would stay with her tonight.

There was one surefire way to stop the painful reminiscing. After eighteen years of practice, a host of sabotaged relationships, and two failed careers, Lexi had cracked the code to timelessness. She considered herself a magician, capable of freezing the clock with a few expert moves. She'd discovered how to escape her mind's incessant spinning. Experience only the best sensations, those which didn't induce pesky or intrusive sentiments.

Glancing around the restaurant, Lexi searched for a human-sized diversion.

Prospects were slim. The mood lighting didn't help. Dim wall sconces emitted a faint golden hue, making it difficult to tell if these men and women had lines of ink engraved on their shoulders. Lexi wanted an escape, but not at the risk of killing anyone. She had a few firm boundaries. Ending a life was one of them.

With a sigh, she reached for her phone. Two flicks of her eye reactivated the AutoScan function.

AutoScan – Colin Brennan. I miss you, kid. Emotional night here in Orlando. Lots of memories have been popping up. Some are tougher than others. Lexi sighed and deleted the note. She started over. *AutoScan – Colin Brennan, Orlando's good so far. How's your week going?*

She was about to send the text when a bloodcurdling scream erupted from the opposite end of the restaurant. Lexi dug her fingers into her legs and craned her neck toward the noise.

Beside the bar, a young man convulsed on the floor. Blood oozed from his eyes and nose. His face was covered in burgundy streaks.

"Crap. Autoimmune issue?" Lexi murmured. "Allergies?"

Tamika gripped her shoulder. "That waiter's an AR. His

mouthguard's showing."

Sure enough, a glimmer reflected off the guy's chattering teeth. There was also a bulge above his elbow, evidence of an arm band tucked under his crisp white shirt.

A familiar urge bubbled in Lexi's chest, immediately chased by sheer panic. She dug her fingernails deeper into her flesh. The gnawing sensation crept up her throat. Lexi knew she had to act fast. She needed a mission. A task would sharpen her focus and keep the laughter at bay.

Lexi ended the message she'd drafted for her brother and switched gears. *AutoScan – ContaCan Emergency Hotline, there's an AR who needs help at the Executive Airport Suites in Orlando. Convulsions, uncontrolled bleeding. Hotel bar. Hurry.*

Flashing lights materialized on one side of the restaurant, illuminating a nanoscreen embedded in the wall. The letters were large, at least a foot tall. They shouted their message to the entire room.

Authorities alerted. Ambulance arriving in 2:05, 2:04, 2:03 . . .

As Lexi stared at the nanoscreen, the threat of laughter retreated. She swallowed, grateful for the small victory.

Microscopic air purifiers emitted a whirring sound. Antioxidant-infused oxygen was being pumped continuously, Lexi knew. It was an attempt to dilute the pathogen. For this AR, however, it was too little too late. The poor kid was already infected. Blood continued squirting from every visible orifice.

Lexi turned back to the nanoscreen. While she watched, the letters on the wall rearranged themselves to form a new directive from the ContaCan National Advisory Board.

Begin CPR immediately. Protective equipment kit is located on the east side of the bar.

Lexi craned her neck toward the flashing yellow box near the restaurant's entrance. The plastic container, mounted to the wall, dangled open like a gaping mouth. Someone had already removed its contents.

Glancing back at the bar area, Lexi spotted someone very tall positioned over the waiter. She assumed he was male, based on his broad shoulders and massive hands.

The man was decked out in protective gear from head to toe. He knelt on the ground and began chest compressions. The waiter's spasms slowed, but blood continued gushing from every orifice. A maroon river carved its way down both cheeks, pooling at the teenager's chin before dripping onto the ground.

Soon, all convulsions ceased. As Lexi observed the motionless teenager from across the room, her throat closed up. The waiter's lifeless body carried the weight of a thousand stifled screams. She begged him to move some part of his body. A finger, a toe, an eyelid. Anything.

Lexi knew her silent pleas were in vain. The boy was gone. She felt it in her gut.

Flashing lights reflected off the walls, drawing Lexi's attention to the hotel entrance. The ambulance had arrived. Wordlessly, hotel guests and employees cleared a path. EMTs loaded the waiter onto a stretcher. Their pace was slow. Calm. Indifferent. The lack of urgency confirmed Lexi's morbid suspicions. These medics didn't need to rush, she knew, because the boy would never awaken. Maybe the first responders suspected it before they arrived on the scene. Neon lights swirled, but there was no siren.

As the ambulance drove away, the man who performed CPR removed his containment hood and gloves. He gasped like a marathoner crossing the finish line.

The guy placed one hand on his chest. Fingers rose and fell with each inhalation. Lexi tilted her head to the side, mesmerized by his rhythmic breathing.

In an instant, the man met Lexi's gaze, closing the distance between them.

Lexi was struck by a pang of familiarity.

Where have I seen you? She hunted for an elusive memory tucked deep in the recesses of her brain. *Did we fly together? Meet on a random layover?*

Hotel security swarmed the man, stuffing his contaminated gear into biodegradable antiseptic bags. Eye contact was broken. The moment ended, taking Lexi's nondescript recollections with it.

All at once, the world came rushing back to her. It was a sonic boom against Lexi's eardrums. Clinking glasses echoed off the walls, as grating as nails on a chalkboard. Carefree chatter had never felt so offensive.

Patrons returned to their seats and resumed their casual conversations. Lexi closed her eyes for a moment, processing the obscenity of it all. Life was astonishingly fragile for ARs. Here one moment, gone the next. They left behind a trail of blood and a future cut short. A smattering of stunned observers who cared for approximately five minutes then returned to their own lives. Unbothered.

AutoScan – Colin Brennan, a waiter had an episode in the hotel bar just now, Lexi screamed internally, drafting a new message for her brother. She needed Colin's empathy. He felt things differently. Colin was Lexi's pulsing heartbeat when numbness descended upon her. *It's wild, kid. The AR died in front of our eyes. People are pretending it didn't happen. Or maybe they'd rather not think about it.*

Lexi was about to send the text when Brandon placed a hand on her arm. She shifted her attention to her coworker.

"Crazy, huh? I hope that AR is okay," Brandon murmured.

Lexi nodded, even though it was obvious the teenager was irreversibly fucked. No chance he had survived. "Me, too."

Tamika excused herself to get another drink. "Want anything, Lex?"

"Nah, I'm okay."

"Thank goodness someone called an ambulance," Brandon reflected. "I was too stunned. Deer in headlights."

"Making the call was easy. That dude who performed CPR was the brave one." Lexi glanced back at the man who risked everything to save a stranger. While she watched, security guards gestured toward a narrow hallway. Lexi guessed the man would be escorted to a post-exposure sanitation room.

How do I know you? Lexi marveled at the man's smooth dark skin and the perspiration dotting his forehead. Surrounded by a huddle of hotel employees, he walked down the hall, offering no response.

Chapter Three

"Stay with me," Jason instructed, his voice muffled by a thick containment hood. The contraption was stuffy and uncomfortable. Sweat dripped down Jason's forehead, burning his eyes. He continued the task at hand.

To his dismay, the waiter's spasms slowed.

With a grunt, Jason pressed his palm into the stranger's chest. There was a faint crack, barely audible through the medical-grade helmet. Jason had snapped the kid's ribs. That was par for the course during CPR—Talia had drilled that lesson into Jason's head over the years. Broken ribs would heal, she'd always reiterated. Keeping the heart pumping was all that mattered.

Jason kept pushing.

Blood oozed from the waiter's eyes, ears, and nose. It wasn't a thin stream. This was clotted blood. Thick as peanut butter, with globs of snot and unidentifiable matter. The waiter grew still. Aside from the blood leaking from his eyes, his body was motionless.

Jason refused to quit. He grabbed an automated breathing device and placed it over the kid's mouth to form a seal. A red light illuminated on top of the apparatus. Jason jabbed the round button. Hard. The machine was more powerful than he'd expected. His muscles tensed as he held it in place, administering oxygen to the unmoving stranger. Then Jason grabbed an antioxidant solution and removed the cap. He jammed the syringe into the boy's arm.

Someone reached under Jason's hand, releasing his grip on

the needle. The paramedics had arrived.

The EMTs lifted Jason from the scene, thanking him for his attempt to save the AR. A message illuminated the visor of the containment hood.

Good job. Your assistance is appreciated.

A petite woman with the number 64757 embroidered on her uniform nodded at Jason, so he assumed the anonymous digital note had come from her.

Hotel staff will escort you to the post-exposure sanitation room. Monitor yourself for symptoms and call the ContaCan Emergency Hotline if you exhibit symptoms.

Jason stood up. His legs felt like noodles after kneeling for so long. As he flexed his tired muscles, he wondered how the rest of the evening would unfold. Talia had explained the protocol for situations like this, but that was several months ago. When they were still talking. He couldn't remember any details, or maybe he'd subconsciously erased that conversation along with many others they'd shared.

Quickly, Jason composed a message to the paramedic.

AutoScan – Orlando EMT 64757, can I use the sanitation room privately? Also, what's this guy's chance of survival?

Even though Jason knew the waiter was a lost cause, he wanted some good news. Any glimmer of hope would have sufficed.

He tried to send the message with a double blink. A dull thud in his ear reminded him the AutoScan function had been turned off. Preventative gear always disabled that service. Any messages needed while sporting the heavy-duty hood would flash across the visor. Communication only flowed in one direction until the helmet was safely removed.

Jason sighed and walked toward the lobby. Hotel security guards were waiting for him. He pulled off his containment hood and glanced back at the restaurant. The waiter had been loaded onto a stretcher, but it looked like a formality. The paramedics took their time wheeling him toward the ambulance.

Jason couldn't watch the sad display. He averted his gaze, desperate to see something other than his failed attempt to save an unlucky teenager.

When he turned his head a fraction of an inch, green eyes pierced through the void. Jason recognized those eyes. He'd seen them at the SkyLine Company-Wide Celebration of Life in 2037, honoring the eleven crew members killed by the meteor shower.

She had been there, this striking redhead. Jason remembered that afternoon clearly.

Like Jason, the woman had arrived early for the program rehearsal. Also like Jason, she'd prepared a speech for a fallen friend. She'd walked into the Seattle auditorium wearing bulky sunglasses even though it was drizzling outside. Typical Seattle gloom. No trace of sunshine for hundreds of miles.

Her visceral agony had shaken Jason to his core.

From beneath the oversized eyewear, tears poured down her cheeks, carving a tortured path to her chin. She hadn't bothered to wipe her face. The woman presented herself as calm and self-assured, yet her tears betrayed her confident demeanor.

By the time the green-eyed flight attendant had ascended the podium and removed her shades, her eyes were rimmed with red. Her cheeks were flushed. The waterfall had ceased, though.

Jason would never forget the evenness of her tone. Her voice didn't crack or falter as she described her closest friend to a room full of grieving employees. She remained stoic while recalling her first Thanksgiving away from home. That was when she'd met Jorge, on a delayed flight from San Francisco to Denver. Somewhere above the clouds, she'd found her kindred spirit. They were like siblings. Their bond was instant and eternal. Until the meteor shower severed it.

Jason had left the auditorium halfway through her speech. He wasn't proud of the cowardly exit, but the woman's anecdote hit too close to home. He had to maintain his composure if he wanted to pay his respects to Colleen. He couldn't risk falling apart, not during a moment of such magnitude.

He'd paced the hallway beside the auditorium. Sent a message to Talia. When she didn't respond, he summoned an album labeled *Vel* through AutoScan. Countless videos flashed across his cornea, vestiges of a happier time. He'd rescued the two-year-old mutt at the beginning of the year and named her Vella, short for Velocity, because of her boundless energy. Talia had given Jason so much crap for that name. She claimed it was dorky, but Jason couldn't bring himself to choose a different moniker for the dog. Vella suited her too well.

The photos and videos brought Jason's blood pressure down to a manageable level. Vella's antics were hilarious. The dog was hyper, sure, but she guaranteed life would never be boring. She was incredibly affectionate, too. Vel didn't have an aggressive bone in her body. Thirty pounds of pure love.

Jason issued a directive for AutoScan to close the photo album, then he checked Vella's daily activity through her remote bio-tracker. She had gotten an extra walk around the block with the dog sitter that morning and followed a few commands to earn herself a bully stick. Jason's pup was doing great, which calmed his nerves. He'd return home to rub her belly within a day or two.

Inhaling sharply, he had re-entered the auditorium slightly less rattled. A different employee stood at the podium, describing his favorite layover with the First Officer of Flight 2434. Soon it would be Jason's turn to deliver his speech for Colleen.

He never got the chance.

One hour into the practice run-through, lockdown was initiated. ContaCan had spiraled out of control. There was speculation it might be an intergalactic weapon created by aliens, possibly with the intent to eliminate the human race. Infectious disease experts predicted an extinction event unless a cure was discovered within the next few months. The survival rate was fifty-fifty, but those odds diminished each time the pathogen evolved. This bug was smart. Like an artificial intelligence system, the pathogen taught itself to solve complex problems. It appeared to gather data and learn from each kill. ContaCan was transforming itself to become more deadly, it seemed.

Everyone was sent home. They were forced to use ground transportation. Full-body scans upon entry and contactless pods with private lavatories. Personal biodomes were encouraged, the skintight ones composed of synthetic materials. But those suits were expensive, and there had been a few worrisome malfunctions in the past. Plus, they were hard to come by. So that wasn't a viable option, not really.

Jason's train ride back to Nashville took two days. The whole way, VirtuAlarms announced the rapidly-deteriorating state of the world.

By the time he arrived at his apartment in Lockeland Springs, a hundred million Americans had perished. Gruesome deaths. ContaCan was eating away at their flesh with a speed that could only be described as meteoric, ironically.

SkyLine had hosted a half-assed virtual ceremony a month later, but the redhead hadn't participated. Maybe one attempt to commemorate her friend had been difficult enough. Perhaps she'd expressed herself thoroughly that ill-fated day in Seattle. Maybe there was nothing left to say.

I'm sorry. Jason silently apologized to the woman, maintaining eye contact from across the room. Sweat continued to drip down Jason's forehead. He didn't bother reaching up to wipe it off.

He hoped that even from across the hotel, his eyes

conveyed sympathy. He lost someone to the meteor shower, too. Captain Colleen Johnson had helped him in ways he couldn't fully articulate. At the regional airline, Colleen had taken Jason under her wing. Her family embraced him when he needed it most. Years later, Colleen wrote Jason's recommendation letter for SkyLine Airways. She was one of the reasons SkyLine took a chance on him. Older guys had more experience, but Captain Colleen's praises had set him apart.

I know your grief. Jason tried to convey the message to the green-eyed gaze latched onto his. Pain was never unanimous, he realized. This stranger's experience undoubtedly differed from his. Still, loss was woven into his soul. It was etched onto his skin, engraved in the fine lines around his lips and eyes. It flitted through his mind like dust particles in sunlight. The past year had entailed one devastation after the next, including the death of a waiter tonight. In Jason's arms.

A security guard removed the containment hood from Jason's hand.

Jason glanced at the hotel staff forming a huddle around him. He sucked in a breath of air and handed over the requested items. They were tossed into an eco-friendly biohazard waste bag.

When Jason glanced back at the woman in the restaurant, she'd turned her attention to the guy sitting beside her. Her green eyes were no longer Jason's portal to the previous year.

Tilting his head down, Jason followed the security guards to the post-exposure room. He anticipated an excruciating sting from the sanitation shower. That device was basically a human-sized pressure washer. Talia had described the agony of the scalding torrent on countless occasions. Jason predicted pure misery in his near future.

But physical discomfort was the least of his concerns.

He'd be forced to peel off his shirt before stepping into the barbaric shower. Harsh accusations and judgment would follow. Jason figured he'd be interrogated like a murderer. It wouldn't be the first time that happened to him, thanks to the smeared inscription on his skin. He knew it also wouldn't be the last.

CHAPTER FOUR: OCTOBER 5, 2038

Lexi received an incoming call at two-thirty, several hours before her Soothe Alarm was set to go off. She opened her eyes, taking in her surroundings. The bed was king-sized, noticeably bigger than her own bed in Sacramento. There was no suitcase in the corner of the room. In her sleep-infused daze, that struck Lexi as odd. She always placed her roller-bag near the door on layovers. That made it easier to grab the suitcase when it was time to head to the airport.

Moonlight trickled in through a gap in the curtains, illuminating Lexi's Instructor-In-Training badge dangling from the dresser.

Hotel room, Orlando, training week. She waited for the mental fog to dissipate. She'd put her roller-bag in the closet since she would be in Orlando for several days.

The phone rang again, a shrill tone jolting her eardrum. One word flashed across her eyelid—*Mom.*

Lexi's pulse quickened instantly. She'd been dreading this middle-of-the-night phone call since age sixteen.

Suddenly wide awake, Lexi jolted upright, blinking twice to accept the call. "What's wrong?"

Erin Brennan sucked in a gulp of air. "Lexi, it's your brother . . ."

"What happened?" Lexi could imagine the tears streaming down her mom's face.

"Colin's not okay."

Lexi swallowed. *He's never been okay.*

She wished her brother were within arm's reach. She ached

to scold him, shake him, hug him as tightly as possible while shouting obscenities and apologies.

"Where are you right now?" Lexi asked. "Where's Dad?"

"Your father's here with me. We're at Lutheran Hospital Midtown. Behavioral Health Unit. I mean, we aren't allowed inside because . . . you know. Precautions. In case there are undeclared ARs. But we're in the containment room."

"How's Colin?"

"Stable. He's asleep."

"They sedated him?"

"Yes. He took some pills, then changed his mind and called for help."

"Dammit. The doctors should've inserted a slow-release pack." Lexi groaned.

"I agree. Colin doesn't regulate his meds very well."

"How long are they keeping him?"

"We haven't been given a release date. Colin was confused when he arrived. His story kept changing, so nobody's sure what really happened. They pumped his stomach an hour ago."

"Wow. Okay."

"It sounds like he's been having intrusive thoughts again. Obsessing about certain things. He told them he was in danger. Really bizarre claims."

Lexi sighed. "It's good he sought help, right?"

"I think so. He couldn't complete an intake assessment, but they plan to do it once he's awake. Guessing he'll be here at least a week."

"Longer than last time."

"Yes, because of his history."

"Okay. I'll fly home today." Lexi began planning the steps to attain a space-available ticket from SkyLine. She knew there would be cabin seats available, so she wouldn't have to ride the jumpseat. Lexi hadn't worried about oversold flights since 2037. Pre-ContaCan days. Back when intelligent space pathogens only existed in nightmares.

"Will SkyLine let you teach the class if you leave training?"

"Doubt it," Lexi admitted. "That doesn't matter. I'd rather be with you."

"Stay in Orlando, baby. There's nothing we can do right now. We'll visit Colin later this week."

"No. I need to come home," Lexi argued. "Training ends Friday. I can't wait four more days."

"Finish the course in Florida. You can fly home after. Don't throw this opportunity away. Colin is in good hands."

Lexi internally reflected that hadn't helped Colin very much in the past. She swallowed. "How are you holding up? How's Dad?"

Her mother cleared her throat. "We're both glad Colin's safe. It feels promising that he changed his mind after taking the pills. He wants to get better. Also, the social worker thinks it was a cry for help. He didn't take enough meds to cause long-term damage."

"Ugh. Mama, I need to be there."

"You're exactly where you should be, Lex." Her mother's voice was quiet but firm. "You eventually want to transition to the training department, right? This is step one. Focus on the task ahead. Fly home Friday. We'll do dinner Saturday."

"Deal. My place?"

"Ours. Monty will be excited to see you."

Lexi nodded, always eager to spend time with her parents' dog. "When will we visit Colin?"

"Saturday or Sunday, I would imagine."

"Okay. I love you, Mom."

"Love you, too, Lex."

With a double blink, Lexi closed out the call. Bile rose in her throat. She needed to communicate with Colin.

Lexi was fully aware her brother had zero access to

technology. In the past, the hospital deactivated AutoScan and confiscated every personal item upon arrival. Cell phones, tablets, and clothing were stored in a separate room, inaccessible to the patient. Lexi figured that nowadays, they were probably incinerated.

ContaCan kept morphing. The government blamed ARs, insisting there was no way to slow the pathogen's evolution when part of the population continued to catch the deadly bug. As a result, extreme measures were taken, which just incited more animosity. Personal property was destroyed. Government-issued cameras were placed in bathrooms and locker rooms. Privacy was a concept from a different era. It no longer existed, thanks to ContaCan.

Colin's phone could be a pile of smoldering ash by this point, Lexi reasoned. Yet she was determined to send her brother a message. Resolve coursed through her veins.

AutoScan – Colin Brennan, I love you, kid. Things might feel unbearable, but you've pulled through before, and you'll do it again. Plus, you're not alone. You're stuck with me as a sister. I'm in your corner, and I won't quit. Not now, not ever.

You are brilliant and fierce, Colin. Remember your worth. Never forget that you are so, so loved. I'll see you soon.

She sent the text with a double blink. A dull thud indicated Colin's phone was off. It didn't matter. Lexi had stated her piece. Part of it, anyway.

The words felt fragmented and incomplete. They only captured a portion of the wild thoughts that had been spinning in Lexi's mind for nearly two decades. The sentiment was authentic, though. Which was the best Lexi could offer her brother.

Lexi stepped onto the balcony.

A band of orange haze lingered in the distance, slicing through the sky like a celestial partition. Automated cars zipped toward the airport, programmed to drop off passengers at various terminals. It was a welcome sight after months of wondering whether anyone would survive ContaCan, let alone take a chance on commercial flying.

Lexi knew she should be excited by this display of resilience. The morning aviation rush was back in full force. People were traveling once again, for business and even for leisure.

A week earlier, Lexi would've smiled at the dawning of a new day. She would've admired the view, allowing herself to feel something other than complete despair. But in the aftermath of last night's phone call, all positive thoughts felt foreign and out of reach.

Colin was hurting. Lexi couldn't help him. She was useless and helpless. A waste of oxygen, really.

With slumped shoulders, Lexi returned to her hotel room. Clothing dangled from an open closet, beckoning her to get dressed. Her company-issued tablet rested on the windowsill. Its flashing green light indicated the solar-fueled battery was charged to full capacity.

A morning alarm seeped through the hotel walls. This wasn't soft and comforting like Lexi's Soothe Alarm. It was an old-school beeping, programmed to shock someone into consciousness instead of vibrating politely inside their Ear-Link.

The noise shook Lexi to her core.

She sat down on the hotel bed, waiting for her neighbor's alarm to cease its tortured symphony. Her fingernails sliced into her thighs. Lightly, then with more pressure. When the indentations turned white, Lexi lifted her hands and sat on them. She wouldn't pierce the skin today. Life was broken enough without additional flesh wounds.

Fuck. She was desperate to summon her classic brand of sorcery. She needed a release. She'd gone too long without one. But there was no nameless man or woman nearby.

There was no way for Lexi to forfeit her soul, suspending

time in the process. Her superpowers had been fading for months, thanks to ContaCan and its threat of sudden death. Lexi doubted her talents even worked anymore.

She would have to suffer through each second, minute, and hour the traditional way—by being fully present. There was no chance for wizardry here in Orlando. To Lexi's dismay, her magic powers were null and void.

Lexi applied a second layer of concealer under her eyes, this one thicker than the first. A quick glance in the mirror informed her that she looked like a powdered donut.

She smiled at her reflection. It was a nightmarish grin, skeletal and empty. Tamika would see through her weak attempt to mask the truth, she guessed. The façade was flimsy at best.

Lexi grabbed her backpack and darted into the hallway.

Every booth at the restaurant was full. Waiters lingered on the periphery, swooping down to refill water and orange juice as needed. One of the servers was a striking brunette, a gorgeous girl who reminded Lexi of her first college romance. Blair had been mesmerizing. Long, lean, and graceful, she had brightened every room she entered.

Lexi sighed. Blair was long gone. She'd passed away five months ago. Lexi glanced at the stranger's lips, curious if they felt as soft as Blair's had, once upon a time. Back in a different decade and a long-lost era of carefree trysts.

As Lexi watched, the woman's teeth shimmered. She was wearing a mouthguard. When Lexi realized the implications of the unnatural shine on the woman's teeth, her heart seemed to stop beating.

Her eyes traveled to a bulge above the woman's elbow, proof of the armband nestled beneath her sleeve. The waitress turned toward the breakfast bar to reorganize a stack of cereal boxes.

Through her white shirt, Lexi spotted the insignia on her

left shoulder, midnight ink etched into porcelain skin. This marking would remain with her for life. Like the AR last night, this woman was branded. The permanence of the waitress's tattoo screamed out to Lexi. A thought flitted across her mind, evaporating before she could decipher it.

Finished with her task, the server whirled around and positioned herself beside the juice machine. Briefly, Lexi met her gaze.

I'm sorry you're out in public. Lexi attempted to guess the waitress's age. Maybe she was paying her way through grad school. Perhaps she had no choice but to work at that hotel, surrounded by tons of people. Opportunities for ARs were few and far between. Most companies refused to hire them. The ones that did wouldn't provide benefits since ARs had astronomical medical bills. Those businesses typically made work conditions so miserable that ARs could only tolerate the job for a few weeks before giving up.

A pang of sadness sliced through Lexi. She wondered if this girl had any family left. The abnormal gene skipped a generation sometimes, but not always. Her relatives were probably dead. Or exiled to AR containment facilities, which was usually the last stop before the morgue.

Sighing, Lexi glanced around the busy restaurant. She couldn't handle additional melancholy. Not today.

From the left side of the room, Tamika lifted her hand. A mug rested in front of an empty chair, steam rising from the rim. Lexi marched toward her friend.

"Thanks for getting me coffee," Lexi said, gulping down the hot liquid.

"Sure thing. Bacon's hella crisp. Try some."

"Nah, I'm not hungry."

"Hmm. Because of what happened last night? Awful. I hope that guy is okay."

"He isn't."

Tamika nodded. "I figured as much. Did it hit you hard?"

"Kinda."

"Looks like you didn't get a lot of sleep. No offense."

"None taken. I'm exhausted."

"If it makes you feel better, shit went down quickly. Maybe he didn't suffer too much." Tamika's voice was ardent, bordering on enthusiastic.

It dawned on Lexi that she was trying very hard to convince herself of those compassionate falsehoods.

"Hopefully the guy wasn't in pain long."

"That's not the reason I look like trash. There's something else," Lexi admitted, staring into her cup. She swirled around the last few drops of coffee. "My parents called me in the middle of the night."

"Oh, no. Bad news?"

Lexi nodded, her stare fixed on the ceramic mug.

"I'm sorry, Lexi. What's wrong? Can I help with anything?"

Lexi glanced around the restaurant. Her classmates appeared to be in good spirits. At a table by the window, two Philadelphia-based flight attendants split a Belgian waffle drenched in maple syrup. A man and woman based in Richmond waited in the omelet line, chatting with each other.

"It would take forever to explain," Lexi told Tamika with an apologetic frown. "The condensed version is that my brother's been sick a long time."

Tamika's eyes widened. "He's an AR?"

"Not that kind of sick. Emotional stuff. With Colin, there are good times and bad times. This is a bad time."

"You should fly home. Listen, nobody wants to see you complete instructor training more than me. But family is more important."

"That's what I told my parents. Mom convinced me to stay here and finish training. She said we can't do much until

Saturday, then we might be able to visit him at the hospital."

"I see," Tamika said, sympathy evident in her dark brown eyes. "Can I help at all?"

Lexi shook her head. "Thanks, though."

"Don't worry about studying," Tamika instructed. "I'll take the best notes of my life. Classes don't start for a few weeks. We can go over the teaching templates together."

"That means a lot. I appreciate it, Tamika."

"Wish I could do more."

The shuttle screeched to a halt in front of the hotel. Lexi and Tamika glanced at the vehicle taking them to SkyLine Headquarters for another ten-hour day of instructor training.

Lexi grabbed her backpack and rose to her feet.

"Shoot, I missed that. Did you catch it?" Brandon whispered, scooting his chair closer to Lexi's. His micro laptop rested on the table, the cursor blinking steadily.

Lexi shook her head. The notes section of her tablet was bare, aside from a couple comments she'd jotted down yesterday.

Tamika angled her tablet toward Brandon. In the center of the page, overlapping the slide that explained SkyLine's new liability reduction plan, she had scrawled—

Protective equipment doubled on international flights. Per FAA rules, one per crew is mandatory. Highly recommended self-identified AR passengers wear protective hoods, intravenous arm bands, and mouth guards. Cannot ask to see arm bands per privacy laws. Enhanced air-filtration system turned on by the lead flight attendant before each flight, whether or not ARs self-identify.

Tamika brightened and enlarged the font with a couple flicks of her eye. Glowing orange words stood out against a black backdrop.

"Code?" Brandon asked quietly.

Tamika used ocular swipes to compose five letters in the upper lefthand corner of her screen.

After punching in the guest access code, Brandon copied the notes to his own device. Lexi quickly followed suit. Then she turned her attention to the front of the class.

Reggie Hortens was presenting hypothetical situations likely to occur during the first hour of an international flight. He explained procedures for handling sudden illness among passengers. He also detailed the possibility of a flight attendant experiencing a rapid onset of symptoms.

Lexi's phone, face-up on the table, buzzed with an incoming text.

Attachment – Pic.Digi file.

Thought you could use a photo of Cleo. She was very friendly when I checked on her yesterday. How's training?

Katie Hoffmeyer hadn't included any emojis or GIFs. It was a tiny detail, insignificant in the grand scheme of things. After twenty years of friendship, though, Lexi could spot when something was amiss.

While Reggie paced the front of the room, describing how federal regulations varied between domestic and international travel, Lexi discreetly slid her phone to her lap. The photo of Cleopatra was adorable, but Lexi suspected that wasn't the real reason her friend had reached out.

Did Erin tell you? Lexi texted, referring to her mother by her first name.

Katie's response came quickly. *Yeah. When Colin didn't show up to work today, I called him. Then I called Erin.*

Tamika elbowed Lexi's side just below her ribs. The nudge made Lexi grimace. When she looked up, everyone in the room was staring at her. Reggie tapped his finger on the podium impatiently.

"Lexi has been waiting for this moment her whole life. She loves mid-flight emergencies at the tail end of the most devastating crisis in human history," Tamika joked, subtly looping Lexi into the topic at hand. While the class chuckled, Tamika jutted her chin at her tablet. The answer was scrawled in red letters at the top of the screen.

"Okay, so if a passenger is unconscious without a pulse, one flight attendant begins CPR. Of course, that flight attendant must wear full protective gear."

"No visible inscription?" Reggie asked, cutting Lexi off.

She blinked. It took her a second to realize Reggie was referring to a tattoo, the same one etched on the beautiful waitress at the breakfast buffet this morning. And the AR who died last night. Six bold lines of ink, which sparked a human rights firestorm.

"Doesn't matter. We can't take chances, so we'll use a protective screen and mouth guard whether they have the AR tattoo or not," Lexi said. Her mind flashed to the semi-familiar man, decked out in preventative gear while resuscitating that doomed adolescent. He'd done everything right, used every precaution in the book. Yet nothing could save the poor teenager. "A second flight attendant calls the pilots. They connect to FlyingMed. If the nanoscreens or earpieces fail, we page for medical assistance. See if there are doctors or nurses on the plane. That's our absolute last resort. Minimize contact. Involve as few people as possible."

Reggie nodded. "Who verifies credentials? What liabilities are involved?"

"We use our best judgment. In terms of liabilities, medical professionals signed a ton of releases at the start of ContaCan," Lexi recited without glancing at Tamika's notes. "It's all included in their database profile. If they are licensed and actively practicing, which we will see when we ask for documentation, they should have up-to-date liability protections."

"Excellent. What happens after a few minutes of chest compressions?

"Trick question! Depends on the phase of flight. Are we descending? Continue CPR until we land and EMTs meet the plane. Cruise altitude? Follow instructions from FlyingMed.

After the passenger has been taken off the plane by EMTs, we can self-quarantine for five days to protect ARs. It's optional, but most people choose to take paid leave. It's also recommended we get the latest round of the antidote. What's the minimum requirement, modification number three?"

"Four, I believe. Next month it will jump to five because of a rare frameshift mutation, which is important if you're in close contact with an AR. Anything else?" Reggie pressed.

Lexi tilted her head to the side. "Yeah. Antibody cocktail wouldn't hurt, along with a few IVs of fluid. Routine biometric screening for abnormalities. No heavy exercise. It's also recommended that we avoid alcohol for two or three days following the incident, although that feels a little excessive."

"Whiskey has medicinal properties," Tamika chimed in, eliciting a few snickers from around the room.

"Correct, for the most part," Reggie said. "Lexi, great job. You're well-versed in these protocols. I assume you've had a couple medical emergencies on your flights."

"I've got terrible luck. Even though I'm junior, I've had twice as many medicals as some senior flight attendants," Lexi explained.

"Haven't you been a flight attendant for eight years?" Monica, a Seattle-based flight attendant, asked from two tables away.

Lexi bit her lip. "Did I say that? Small exaggeration."

"Listen, I've been in this line of work for a long time. Everyone does it." Reggie lifted a slim, tailored eyebrow. "It's a rite of passage for flight attendants to brag about being more senor than they actually are."

As Reggie transitioned to the next lesson, Tamika turned to Lexi. "Nice work. You nailed it, girl."

"I had some help," Lexi responded, resting her head on her friend's shoulder.

Lexi glanced at the holographic clock above the cafeteria's entrance, quickly calculating the time in California. *AutoScan – Call Katie Hoffmeyer.* A dull thud sounded in her ear, reminding her the function had been turned off for class.

"Shit," she murmured, whipping her phone from her pocket. With ocular swipes, she dialed her closest childhood friend. While Katie's phone rang, Lexi paced the hallway.

"Hey, Lex," Katie responded after the third ring.

"Hi. Are you on lunch?"

"Yep. I picked up sweet potato fries at Pete's Downtown Eats. Heading back to the office now."

"Jealous. Those things are addicting."

"Agreed. How are you, girl?"

Lexi paused. "Okay, I guess? Not the best. Trying to fake enthusiasm, but I doubt anyone's buying it. Time passes slowly, then quickly. Nothing makes sense."

"Wish I could hug you," Katie murmured.

"That makes two of us." Lexi chewed on her nail. "Did you notice anything at work recently? Was Colin acting weird?"

"Not really. I can usually spot the warning signs, but Colin seemed all right. A few complaints here and there, sure. Which is normal this time of year. We have a bunch of deadlines coming up. We didn't eat lunch together yesterday. I just figured he was busy."

"Sometimes he gets distant before things take a turn, but not always," Lexi reflected. "He misses Marco, I bet."

"Breakups are the worst."

"Did he mention Marco?"

"Not a word. Honestly, Colin seemed normal for the most part. I'm sorry, Lex. Wish I'd seen something."

"You did everything you could. And I appreciate that. It's a never-ending rollercoaster with Colin. This is nothing new, but I'm farther away this time."

"Right. Literally all the way across the country. How's training?"

"This instructor course would've been fun a week ago," Lexi said, approaching the oversized window at the end of the hallway. Palm trees glistened under the blazing sun. Lizards darted from one branch to the next, weaving around each other in search of food or friends or some other small delight. "I thought it would be a nice break from the shitshow this whole year has been. Life is finally improving, right? I've been excited about this training since I was selected, way back in the spring. It felt symbolic."

"This is your moment, Lex. You've wanted this for a long time."

"Ever since I became a flight attendant. Wasn't sure they'd pick me to teach classes."

"Are you kidding? They're lucky to have you. You'll be the best SkyLine instructor of all time. I would know! Remember junior year of high school when you tutored me in exchange for stolen booze?"

"How could I ever forget? I'm still amazed *and* appalled that your dad drinks brandy," Lexi mused. "We mixed that garbage with everything we could find. It was gross."

Katie laughed. "Which didn't stop us from getting hammered. Point is, I would've failed English Lit without your help. You're good at explaining things. No wonder you were an education major in college."

"Thanks. You were a great student. Well, *great* is a stretch. You were an okay-ish student, for sure." Lexi smiled, the first genuine grin of the day.

"Accurate. I'm braindead when it comes to poetry and classic novels. I hate reading unless it's a meme or a funny t-shirt."

"Obviously. You're a graphic artist. Plus, reading is way more fun when you're in a book club," Lexi noted. "Which is more about the wine than the books anyway."

"Didn't you get kicked out of book club?"

"Yeah, the leader was pissed that I slept with her girlfriend a million years ago. Which is ridiculous. It was right after college, and we were both single at the time. Who cares?" Lexi snickered. "Sacramento is way too small of a town. How am I supposed to find a group where I never banged anyone's girlfriend in the past? Or boyfriend, for that matter. I won't apologize for being good in bed."

Katie chuckled. "You shouldn't have to. Some people need to loosen up."

"Exactly. There are bigger issues in life than wild, reckless hookups from ten years ago."

"God, I miss those days."

Lexi released a wistful sigh. "Same here."

"Shoot, I gotta get back to work. I'm finishing up a big design for the website rollout next month. Gotta tweak a couple logos."

Lexi tapped her fingers on the window, drawing attention from one of the lizards. He tilted his neck to the side and stared at her. "That reminds me, I had this random idea today. Maybe it's stupid. Would you be willing to design a tattoo? I'd like to get one to honor my brother."

"It's not stupid, Lex. I'd be honored. Let me know what you want, and I'll send some sketches your way."

"Thanks, Katie. I've thought about getting a tattoo for years. This feels like the right time."

"I think it's a great idea. I'm happy to help, Lex."

Lexi glanced at the clock hovering above the cafeteria. "I appreciate it. And thanks for the Cleo photo."

"She's adorable. I'll check on her tonight and send more updates. Thursday night, too," Katie promised.

In truth, Katie didn't need to look after Cleopatra. The cat's RFID chip refilled her food and water bowls twice a day. Lexi could also track Cleo's biometrics from anywhere on the planet to verify the cat was safe and healthy.

But it was a favor, an act of kindness. Katie went to Lexi's apartment and snuggled the kitty as a sign of solidarity. Lexi knew that. It was Katie's way of showing support.

"You're the best," Lexi told her friend. "I owe you a bottle of wine."

"You'd do the same for me. Besides, I find it hilarious that my best friend has become a hardcore cat lady."

Lexi bit her lip. *Not by choice*. Still, she'd grown fond of Jorge's tiny feline. Cleopatra was a decent roommate. "Miss you, Katie."

"Miss you more. I love your family like my own."

"It's mutual. Bye for now." Lexi ended the call and tucked her phone back in her pocket.

Someone snuck up behind her, wrapping an arm around her waist. Lexi whirled around to find Luis, a Fort Lauderdale-based flight attendant, grinning sheepishly.

"I'm glad you're still out here," he said. "We can return to training together since we're five minutes late. It looks better when there are two of us."

"Oops. I lost track of time," Lexi said as they walked toward the classroom.

"Same. My man wanted SkyLine gear from the gift shop," Luis explained. "He made a pre-recorded PersonableSpin video with memes and floating quotes."

"If the request comes through PersonableSpin, you have to honor it," Lexi reflected. "That requires a certain level of determination."

"Maybe." Luis laughed. "Or maybe he's just needy."

When they reached the classroom, Lexi opened the door gingerly. Reggie paused his lecture as she and Luis slid into their seats. After a disapproving glance in Lexi's direction, Reggie continued discussing the merits of an abbreviated drink service on international flights. Tamika jotted down notes furiously. Meanwhile, Lexi contemplated tattoo designs and periodically forced herself to listen to Reggie's presentation.

"They definitely work for SkyLine," Carrie, a Seattle-based flight attendant with long blonde hair, mused. She gestured toward the table at the other end of the restaurant, occupied by a dozen men and a handful of women. Their lighthearted banter echoed throughout the room.

"That one's the CPR guy from last night," Tamika said, jutting her chin at the group.

Lexi squinted to see across the restaurant. She watched the man converse with his coworkers. He seemed amicable, despite the harrowing events from the day before. A laugh here, a smile there. No traces of lingering sorrow. Lexi couldn't decide if she found that reassuring or tragic.

She bit her lip, attempting to summon the memory of her previous encounter with this man. They'd seen each other before, she knew. But no matter how hard she tried, she couldn't recall any details. That was alarming, because her memory was usually razor-sharp. Unless she was hammered.

"Pilots?" Lexi murmured, drawing the only logical conclusion. She sipped her drink, the liquor stinging her throat. It was a welcomed sensation. Lexi hoped to achieve carefree lightheadedness as quickly as possible.

Carrie shook her head. Lush golden hair swept across her shoulders. "Don't think so. Could be dispatchers."

"I bet they're supervisors," Taylor, a New York-based flight attendant, chimed in. "They look like they work in different departments. Maybe it's their initial training."

Tamika frowned. "Nah, that group doesn't give off the newbie vibe. I bet they're doing requalification."

"Requalification?" Carrie echoed.

"When employees take a leave for six months or longer, they have to complete a lengthy training before returning to work," Tamika explained.

Lexi swallowed. "Do you think they had ContaCan?"

"Or maybe they were off work because they are ARs," Luis murmured.

"Doubt it," Tamika said. "The survival rate for ContaCan was terrible. And most ARs were forced to transfer to another department so SkyLine could track their interactions. Or they were given assignments that could be completed from home. A ton of them died. I heard the remaining ARs were fired, but I hope that was just a rumor."

"Yikes. Well, I don't see any mouth guards or armbands. Or tattoos, for that matter," Luis chimed in. "Those folks seem healthy."

"Yeah. They look normal," Taylor concluded.

Lexi chugged her drink, reflecting on the *abnormal* flight attendants. There had been dozens at SkyLine. Self-declared ARs. Nearly all of them had died by June.

A few had perished mid-flight, leaving passengers and crews traumatized. Nobody talked about those poor souls. It was an unwritten rule. What was there to say, really? Their blood-soaked membranes had spoken loud and clear.

"Maybe they were off work for another reason," Carrie said. "It could've been a major life event. Military leave. The birth of a child."

Lexi downed her drink. She closed her eyes, allowing the toxins to flood her veins. Then she glanced at the table where the semi-familiar guy had been standing. The rest of the group was there, milling around and slapping each other on the back. But the extra-tall mystery man was gone.

Noticing Lexi's empty cup, Tamika tapped her finger on the glass. "Refill?"

Lexi tilted her head to the side. "Sure, why not. Anybody

need anything?"

Luis, Carrie, Taylor, and Tamika assured her their drinks were fine. Lexi headed toward the bar, fumbling in her purse for her phone. Her fingers landed on a tissue, a mint, and a hair tie. She continued searching for the device that would pay for her drink.

With her eyes cast down, Lexi nearly knocked into a stranger. She managed to avoid a collision at the last second.

"Good thing I have quick reflexes," he responded.

Lexi inhaled sharply. *That voice.*

Looking up, she met the gaze of last night's rescuer. He was the tallest person in the whole restaurant, she suspected. The guy stood at least a foot above Lexi. His eyes were every bit as enticing as they'd been from across the room the night before. And they looked even more familiar up-close.

"Have we met before?" Lexi asked.

He cleared his throat. "Kind of."

"Knew it! You're a pilot?"

"Nah. Mechanic," he said, cracking a smile. A dimple materialized on his left cheek.

Lexi frowned. "That's weird. You're the youngest mechanic ever. They're usually ancient."

"Uh, thank you? I'm thirty-six. Got an early start at the regionals right after college and landed a job at SkyLine four years back."

"Four years, huh? You're the same seniority as me, baby mechanic. Initial Class of twenty-thirty-four. Where are you based?"

"Nashville. You?"

"San Francisco. I drive in from Sacramento."

"Cool. I'll be in California soon. I'm switching stations this month," he said. "Moving to San Diego."

Frothy white waves floated through Lexi's mind. Colin's first attempt at surfing, his wild determination to get it right.

She swallowed at the memory. It was a good day. It was probably half the reason she'd applied to school in San Diego a decade later. "Love that city. I went to college there."

"Nice. I'm Jason, by the way," the man said.

"I'm Lexi. So, Jason, why are you doing requalification training? Did you give birth recently?"

"Smartass." He chuckled. "No kids here, just a beer belly."

Lexi's eyes flicked to his impossibly flat stomach. His tight t-shirt did not leave much to the imagination. It was easy to spot every ridge of his well-defined abs. "Yes. I can see you never, ever hit the gym. Daily. What kept you off work, then?"

"I'm not doing requalification. I'm here for special training. Remember all those planes SkyLine parked in the desert, back when everyone figured the airline was doomed?"

Lexi grimaced. "How could I forget? It was chilling. End-of-the-world shit."

"No kidding. I updated my resume in preparation for the worst."

"Me, too." Lexi had revised hers at the start of the outbreak. She'd bridged the gaps between jobs as best she could. Her CV was unimpressive, and she knew it.

"Well, those grounded planes are returning to service," Jason continued. "Somebody's gotta fix the problems that popped up during the interlude, and SkyLine chose me for the job. I'm in the middle of a three-week training where they teach us how to get those airplanes in working order."

"Wow. I'm glad the AirBirds are coming back. Wasn't sure I'd ever see that day," Lexi admitted. "How's class been?"

"Interesting. If you're into that kind of thing," Jason said with a shrug. "Plus, I was thankful to get out of Nashville."

"Really? I love Music City."

"It's a great town. But my ex is there . . ."

"Divorced?"

"Nope. Un-engaged, technically. Things got weird this year. She's an E.R. nurse, so we always had conflicting schedules. We were ships in the night until SkyLine cut everyone's hours. Suddenly, I was home more. A *lot* more."

"Wasn't that something? When the government scaled back commercial flying, flight attendants worked half our normal schedule," Lexi reflected. "I flew about thirty-five hours per month."

"Right. Everything changed so quickly. Suddenly I was with my fiancée, Talia, more than ever before. We realized we weren't compatible."

"Weren't compatible," Lexi repeated absently. "Makes sense. Some things just don't work out."

Colin's fiancé had ended things last year for the same exact reason. That was the term he used—*incompatible*. In truth, Marco cracked under the weight of Colin's illness. Which was understandable. It wasn't easy to love someone who spent his life on the brink of self-destruction. After eighteen years of agony, Lexi could admit that much.

"Are you okay?" Jason asked, his voice soft. "Didn't mean to bring down the mood with my depressing almost-marriage."

"I'm fine. Just thirsty."

"I know the cure for that." Jason nodded toward the bar. "What are you in Orlando for, Lexi?"

"I'm here with forty flight attendants from all twenty bases, training to teach the new health and safety procedures class. It's a post-ContaCan tutorial. Did I mention I was a flight attendant?"

"You did. Also, I already knew."

Lexi bit her lip. "Is that so? How did we meet, anyway?"

Chapter Five

Jason paused, debating how to frame his answer without sounding insensitive or creepy. Insensitivity was a party foul, but creepiness was worse. There was no bouncing back from that. He had to select his words carefully, he knew.

"Well," he began, "It wasn't under the best circumstances."

The woman's green eyes widened. "Was I sloppy drunk?"

He laughed. He certainly had not been anticipating that reaction. "Um, I don't think so."

"Oh. Excellent." Lexi offered a shy half-smile, but Jason got the impression she was anything *but* shy. "Then how bad could it possibly be?"

"Pretty bad," Jason admitted. His mind traveled to the dim auditorium in Seattle. Endless gloom outside the windows. A few dozen employees had assembled to pay their last respects to beloved friends, coworkers, and mentors. "It was the Celebration of Life last year. I was next in line to give my speech when they sent everyone home."

Lexi's eyes moved to something in the distance.

"I'm sorry," Jason said quickly. "I wish we had met at a better time."

"It's fine." Lexi met his gaze, and Jason was taken aback by the mirth in her green irises. It was as though she'd deliberately flipped a switch in her mind. She offered a casual shrug. "We're meeting now, aren't we? Let's consider this our first interaction."

"Deal."

"Nice to meet you, baby mechanic. For the very first time

in our entire lives. And our four-year SkyLine careers."

"We should raise a toast to the class of twenty-thirty-four," Jason mused. He had never met anyone hired the same year as him, aside from the nine men and four women who had been in his initial training class. None of them ended up in Nashville with Jason. They were scattered across the country, repairing planes in various bases and outstations.

"That's a good idea. Hard to believe it's been four years, right? Have you been back to Headquarters since initial training?" Lexi asked.

"Yeah, a few times. Line mechanics have annual training in Orlando. I was here a couple weeks before the meteor shower." Jason immediately regretted his statement, fully aware that era was laced with emotion. The age of carefree, stupid innocence before the sky collapsed and ContaCan was unleashed.

Jason cleared his throat. He added, "But I've also been here for a few special trainings in the past. When we got the Premier AirBird series, things like that. And one awards ceremony. How about you?"

"Nope. This is my first time back since twenty-thirty-four." Lexi paused. "What award did you get?"

Jason felt the heat rising to his cheeks. He didn't know why he'd mentioned that. Just an attempt to talk about something other than the days leading up to the loss of Jorge and Captain Colleen. "It was small. Just a formality. How does it feel to be back at Headquarters after all this time?"

"I like it here," she murmured. Her words had an ethereal quality. They felt musical and delicate. "SkyLine isn't perfect, but there's a positive vibe overall. It's a nice distraction from the hell we endured last year."

"True," Jason reflected. "This place is pretty nostalgic."

The walls outside his training classroom were adorned with grainy old photos from before he was born. There were mechanics, pilots, engineers, and executives. They'd been recognized in aviation publications, and some had traveled to the White House. They were titans of the industry. They'd left big shoes to fill, but Jason appreciated a good challenge.

He smiled. "How long is your training, Lexi?"

"We're here all week. Then we disperse to our bases to teach the class."

Jason nodded. "Sounds ambitious. Does this make you a teacher stew?"

Lexi rolled her eyes. "People only use the term *stewardess* when they're being sarcastic or condescending. But sure, why not? I'm a teacher stew."

"Okay. Let me buy you a drink, teacher stew." Jason sucked in a breath of air, waiting for her response.

She held up her phone like a prized possession. "No need, baby mechanic. That's why I slammed into you. I was searching for this thing."

In one swift motion, Jason grabbed the device from her hand and tucked it in the pocket of her jean shorts. "This round's on me."

She bit her lip. "I don't like being bossed around. However, I appreciate free drinks. So I'll make an exception this one time."

"Fantastic," he said. His gaze traveled to Lexi's pocket, where her phone rested snugly against her hip. "Do you still pay with your phone?"

"Yeah, I'm a rebel. My brother gives me hell. He's had ThumbPay for years. One time I read an article about how the government could hold it against you, and that really stuck with me. So I kept doing things the old-school way."

Jason tilted his head to the side, searching for a glint of metal inside the woman's ear. He spotted the implant almost immediately. "You use AutoScan, right? And it looks like you've got an EarLink."

"Okay, I see where you're going with this."

"It's just interesting you'd allow someone to scan electrodes in your brain and permanently insert a device in your ear canal, but a thumb-scanning payment method is where you draw the line." Jason grinned, certain his logic was spot-on.

"Touché," Lexi admitted with a shrug. "It became my weird quirk. My claim to fame."

"How's that?"

"I'm the last person in the world who *only* uses her thumb for certain activities. Fun ones."

Jason lifted an eyebrow. He'd never heard anyone discuss ThumbPay and foreplay in the same breath, especially five minutes after introducing herself. "Hmm. Anything in particular?"

"Use your imagination." She kept a poker face, but her green eyes shined with amusement.

Jason swallowed. "Are you this straightforward every time you meet a guy?"

"Who says I only meet guys?"

"Oh, gotcha. So you're—"

"*Open-minded,*" she filled in before Jason could complete his train of thought. "Yeah. I like people. All different kinds. It's mostly about a person's energy. I'm attracted to vibes, not anatomy."

"That's cool. How's my energy so far?" Jason asked.

"Not sure. I'll know more after another drink."

"Then let's not waste time," he said. "What will it be, Lexi?"

"Vodka soda. You?"

"I usually drink scotch."

She groaned. "Scotch is the drink of grumpy old men, Jason. Geriatric dudes love that stuff."

"Fine, I'll branch out." Turning toward the bartender,

Jason ordered two vodka sodas, then held his thumb above the scanner embedded in the bar. "This is just to impress you, Lexi. If I don't like this drink, you're to blame."

"Sure, blame the flight attendant. Everyone's favorite scapegoat." She clinked her glass against his. They took a swig in unison. "It's good, right?"

Jason tilted his head to the side. The drink was overly carbonated and at least two-thirds vodka. It wasn't great, but it wasn't terrible. "Could be worse. Listen, we're heading to the bar across the street. They've got decent food, and some of the guys want to play darts."

"Who's in your group?"

"A bunch of re-qual pilots, a couple mechanics, and a dispatcher," Jason explained. "Oh, and two first officers upgrading to captain."

She cast a brief look at a table at the far end of the restaurant. "I should head back to my team of teacher stews. They're probably wondering why I haven't returned yet."

"Invite them to play darts," Jason suggested. He considered reaching for her arm, then decided against it.

"Not sure I have the energy. I barely slept last night."

"We won't stay long. I'll have you back here in an hour."

She sighed. "I've heard that line before. Then, all of the sudden, it's four in the morning, and I'm calculating how many minutes of sleep a person needs to survive."

"Well, you've never hung out with me before," Jason reminded her. "I do things differently. You wouldn't know. Since we just met tonight for the first time."

"Duh," she said with a casual flick of her wrist. "But, also, stranger danger."

Chapter Six

Lexi walked back to her table, savoring the weightlessness of each step. She sipped her drink and sat down beside Tamika.

Luis was in the middle of a story. His eyes lit up as he described a luxurious all-inclusive resort in Grand Cayman where he'd been stranded for forty-eight hours, thanks to a slow-moving hurricane. It happened several years earlier. The pre-ContaCan era. All flights had been canceled in anticipation of the storm. Luckily for Luis, the hurricane bypassed Grand Cayman. So he did what any decent flight attendant would do—partied his ass off.

Luis's Caribbean excursion sounded like a drunken blur, a blissful haze typical of the old days. Back when it was possible to forget every single problem after a couple shots of your preferred poison. Three or four drinks in, everything bad vanished. Poof. There was no lingering remorse. No incessant worrying over gravity-defying meteors or the toxins they had carried with them.

"You were gone a long time," Tamika hissed in Lexi's ear while Luis recalled the resort's swim-up bar. Lexi tried to picture the bartender exactly as Luis described him—long and lean, covered in tattoos. Dark hair that grazed his shoulders. An addictive laugh.

"I saw you chatting with that guy from last night. He's cute," Tamika pressed.

"Yeah. Seems nice."

Tamika offered a devilish laugh. "I bet."

Lexi snickered at the excitement in Tamika's voice. "I'm careful about this kind of thing. What's the old saying? I don't do naked gymnastics where I work."

"Nobody says that, but ten points for creativity. You've never hooked up with anyone at SkyLine?"

"Nah. There was this one superhot gate agent in Portland who kept flirting. I considered asking her to grab dinner but decided against it. Too much drama. My life is already confusing enough." Lexi polished off her drink, setting the empty glass back on the table.

"First time for everything," Tamika pointed out with a grin.

"I'll try anything once, or even three times. Just to be sure. Don't tempt me."

"That's what I'm here for. You're welcome."

Chuckling, Lexi rose to her feet. "Hey, everyone. Jason invited us across the street with his group. Mostly pilots, also a couple mechanics and dispatchers. They want to play bar games."

"Not me," Taylor said. "I'm beat. Sorry to be a buzzkill."

"Same," Brandon admitted with a yawn. "See y'all in the morning."

"Could be fun," Luis reflected. "Okay, I'm in."

Tamika nodded. "Let's go play darts."

"Why not?" Carrie mused. "Sign me up."

The group of four marched toward the hotel's double doors. Once they were outside, Lexi glanced across the street and spotted the sports bar immediately. Neon signs illuminated frosted windowpanes. The building was crescent-shaped with the concave side facing the hotel. Lexi charged ahead.

"So your new friend is a pilot?" Carrie asked, nudging Lexi's side. As they passed under a streetlamp, she swatted at a mosquito, tangling her finger in her long blonde hair.

"Nope, a mechanic. Currently lives in Nashville but moving soon," Lexi supplied. "His name's Jason. He'll be based in San Diego next month."

"Great city," Carrie noted.

"Hey, do you think they'll have pool tables here? Retro video games?" Luis interjected as they approached the restaurant's half-empty parking lot. "And I wouldn't turn down a bacon burger."

They entered the building, chatting about appetizers and competitive bar games. Lexi searched for Jason's group.

Briefly, her focus landed on a cute blonde bartender. The woman was chatting with a few guys saddled up to the bar. She seemed friendly in a typical hospitality industry way, sporting the same practiced grin Lexi often donned at work. There was a distinct pattern to the way the bartender reached for empty glasses or smoothed out the rising hem of her shirt.

This was not her true self. Lexi could relate to that. The job was a performance. It was theater. For some folks, it was also a means of self-preservation, Lexi knew.

The nanoscreen behind the bartender flashed bright red with a news update. Something about a group of ARs in Alabama who had dodged the tattoo requirement. There would be hell to pay, it seemed. The bottom of the screen posed a question—

DefenderTech to blame for this threat to national health and safety?

In the center of the display, the White House press secretary was launching into another tired old rant. He was a mummified human with beady eyes and flushed cheeks. His bulbous nose was four times too big, dwarfing the rest of his face. The guy certainly had a lot of energy for being a thousand years old. He lit up when discussing the prospect of violence against ARs. The dude was downright gleeful as he insinuated one-tenth of the population must be stopped by any means possible. Lexi couldn't be sure, but the creepy old demon seemed to climax when he suggested bodily harm against all ARs.

While Lexi watched in disbelief, the press secretary suggested utilizing the newest form of domestic terrorism—autonomous explosive devices that embedded themselves inside a victim before detonating.

Lexi grimaced at the thought. The tiny floating explosives were a sinister and cowardly way to conduct an execution.

The nanoscreen displayed another message chastising DefenderTech for the incident.

Lexi didn't know much about the humanitarian tech group, but she knew their history was far less malicious than the current administration's. The president's cronies loved to rally a crowd of bloodthirsty idiots. DefenderTech wasn't like that.

A decade and a half earlier, the hackers had saved the lives of several vulnerable families in Texas. They crashed a website designed to oppress women. The smug politicians who had launched the war on reproductive freedoms were too stupid to figure out how to repair the site.

In 2022, after the nation's highest court deliberately revoked human rights on a federal level, DefenderTech fought back once again. The organization linked women to discreet healthcare access by purchasing plane, bus, and bullet train tickets on demand. They set up appointments at clinics. A network of humanitarians greeted the women at each step of the process, offering shelter as well as emotional support. DefenderTech wiped all records clean to ensure everyone's safety. It was a Freedom Trail of a new era, a rebellion born of compassion and respect.

Lexi inhaled sharply as a new note cascaded across the nanoscreen.

Which brave Americans will rise to the challenge and eliminate ARs transgressions? This abomination requires immediate retribution! Sins of the AR community will not be tolerated in this sacred land, cleansed by the blood of our gallant forefathers.

She rolled her eyes at the absurd terminology. Separation of church and state had ended years ago, when the Supreme Court began ruling on cases using a narrow interpretation of a book written two thousand years prior. All at once, the Constitution was abandoned in favor of religious dogma.

Since that shameful moment in American history, over-the-top Biblical language had been inserted into every new law, press release, public statement, and mandate.

Lexi hadn't known what an *abomination* was until DefenderTech leaked a memo from the court's biggest neo-Nazi, the Amy chick, whose appointment was confirmed after a string of lies under oath. The lady had no soul. None.

In 2025 or 2026, Justice Amy's top-secret pep talk to a group of Christian incels had been exposed online. She'd urged for a new sort of ethnic cleansing. She aimed to rid the country of so-called abominations such as homosexuality, birth control, vegans, Peace Corps members, edible underwear, and dildos.

The woman was a bona fide psychopath.

She had an ax to grind with anyone and everyone, it seemed. She hated her own uterus enough to ensure all other women were enslaved by theirs. And her vitriol toward the LGBT community would have been comical if it hadn't caused so much death and suffering. Lexi had looked up the meaning of the term *abomination* and known, even at age twenty-two, that the nation was going to get fucked by violent religious terrorists.

She'd been correct in that assumption.

How people could believe this utter nonsense, Lexi would never understand. It was a joke, except it was the sinister kind where folks died in the end.

The terminology was an obvious ploy to incite anger. And this newest AR incident was the sort of event which checked every box for the religious fanatics and fascists. It gave them another log to add to the burning fire of resentment. They wanted someone to blame. ARs were an easy target. The self-righteous religious crowd had already launched a war on women, minorities, and the LGBT community. Those causes were old news. Now, extremists could channel every ounce of their seething hatred toward a new target. They had a brand-new moralistic crusade, a specific group of individuals to harass and harm. With the government's blessing.

In July, the nationalists had lit a repurposed elementary school on fire with hundreds of ARs inside. Lexi shuddered at the memory. The photos had leaked online, most likely the work of DefenderTech. Lexi would never forget the images. Brutal scenes. ARs jumping from five stories above ground in a desperate attempt to die on their own terms. Kids trapped behind smoky windows, helpless and powerless.

Crowds of self-professed patriots had cheered while folks roasted alive. The photos captured humanity at its absolute worst.

The nanoscreen went on to declare—

ARs and their allies must be held accountable. Extreme action will be taken to maintain national security. America's future depends on it.

Shaking her head, the bartender pulled up a Holoscreen. Her slim fingers swiped the transparent image, then tapped twice.

Instantly, the nanoscreen disappeared, taking its ominous warnings with it. All that remained was a bare wall, the same shade of green as every other wall in the restaurant.

Lexi swallowed. Nausea washed over her. She vowed to drink more water and less alcohol for the next hour.

Sighing heavily, she swiveled her head in search of Jason. His group was gathered around a high-top at the far end of the room. A dartboard hung in front of them, scarred by years' worth of stab wounds.

Lifting a hand, Lexi signaled the flight attendants to follow her lead.

"You made it," Jason announced as they approached the table. A red dart rested in his hand. "Glad you changed your mind, Lexi."

While Tamika, Carrie, and Luis introduced themselves to everyone, Lexi slid closer to Jason. His breath felt warm against her ear as he asked if she needed a drink. Lexi tilted her head. She stared into his mahogany irises before offering a response. "Nah, I'm good. I'll take some of your water, though."

"Sure. How about food?" Jason pressed. "I lived in Orlando years ago . . . this bar has the best wings in the city."

"That's okay. I'm not hungry."

"No food, no alcohol? You're a cheap date," Jason declared. He grabbed her hand in one swift motion. "Let's play darts, then. You're on my team."

"That's how it's done!" Luis exclaimed, pointing at the dart wedged in the bullseye. He swung around to face everybody, spilling his beer in the process. Ice-cold liquid splashed across Lexi's sandals.

Jason leaned against the wall, one hand gripping a beer mug. Lexi stepped back and sank easily into his chest.

"It appears we lost the game," Lexi noted.

"Nothing about tonight feels like a loss," Jason responded.

"Buy me a drink!" Luis demanded, slamming his beer on the table. "We kicked your asses. That was the deal, right?"

"Those were the terms," Tamika confirmed. "You owe us. I think it's last-call soon."

"Damn, last-call?" Lexi echoed. "What time is it?"

Before she could summon AutoScan's worldwide clock, Luis informed her it was nearly midnight.

"We were supposed to be back at the hotel an hour ago. You tricked me." Lexi groaned. She grabbed a nacho from the plate in the center of the table and crunched down. Then she reached for her purse.

"I didn't want to interrupt the game," Jason explained.

"You should have. We lost," Lexi pointed out. "Badly."

"Technically, we came in second place."

"Out of two teams."

"Second place," Jason repeated with a chuckle. "Let me pay for their drinks, then we can walk back to the hotel." He held his thumb to the scanner in the center of the table, ordering another round for Luis and Tamika.

Then he grabbed Lexi's hand and headed for the exit.

Lexi glanced back at Tamika just before reaching the door. From across the bar, Tamika winked, raising her glass in a one-sided toast.

Warm, humid air washed over Lexi when she stepped outside. Streetlights flickered overhead, makeshift disco balls piercing the onyx sky.

Jason's fingers were laced through hers. At the edge of the parking lot, with the hotel towering above them, he paused. Lexi stopped mid-step. Her entire world seemed to stand still. Murky darkness wrapped itself around her like a childhood blanket, warm and cozy.

Jason's fingers slid up her arm and landed on the side of her neck. His body tilted toward hers. The feeling was at once familiar and foreign, brimming with hysteria. A collision of emotions, all of them pleasant, hit Lexi hard.

Lexi stood on her tiptoes, eagerly approaching Jason's mouth. Her spine tingled with anticipation. This sensation had been ignored and silenced over the past year. But it wasn't dead—it was merely dormant, waiting for an opportunity to awaken. The magician in Lexi still existed, after all. She felt her old self returning with each fluttery heartbeat.

Lexi kissed Jason. Her tongue traveled to every crevice of his mouth. The tingling in her core grew stronger.

Where there had been ice, a bold flame now burned. It

would grow and grow, Lexi knew. This was her biggest talent. Lexi had mastered clocks and brainwaves in one fell swoop.

"Maybe we don't need sleep, after all." The kittenish quality of her own voice rang in her ears.

Jason smiled. "Will you hate me if you're exhausted tomorrow?"

Lexi shrugged. The beer had dried, leaving a sticky film on her sandals. "Not if you make it worth my while."

A buzz sounded in Lexi's ear, indicating Katie had sent a photo. The image flashed across Lexi's cornea. Cleo was perched on a windowsill behind the couch, a plush green toy dangling from her mouth.

Cleopatra looked content. She was comfortable in Lexi's apartment, claiming certain spaces as her own. But nothing would ever compare to her previous domain, Lexi knew. The cat had already lived in the best home. With the best human. She was the luckiest feline in the whole world, until the day her father was obliterated. On a flight that Lexi was supposed to work.

A tidal wave of regret smacked Lexi, weakening her knees. She loved Cleo so much. Then again, the cat was a furry ten-pound reminder of Lexi's vast and unforgivable shortcomings. It was a complicated relationship.

She glanced up at Jason, hoping to rekindle the flame inside her. But adrenaline had been replaced by something else. Emptiness, perhaps. A distinct sense of absence. Her veins ran dry, as far as Lexi could tell. She was a shell of a human.

The liquor was wearing off. Lexi knew she needed another drink to keep the sadness at bay.

AutoScan flashed across her cornea once more. This time, it was an annual reminder. The clock had struck midnight, which meant it was officially Jorge's birthday. She hadn't had the heart to delete the recurring date from her calendar after

J.R.'s death in 2037.

Well, fuck.

Lexi couldn't recover from this. Her mood had flipped, and there was no going back. Curiosity nagged at her. She didn't want to know. She really didn't. But, also, she did.

Lexi swallowed. She willed herself not to speak, yet the burning question proceeded to fall from her lips. "Um, Jason? Who did you lose that night?"

Chapter Seven: October 6, 2038

"Details, please," Tamika instructed, slicing a hard-boiled egg in half.

The yolk was a dark shade, halfway between a blazing California sunset and a ripe papaya. Lexi averted her gaze. The faint buds of a hangover tugged at her.

She grabbed her water from the table and chugged until she'd drained the glass. "We kissed."

Lexi turned to observe the SkyLine employees meandering through the breakfast buffet. Taylor was wearing a blazer with sky-high heels. Lexi observed her style, equally curious and impressed. Manhattan radiated from Taylor's skin. It was practically woven into the fabric of her fitted plaid pants. Lexi appreciated that sophisticated appeal even though her own taste in clothing couldn't be more different.

"That's all?" Tamika furrowed her brow. "It's okay. Sometimes the chemistry isn't there."

Lexi shook her head. "Chemistry wasn't the problem. I asked a tough question. Then things took a weird turn. We drank wine in his room until two in the morning."

"What did you talk about?"

"Jason lost someone during the meteor shower, too," Lexi said, her voice hushed. "All the emotions I've kept inside, they were suddenly out there. I can't explain it. Jason's memories felt familiar. Finally, someone could relate to what I went through. I haven't experienced that depth of understanding since he was killed."

Lexi didn't mention Jorge's name. She didn't have to.

Reaching over, Tamika placed a hand on her arm. "I'm glad you were able to find some peace last night. You've been through a lot, Lex."

"One blow after the next. I still can't talk about it very much. It's too hard." Lexi sighed. "But I can listen. And Jason jumped right in. Maybe he'd been waiting to share all this stuff with someone. Maybe he was sick of compartmentalizing. He was friends with the captain of one of the doomed planes."

Lexi's mind returned to Jason's very specific, very compelling description of his mentor. There'd been an edge to his voice, a fierce longing that struck a chord in Lexi. This wasn't just a coworker. Captain Colleen was Jason's hero. He'd repaired the plane she flew that terrible night. Jason had patched it up a week before the meteor ripped it to shreds. No amount of maintenance could've prevented the plane from exploding on impact.

A burst of laughter erupted on the opposite end of the restaurant. Beneath her cardigan that was buttoned all the way to her neck, Lexi shivered.

Then the words tumbled from her mouth, snowflakes cascading to the ground in an unexpected blizzard. "For me, ContaCan wasn't the end of the world. The apocalypse happened way before then. I was supposed to be on that plane with Jorge. I miss him so badly my chest hurts. I still see his face when I look at Cleo. Or my uniform, for that matter. Or my improved spot in the seniority line after seven flight attendants died in the meteor shower and seven *thousand* died from ContaCan."

Tamika nodded thoughtfully.

"Jason and I met at the Celebration of Life. He spotted me during the rehearsal," Lexi continued quietly. "He heard the speech I wrote for Jorge. Which was the last time I've ever talked openly about him until right now."

Tamika tilted her head to the side. "I'm here for you. You know that, right?"

"Yes. I appreciate it." Lexi stared into her coffee cup. "Jason and I talked for a long time. We polished off a bottle of wine, then fell asleep. It was fairly innocent, which was surprising because I've waited forever for a good hookup. ContaCan really messed things up."

"Tell me about it," Tamika agreed. "San Francisco was a ghost town. I didn't meet anybody for, what, eight months? Not a single interaction."

Lexi nodded. "Back in December, this random chick I found online started convulsing right as she got to my apartment complex. She fell in front of the building, blood gushing from her eyes."

"Jesus. Did you call the ContaCan Emergency Hotline?"

"Yes. The girl was dead by the time I'd finished describing her symptoms to the operator," Lexi recalled. "Afterward, I drank alone until I blacked out. Technically not alone. Cleo was there with me."

"Animals count."

"Yeah. Thankfully, I placed the call anonymously through an untraceable app that Colin installed for me. I could've been fined if the government found out that girl had been coming to see me. If she'd set foot in my apartment during lockdown, they would have tossed my drunk ass in jail."

"Assuming they'd had time. You might have died instantly," Tamika reflected. "Imagine if she'd made it another hour, and her symptoms emerged while you were together in your apartment."

"Fifty-fifty chance," Lexi murmured aloud. "Significantly less than that once the pathogen started to evolve. What did it get reduced to, a thirty percent chance of survival?"

As soon as she said it aloud, her mind traveled to Colin. To the support group, many years ago, where a therapist casually mentioned the low odds of survival for someone with Colin's smattering of diagnoses. Lexi had been outraged. What kind of counselor presented those grim statistics without suggesting a way to improve one's prognosis? The rest of that week was a blur for Lexi. An array of fuzzy nonsense punctuated by white sheets and tangled legs. She couldn't remember whom they belonged to. She couldn't even remember what year it had happened. Maybe college, maybe after.

"Back then, it was Russian roulette to hook up with a stranger," Lexi reflected, forcing her thoughts back to the nameless woman who died on her walkway. "But I risked it anyway. Until that night in December when I took a gamble and a girl dropped dead. The next day, I woke up with the worst hangover of my life, and I just *quit*. Cold turkey. I put on an invisible chastity belt or something."

"Most of us felt that way. The world flipped upside-down. Nothing made sense."

"It's been brutal, right?" Lexi exhaled loudly. "All this pent-up angst. After a while, you get used to solitude. Eventually, you can't remember what excitement felt like. Everyone talks about how we've been in survival mode for a year, but nobody mentions how goddamn *boring* it's been."

Tamika nodded. "ContaCan wrecked everyone's serotonin levels."

"Yeah. Last night felt thrilling for a while. I was sure we would get it on. I was ready to break my no-SkyLine rule, which was never really set in stone. More like a suggested guideline. Proceed at your own risk," Lexi said. "But the atmosphere changed. AutoScan sent me a reminder about Jorge's birthday, and whoosh. My mood flipped. I needed to know about the meteors. About Jason's loss. Something nagged at me."

"I'm glad you followed your gut," Tamika said. "You've got plenty of time to get your freak on later. And you can do it with zero guilt, thanks to the antidote. We've got a national AR database and visible tattoos and stuff. Lots of warning signs so you never have to watch a random chick die in front of your apartment again. We're free to bang strangers again. Just like the old days."

"Strangers *and* coworkers," Lexi pointed out with a snicker.

"Get it, girl. We could all use a release. We sure as hell didn't get one during ContaCan." Tamika lifted an apple from the basket in the center of the table and tossed it in her backpack. Her eyes flicked to the nanoscreen on the wall displaying chronodata, including a global clock. "It's that time. Another day of training awaits."

"I'm gonna grab a yogurt first," Lexi said. "Save me a seat on the bus."

"Duh." Tamika smiled and headed toward the lobby.

Lexi maneuvered through the crowd near the omelet station. A metal bowl rested on a bed of ice, filled to the brim with individual Greek yogurts. She snatched a strawberry-flavored container and shoved it in her tote bag.

"Salted caramel is better," someone said.

Lexi turned to her left, where Jason was standing with his hands tucked in his pockets. There was a black bag strapped over his shoulder.

"Thanks for the insider tip," Lexi replied with a grin.

"No problem. Next time, I'll buy you a real breakfast. Pancakes and bottomless mimosas. The works."

"I'm late for my shuttle to Headquarters," Lexi told him, nodding toward the lobby. "But I hate to turn down that offer. Mimosas are my favorite fruit."

"Same here. Have a good day, Lex. Hopefully, you're not too tired."

"I'm exhausted. Stayed up past my bedtime playing darts. And I didn't even win." She chuckled and jogged to the exit.

Reggie was lecturing about medical conditions which required cabin seat upgrades when Lexi's phone lit up with an incoming call. She darted out of the room and tapped her EarLink.

"Mom," she breathed, pacing the hallway adjacent to the cafeteria. The smell of fried chicken wafted toward her nose, and her stomach rumbled. Lexi hadn't noticed she was hungry. There was a yogurt tucked somewhere in her bag, but she'd forgotten to eat it.

"Sorry to bother you, Lexi. I know you're at training."

"It's fine, Mom. What's up?"

"Colin might come home in a couple days. He'll stay with us for the first few weeks until he's back on his feet. The doctors adjusted his meds. They promised to insert a slow-release pack soon. There's a social worker helping him, an intern. She seems to be making a lot of headway."

"Awesome."

"If he continues to do well, they'll release him maybe Thursday or Friday. He'll be in outpatient therapy for a while."

"Wow. That's good news," Lexi murmured. "What a relief."

"Don't rush back to Sacramento," Erin Brennan instructed before Lexi had a chance to formulate a plan. "Nothing's official yet."

"Mom, I want to be there as soon as he's discharged."

"No need, baby. He'll probably sleep most of the time. Just come home on your original flight on Friday."

"You sure? I—"

"Lexi," she interjected, "Colin wouldn't want you to quit this training. Stay where you are and finish your program."

"Okay. I wish I could talk to Colin."

"Your brother knows how much you care about him."

"If you change your mind and want me home tomorrow, I'll be on the first flight back to Sacramento."

"Focus on your instructor training. I'll reach out as soon as we get an update."

"Okay. Love you, Mom." Lexi ended the call. A dull pain traveled down her left hand, from her wrist all the way to her pinkie. She realized she'd been clenching her fist. Her muscles had turned to cement.

She rolled her shoulders, relieving a fraction of the tension. A heavy sigh escaped her lips. Lexi was about to march back into the classroom when she noticed a flash of movement at the end of the corridor. Down the hall, near the exit, Jason was waving his arms. Curious, Lexi advanced toward him.

"What in the world are you doing, baby mechanic?" she asked.

"Coming to see you. Class just let out."

"Already? It's barely noon."

"We finished early. Figured I'd drop this off before heading back to the hotel." He handed her a SkyLine ballcap, the price tag still affixed to it. The hat was red and black with the company's emblem etched on its side.

Lexi held the cap for a moment, acutely aware of its smooth feel in her hand. The tightness in her body had been replaced by a stinging. Her appendages were waking up after their dance with paralysis. "This is cool. What's it for?"

"Figured you'd need it tomorrow."

"Tomorrow?" Lexi echoed. *Thursday. Second-to-last day of instructor training. Early release day since SkyLine hosts a weekly company-wide bonding session.* "The pep rally?"

Jason shook his head. "Nah, not that. One of the pilots rented a car to drive to Cocoa Beach. Bring your swimsuit to training. We'll leave for Cocoa right after. What do you say?"

"I'll see if I can swing it."

"Renee wants you there," Jason insisted, referring to the outgoing, energetic female pilot Lexi had met briefly at the bar last night. "She's tired of being the only woman in the group. And she thinks you're fun. All the pilots do."

Lexi raised an eyebrow. "Just the pilots?"

"And the dispatchers. And one baby mechanic."

"Oh, good. I'm surprised they approve of me after seeing how much I suck at darts."

"Your dart skills have been forgiven," Jason noted with a half-smile. "Please come tomorrow. How long has it been since we all relaxed? Kicked back and enjoyed ourselves?"

Lexi's mind traveled back to Jason's disclosure the previous night. He'd spared no detail. He had delved into the bond he shared with Captain Colleen, the mark she'd left on him, the misery he experienced after her death. It was the therapy session Lexi hadn't known she needed. The one she'd put off for a year.

"Tomorrow can be a mini vacation. A chill beach trip," Jason continued.

"Sounds fun," Lexi admitted, mulling it over. She placed the ballcap on her head. "How do I look?"

"Like someone who's about to get a badass tan."

"Or someone who would feel guilty leaving Renee all alone in a sausage fest," Lexi mused. "Sure, why not? Let's do it."

"Great. I'll bring sunscreen. Safety first." Jason wrapped her in a hug, sweeping her feet off the carpeted floor.

"Sunscreen?" Lexi asked, still tangled in his arms.

He chuckled, the vibrations echoing through his chest. "Black people can get sunburned, you know."

"Right. Duh. Of course." Lexi smiled and sank deeper into his shoulder. "You're very persuasive, Jason."

"I can be that way when I really want something." His breath was warm against her ear.

After the embrace, Lexi held her new baseball cap in front of her. "Shoot, I can't go back to class with this. I'm on thin ice with our instructor, Reggie. He'll think I left in the middle of his lecture to do some shopping."

Jason peered over her shoulder at the closed door leading to Conference Room 116. "Why'd you step out, anyway?"

"Got a call from my mom. We're supposed to disable AutoScan during the day, but I might break the rules and turn it back on. Can't afford to miss anything important."

"Is everything okay with your family?"

"No," Lexi confessed. "It's a long story. And a grueling one."

"Got it. Like our chat last night," Jason noted. He accepted the hat, placing it backward on his head. The tag dangled over his left ear. "Know something? It felt good to talk about Colleen. After bottling it up for ages, it was nice to release everything."

"I'm glad you opened up," Lexi said quietly, and she meant it.

Jason nodded, tucking the tag into the cap's hem. "I'll hang on to the hat. This works better, anyway. You can get it when you return to the hotel tonight. It'll be collateral."

Lexi snorted. "Sure. Whatever."

"Come find me later." He lifted a hand to wave.

With that, they headed in opposite directions.

"Lexi, can you stay behind?" Reggie asked at six o'clock. Throughout the room, flight attendants discussed dinner plans while gathering their belongings.

Lexi forced a thin smile. "Sure."

The conference room cleared out within seconds. It had been a long day, and everyone seemed eager to return to the hotel. Tamika shot Lexi a sympathetic look as she headed through the door.

"I'm sorry I left the room during your lecture," Lexi blurted out before Reggie had a chance to scold her. "It was rude. It won't happen again."

He frowned. "Is something wrong? I vouched for you when you interviewed for this position. You seemed enthusiastic."

"I was." She cleared her throat. "I *am*."

"Is that so? You've been preoccupied this week."

Lexi bit her lip. Through the window behind Reggie, she watched the shuttle depart for the hotel. She ached to be on that solar-powered van, cracking jokes with Tamika and planning the night ahead. "I'm scattered right now. Sorry."

"If you don't want to teach the class, we need to know immediately so we can find a replacement."

Lexi sucked in a deep breath.

"I *absolutely* want to teach this course," she began, meeting Reggie's gaze. "Education was my major in college. After my sophomore year of high school, I realized my academic classes couldn't answer the biggest questions in my life. I decided I'd change that someday. Maybe design my own curriculum. Give people information they could actually use."

Reggie crossed his arms, his oversized muscles stretching the sleeves of his crisp white shirt. "What changed?"

Nothing. Lexi's life had always been a disaster. This was no different than before.

Bad luck followed her like an ancient curse. She'd climb steadily toward a goal, then lose her footing halfway through. She never managed to achieve what she set out to accomplish. Every endeavor was doomed from the start.

Lexi shifted her gaze to the floor. The carpet, red with black and gold accents, had been designed to match the fuselage of a SkyLine AirBird. It was nostalgic and sentimental and completely overwhelming. The colorful kaleidoscope matched Jorge's work sweater. At home, Lexi cradled his uniform every night. She was comforted by a dead man's sweater. It was one of the few remaining items that had belonged to her best friend. His airline sweater and his cat. Lexi had inherited both.

Tears sprang to her eyes, which made her angry.

She willed herself to pull it together.

"On Tuesday morning at the crack of dawn, my mom called to let me know my brother was hospitalized." Lexi blinked until the excess moisture in her eyes retreated.

Reggie's demeanor softened. "Sorry to hear that. He's an AR?"

Lexi shook her head. "No. Colin's in and out of the psych ward all the time. Bipolar, OCD, generalized anxiety disorder . . . you name it. He does well for a while. Then things fall apart."

"That's a lot to deal with, Lexi."

"It's all I've known since adolescence. My brother was surprisingly calm throughout ContaCan. Weirdly, a global emergency centered him. He seemed more focused, like he had a mission. Staying healthy, I guess? I thought maybe things would change for good."

Reggie's lips curved into a sympathetic frown.

Lexi swallowed. "I can't save him, Reggie."

"That's not your responsibility."

"You don't understand. Eventually, I'll lose him. I can't keep anyone safe."

"Anyone?" Reggie repeated.

Lexi could not formulate a coherent response, so she nodded.

"Have you ever talked to a professional? About losing Jorge," Reggie clarified.

Lexi blinked. It took her a moment to remember that Reggie had helped organize the Celebration of Life last year. He'd been in the auditorium that day with a handful of other administrators. He'd had a front-row seat during her speech.

Reggie knew. He understood that Lexi was powerless to help the two most important men in her life.

Lexi cleared her throat. "I've gone to family therapy with my brother a few times."

"That's a good start. Maybe your own grief counselor would help. SkyLine has employee assistance programs, you know. They'll connect you to a support group or therapist. Your emotions are valid."

"Thank you. Jorge was such a big part of my life. It hurts like hell. He's still everywhere, in a sense. But he's also long gone in the ways that matter most."

"Having a strong community helps. You shouldn't go through this alone. Now that your brother's sick, the pain is intensified," Reggie surmised. "My dad was diagnosed with cancer fifteen years ago. I became his primary caregiver. Suddenly, my whole life revolved around his illness. I grew angry and bitter. It put a strain on my relationship. I didn't think Kevin and I would make it."

"Are you two still together?"

"Yes. Things got better. I joined a support group, which saved my career and my marriage. Not to mention my mental health."

"I'll look into it."

"There are so many ways to heal, Lexi. Choose the path that works best for you. You've been through a lot. The sadness is twice as big when you're battling it alone."

Lexi nodded sharply, determined to avoid Reggie's piercing gaze. He meant well, she knew, but his pity was searing and oppressive.

"I have one more suggestion," Reggie began. "Would you like to try Predictive PersonableSpin? SkyLine purchased the upgrade last month. Research has shown it can help."

Lexi's breath got caught in her windpipe. She'd read several articles. She'd heard about the studies that were conducted with parents and siblings who had lost family members to ContaCan. Some folks had amazing results. The reviews were still pouring in, but Lexi had mostly decided it was not a viable option for her. After all, what could she say? No words could capture the apology Jorge deserved.

"What if I forget stuff, or it comes out wrong?" Her bottom lip trembled against her will. She couldn't force her body into submission.

"You can't mess it up, Lexi," Reggie assured her. "That's the beauty of friendship. As long as you're honest . . . as long as you care about the other person, you'll do it right. Every time."

Lexi shrugged, unconvinced.

Reggie placed a hand on her shoulder, speaking in hushed tones. He guided her through the unfamiliar technology. He demonstrated each step of the process like a shaman, explaining how long it would last and the expected outcome. Apparently, it would take a few minutes for the app to sync all visuals, the documented ones as well as those committed to Lexi's memory. Then a global scan would be conducted, sifting through every public article and VirtuAlarm with information about Jorge's life, history, and personality.

Lexi inhaled sharply and got to work.

First, she activated AutoScan. In one fell swoop, she synced it to the PersonableSpin app on her company-issued tablet. With a few unspoken commands, Lexi uploaded every video, photo, and conscious memory of Jorge. The system rang in Lexi's ear, informing her the sync would take ten minutes.

Lexi sucked in a breath of air. PersonableSpin needed ten minutes to analyze Jorge's movements, mannerisms, speech patterns, and documented history. The program would sift through every relevant article, comment, photo, video, and expression. It would scrutinize the tone of his voice. The way his eyes lit up when he talked about Cleo.

Jorge's whole life and personality would be condensed into a handful of seconds. Ten minutes worth, to be exact.

Predictive responses would be generated using his past behaviors, Lexi knew. But she doubted the artificial intelligence program could fully capture her best friend's essence. Jorge was absurd in all the best ways. He was quirky and loud and thoughtful. He was irreplaceable.

"I'll leave you to it. Predictive PersonableSpin usually has a fifteen-minute range before it starts to fade," Reggie said while the app sorted through every image of Jorge. "I'm going to order you a *Swyft*. It will be here in twenty minutes. That's enough time, right?"

"Yes," Lexi said. A red rectangle appeared on the left side of the room, displaying the countdown until the *Swyft* would arrive to take Lexi back to the hotel. Lexi breathed a sigh of relief, grateful that Reggie had selected the rideshare service with a fully-automated fleet. That way, she wouldn't have to make small talk with a stranger.

Reggie gathered his belongings, dimming the lights on his way out. When he reached the doorframe, he turned to face Lexi. "You should relax tonight. Do something fun to take your mind off things. Tomorrow is a new day, and you can hit the ground running. Deal?"

"Thanks, Reggie. I'll try harder in class," Lexi vowed weakly.

"You've got a lot on your plate right now, but you'll make a great instructor. I saw something in you during your interview. It's still there. We just need to tap into it."

Lexi nodded, unable to find anything meaningful to say. Reggie exited the room and left her to converse with her dead best friend.

A ripple coasted across Lexi's scalp, indicating the app was ready.

Lexi, however, was not.

Closing her eyes wouldn't buy additional time, she knew.

The app would cast Jorge's image onto her cornea in full technicolor. A closed eyelid wouldn't delay the image. If anything, it would enhance her best friend's avatar.

Lexi swallowed. She practiced deep breaths like Colin's therapist had taught her.

She felt Jorge in the room before he materialized in front of her, thick black hair swept into a pompadour. His shiny purple crop top had kittens all over it.

"What the hell are you wearing?" Lexi blurted out.

Jorge smiled that toothy grin that felt like home. "Babe, this is how we dress in Gay Heaven."

The familiarity of the voice took Lexi by surprise. Jorge's words were velvety smooth. Exactly as she'd remembered. Lexi's bones screamed that it was Jorge in the flesh, even though her head knew better.

"Is Gay Heaven strictly gay, or do they allow *wavy* folks?" she inquired.

"Gay Heaven is inclusive. All adults are welcome, except jerks. There's a big bisexual population here. You'd fit right in."

"Sign me up."

"Done. I'll save you a cabana next to mine but don't get any ideas, okay? You're not allowed to join for a minimum of seventy years. You've got a long life ahead of you. When you get here eventually, you'll love it," he informed her with a flick of his wrist. "Crop tops and glitter. Neon body paint. Sometimes we wear nothing at all because it's always tropical weather in Gay Heaven."

Jorge's lips curled up in his classic lopsided grin. Lexi's chest swelled with emotion.

Don't leave me, J.R. Stay here. You're real. We are real.

Jorge's brown eyes filled with muted sadness, the kind Lexi had glimpsed before. Usually, when he'd discussed his family.

"I can hear your thoughts, my love," he reminded her. "And yes, we are real. Closest friend I've ever had. Nobody can take that away, right?"

Lexi shook her head. Their bond was unbreakable. She still felt it all the time. Sometimes it was so powerful that she could hardly breathe.

Jorge exhaled loudly. "But I can't stay long-term. And for that, I'm sorry."

"I need you," Lexi begged, her voice rising.

"You still have me. You've got all the best parts of me. You're taking care of Cleo, babe. By the way, if you ever skimp on her food or buy the cheap shit instead of the grain-free stuff, I will haunt you for life," he added with a hearty chuckle.

"She's a sweet cat," Lexi said. "I love her."

"Of course you do. She takes after me." Jorge smiled.

Lexi reached for her best friend even though she knew his avatar had zero mass, weight, or substance. She wanted to be as close as possible, to hold on tightly enough that he'd come back to life. She wondered how she could possibly face the future without him.

"You're doing fine on your own. You have a bright future, miss. You always wanted to teach, right?" Jorge noted. "Now you're going after it. You're chasing your dream."

"I haven't made it through training yet," Lexi cautioned. "Colin's sick again. The world went to crap after you left. ContaCan, fascist government, lockdowns. It's been a real mess."

Jorge nodded slowly. "We get sound bites in Gay Heaven. VirtuAlarms on the regular. I know it's been hard, Lex. And I'm sorry Colin's sick. Thankfully, he has you. Which is the best gift anyone could possibly have."

Just like that, Lexi's vision blurred. *Dammit. I didn't want to cry, Jorge.*

Let it out, he instructed, this time via electrodes connected to her cranium. *It's okay to break down sometimes.*

"I can't protect my brother." She gasped for air, her words escaping in short bursts. "I keep trying, but I can't help him."

"You can," Jorge argued. "You already have. Just by loving him."

"I loved you, though," Lexi pointed out, swiping at her cheeks to erase the tears. "I loved you, and it wasn't enough. I wasn't there when it mattered, Jorge. I traded off the trip when you needed me most."

"Oh, baby girl," Jorge crooned, pouting. "Is that what's been chipping away at you? If I could do it all over, knowing everything I know now, I'd keep you far from that aircraft. It was my time to leave, babe."

"How can you say that?" Lexi choked.

"Have you checked the Emergency Expulsion Registry, my love?"

"Huh?"

"The EER. Have you seen it?"

Lexi frowned. "Not lately, no. That thing is depressing as hell."

"Look at it soon. Promise me."

"Um, okay? I promise."

"When you do, you'll understand," Jorge assured her. "It was my time, Lex. And that's okay. I would've kicked you off that plane myself if I'd known what was going to happen. But for me, it was a good way to end things. I died doing what I love."

Lexi couldn't argue with that. "You were born to fly, J.R. You've always been a winged unicorn."

"Yes, I was in my element. You would've been so proud, babe. I stayed calm on the outside. I comforted all those passengers as we accepted our destiny. One of the dads on the plane fainted from shock or fear or who knows what. I held his son, just a little boy. Cradled him in my arms until he stopped crying."

"Is he in heaven, too?" Lexi asked.

"Absolutely. He's with his whole family, enjoying each moment in kid-friendly paradise. Gay Heaven is for adults only. Too many boozy brunches and X-rated hookups. Every day is the weekend. With no Monday in sight!"

Lexi smiled through her tears. "Sounds amazing. Drag Bingo?"

"On the regular."

She paused. "Did it hurt, J.R.? Was it quick?"

"Fast and painless. Boom! Bright lights. The feeling of weightlessness, then euphoria. Like Molly times a thousand. And it just keeps getting better, babe. The afterlife isn't what anyone expects. It is so simple, really. It's the freedom to be happy without fear or regret or any of that nonsense. Joy and love on an endless loop. Easy-peasy."

"I'm glad you didn't suffer."

"Not even a little bit."

"Still, it should have been me. Us. Together," Lexi insisted.

"You have work to do here," Jorge said. "You've got big things coming up. Listen, the algorithms are usually spot-on. I can predict what your future holds. You're going to change the whole damn world, Lexi. And in the brightest moments, the ones where you do the *most* good, please remember that I'm with you. I'm rooting for you, babe."

Lexi chewed the inside of her cheek. *I don't deserve you.*

"Ah, but you do," Jorge countered. "That's why we're besties, duh. Only one work wife for me. There's nobody else like Lexi Brennan."

His image cracked and shifted. The pixelated version of Jorge would soon dissolve into thin air, Lexi knew.

"I need you to forgive yourself," Jorge implored, his voice a whisper.

"Show me how."

"Take some of that kindness you've saved for me, or for your brother, and extend it to yourself. You have so much good in you. Celebrate that. Embrace it."

"I'll try," Lexi promised.

"There is this cute little redhead who's my best friend. She's also my fur-baby mama. I need you to stop being a huge bitch to her," Jorge said with a wink.

"I love you, J.R."

"I know. Now go love yourself." Jorge's image sputtered again, lines of static ripping through his body. He lifted an arm to wave goodbye.

And then he vanished.

Lexi stood in Conference Room 116, all alone. On the wall, a countdown ticked away. The *Swyft* would arrive in a few seconds. With tears still flowing, Lexi tied up her hair and snatched a few tissues from the nearest table. She dabbed her cheeks and marched outside to greet the automated vehicle waiting on the curb.

Chapter Eight

Hey, baby mechanic. I believe you have my hat? Lexi texted Jason while exiting the *Swyft*. The hotel lobby was quiet. Lexi figured everyone was upstairs, unwinding after a long day. Changing into comfy clothes. Enjoying a beverage before heading downstairs for dinner.

Jason's response floated across Lexi's cornea as she walked past the receptionist's desk.

Yes, I do. Room 428.

Lexi marched toward the elevator. She pressed the button for the fourth floor. Jason's door was ajar, so she let herself in. He sat on the edge of the bed, his mouth twisted into a goofy smirk.

"What's that look for?" Lexi asked, folding her arms across her chest.

"I hid the baseball cap."

"I'm coming off a rough afternoon. My patience is wearing thin, buddy."

Jason hopped off the bed and wrapped Lexi in a hug. "What's wrong?"

"You're really going to make me search for this hat?" Lexi asked into his shoulder, ignoring the question. Her voice was muffled by his shirt.

"That was the plan. But it can wait. You okay, Lex?"

She nodded wordlessly.

"Are you sure?"

Lexi pulled away and leaned against the dresser. "I don't know. Can I ask you something? You've used PersonableSpin before, right?"

"Yes. More than half our training sessions have included PS."

Lexi looked down at her hands. "Um, did you ever use it to meet up with Colleen?"

Jason grew silent.

"Don't answer that," Lexi said hurriedly. "I'm just pry—"

"No, I didn't. But I thought about it," Jason burst out. "I've got a billion memories and videos with her. Artificial intelligence would've mastered all her mannerisms based on those files."

"What stopped you?" Lexi asked, fully aware it was none of her business.

"I was afraid. Didn't want anything to replace my last memory of her."

"Was it a good one?" Lexi's cheeks grew flushed. She was taken aback by how connected she felt to Captain Colleen, a pilot she'd never met except through Jason's vivid recollections.

Jason nodded. "The best. She was so excited about getting awarded the Denver base. That's where we met, years ago, at a commuter airline. This career hasn't always been easy for me, you know? Colleen treated me like family. I went to dinner with her wife and kids a few times each month."

Lexi paused, stuck on Jason's comment about the difficulties of his job. She couldn't tell whether he was referring to rigorous training, time demands, or something else. "So she helped you feel like you'd made the right choice, becoming a mechanic?"

"I knew I made the right choice long before I met Colleen," Jason clarified. "My internal drive wasn't the problem."

"What was the issue, then?"

Jason shrugged. "Most days, I had to climb Mount Everest while the rest of my peers coasted along."

"Because you're so young?"

"Among other factors. It was hard in the beginning. If I made a comment at team meetings, nobody batted an eye. They acted like I wasn't even there."

Lexi swallowed. "Because you're not white?"

"I didn't exactly blend in with all the other mechanics," Jason responded. "The silent treatment was the easy part. It was worse when they criticized or mocked me."

"Damn. I'm sorry," Lexi murmured.

"I knew my shit. Studied for years, passed every exam, got my licenses and certifications in record time. Everyone tried to suck the confidence right out of me. It was exhausting."

"I bet." In some ways, Lexi could relate to the feeling of being attacked by everyone in the room, even the so-called progressives. She knew what it was like to hear coworkers frame their insults as questions. Countless dudes had told her they'd *convert* her, usually in graphic and violent ways. Women weren't much better. They'd insist Lexi wasn't like them, not really. That she was just experimenting, and she would choose a hetero life in the end. There were very few safe spaces for bisexuals. Lexi had received plenty of criticism over the years.

"I didn't have a ton of support," Jason said.

"Colleen was in your corner, though."

"Yeah. For a long time, she was my only friend in aviation."

There should've been more. Lexi observed Jason's smooth skin and piercing eyes. He'd been fearless, rushing to help a dying AR.

He was also open. Vulnerable in a way that made Lexi feel less alone in the world. Jason had Colin's unyielding compassion for others and Jorge's brave self-acceptance. He had something else, too. Something Lexi couldn't put her finger on. Something rare and incredible.

"I'm glad your last memory with her was amazing," Lexi commented. She reached for his arm.

Jason looked up at her, his face a mosaic of grief. Lexi could sense the nostalgia emanating from his skin, a longing and powerlessness that mirrored her own. For once, she didn't need to suffocate those feelings. She wasn't desperate to summon her magic skills. Her time-tested methods felt irrelevant. The irony was that she'd waited a year for this exact moment. Now that it had arrived, she wasn't interested in sliding down a mystical escape hatch. Not with Jason.

The past was written on Jason's face, and the future was embedded in his eyes. The present was somewhere Lexi wanted to be, not because it was distinct from all other realities but because it was interdependent on them.

We're here now. Lexi reveled in the moment. Beneath her skin, anguish and euphoria mingled together. Adrenaline was countered by a distinct sense of loss and authenticity. It felt validating. She was content to simply exist. For once, she was a living, breathing human with an imperfect history she could accept. And a radiant man standing before her.

It felt as if Lexi had woken up from a deep sleep, one that had lasted twelve months. Or eighteen years, depending on how she viewed the situation.

Standing at the intersection of tragedy and a stubborn hope for better days, Lexi felt alive. Without the use of magic. No dissociation necessary.

She pulled Jason toward her, kissing him with something other than her carefully-curated brand of lust. Lexi reached for the thumb sensor on the wall and dimmed the lights. Then she guided Jason to bed.

"Okay, it's not really hidden," Jason confessed as he ran his fingers through Lexi's auburn hair. "It's out in the open. I was just messing with you."

She repositioned her head on his chest so she could see his face. From below, his chin was majestic. The man was sharp lines and angles. Lexi spotted the first hint of a five o'clock shadow on his cheeks. She reached up, grazing the stubble with two fingers. "The hat, you mean? I almost forgot."

Jason laughed. "Hmm, I wonder why. What could have distracted you, Lex?"

She smiled. "No idea. Nothing to see here."

"Nope."

Her stomach rumbled loudly, and she placed a hand over her navel to silence it. "Guess we skipped dinner?"

"Hell no, we just postponed it. Let's get food." Jason pulled a shirt over his head and walked to the dresser. After rifling through the top drawer, he selected a pair of red boxers.

"Oh, gross," Lexi groaned. "You unpack your clothes in hotel drawers? Do you also clap when the plane lands? And drink the *sink water* in hotels?"

Jason lifted an eyebrow as he slid into a pair of shorts. "Are you judging me for using hotel furniture? No, I've never clapped when a plane landed. Yes, I drink sink water. How else do people stay hydrated?"

Lexi sat up in bed wearing only a tank top and sighed dramatically. "Holy crap. I banged a psychopath."

Jason grabbed her shorts off the floor and tossed them at her. Lexi laughed as she tumbled backward, landing on the pillows.

"First time, huh? I almost married one," he noted with a smirk.

"Not sure what would have killed you first, your crazy ex-fiancée or the trash water you drink. Like a peasant."

"Okay, okay. We can buy some bottled water on the way back from dinner," Jason conceded.

"Bad for the environment, duh."

"Sorry. Hemp-canned water."

"Much better." Lexi hopped off the bed, heading for the bathroom. "Where should we go to eat?"

"Anywhere you want," Jason called as Lexi closed the bathroom door behind her.

On the counter, a bottle of champagne rested in an ice bin. The baseball cap sat beside two crystal glasses. In a flourish, Lexi placed the hat on her head. She cracked open the door and turned toward Jason. He was leaning against the dresser, arms folded across his chest.

"Found it," Lexi declared.

"Told you it was an easy spot. Find anything else?"

"A bottle of champs, but I'd be drunk as hell if I drank bubbly right now. Thanks to my empty stomach and our rigorous workout."

Jason stepped closer to her. "Just one glass? We can save the rest for later."

Lexi sighed. "Sure, okay. Twist my arm. Where did you find those glasses? And what are we celebrating?"

"I made a couple friends at the hotel bar. They were grateful I tried to save their buddy."

"It was pretty heroic."

"Not really. I wish I could have done more. Poor guy didn't make it."

Lexi nodded slowly. "I figured as much. At least you tried."

"And failed."

"Effort counts for something, right?" Lexi wished Jason hadn't confirmed the teenager's death. She'd known, without a shadow of a doubt, that the kid was a goner. But it hurt to hear someone verify that ugly truth.

"Shitty outcome, but I'd do it again." Jason cleared his throat. "As for our mini champagne celebration, we're toasting the fact that you're halfway through training."

"Barely made it. There's a good chance I won't survive the

second half of training."

"What? You're crushing it. Best teacher stew I know."

"You don't have to flatter me," Lexi responded with a sly grin. "We already had sex, baby mechanic. Mission accomplished."

"What if I'm hoping for round two?"

Lexi crossed her arms across her chest. "We're too old for that. Last time I did two consecutive rounds, I was twenty-three and tripping balls. She put in most of the effort."

"Don't worry, I'm a hard worker." Jason grinned. "And how are we too old? You said I was the youngest mechanic you'd ever seen."

"The bar was really low," Lexi retorted.

"Ouch."

"Did I mention you were the best-looking mechanic I'd ever seen?"

"No, I would remember that."

"Oh." Lexi cleared her throat. "Well, I don't want to blow up your ego."

"I think there's a compliment hidden in there." Jason chuckled.

"Sure, maybe. I guess we'd better drink this champagne before I get kicked out of training and there's nothing left to celebrate." Lexi paused. "Reggie kept me after class today to scold me. I'm the weakest link. My head's not in the game."

"Hmm. Reggie's a local celebrity, right? The mastermind behind SkyLine's updated training process?"

"Yes, he's been busting his butt for a decade. From what I understand, Reggie worked in San Jose for a while, at the Special Projects Building. A couple years ago, he transferred to Headquarters as the Head of Inflight Training. I'd love to follow a similar path."

"Seems like a decent plan." Jason leaned forward, displaying acute interest in Lexi's fantasy world.

Lexi knew she could never follow Reggie's footsteps, not in real life. She shouldn't have mentioned it. "It won't happen, but that would be my path in an ideal world. A parallel universe that's way different from this one."

"You're already on the right track, though. Don't you have a background in education?"

"I do. Before I got hired at SkyLine, I designed a leadership program for Sac State Community College," Lexi explained. "It was a hybrid class, referencing case studies from different corporations and underappreciated historical figures. I never got to teach. Still, it was cool to lay the groundwork for a brand-new course."

"Why didn't you teach?"

"My brother got sick. When I joined the airline four years ago, my plan was to eventually return to academia part-time. I still feel like that might be my calling. Who knows."

"Sounds like you've thought about this a lot."

Lexi shrugged. "I've had a few sleepless nights. Nobody offered a class when I really needed it, when I was a teenager and my brother tried to hurt himself. Nothing I learned in high school or college helped me cope. There should be practical guides for people. Easy-to-follow support services, like caregiver tutorials or mental health videos. I mean, I learned all about *parallelograms* in high school, but nobody ever mentioned healthy coping skills or family supports for mental illness. Not once."

"You could change that, Lex." Jason was mere inches away from Lexi now, close enough for her to smell traces of peppermint on his tongue. She loved the scent.

"Maybe. We'll see." Lexi said. "I want people to have easy access to important information. Fuck the parallelograms. Let's learn stuff that actually matters. Maybe other people wouldn't have to feel so clueless in difficult times."

Jason was silent for a moment. His eyes met Lexi's,

reflecting a depth of understanding she wasn't used to. "I'm sorry."

No other words followed in the wake of his apology. None were needed. It was as though he grasped the angst of Lexi's teenage years, the lack of resources in a time when she'd felt most helpless. Lexi held Jason's gaze until the empathy became too potent to bear.

She swiveled around, reaching for the bottle of champagne. The cork popped easily, as though the bottle had been waiting all day for that show-stopping occasion.

She filled both glasses with champagne and handed one to Jason.

"Cheers, Lex. To your wild, completely achievable goals. You're going to change things for the better. I can tell."

Lexi shrugged. She clinked her glass against his before taking a modest sip. The bubbles danced in her throat. She tossed back another swig, this one much larger.

"When are you moving to San Diego?" she asked Jason, already feeling a head rush. "God, what a fun city. I went to college there. You're so lucky."

"SkyLine wants me in S.D. right away. I'll move when this training ends. The airplanes are parked in the desert, which is a two-hour drive. The company pays for my hotel on the days I work. And they've approved a permanent transfer to the San Diego base once those AirBirds are patched up and ready to return to the sky."

"Did you buy a home?"

Jason reached over the counter, grabbing the bottle of bubbly. He filled his cup to the brim and gestured toward hers, which was half-empty. Lexi nodded in approval.

"I did," he responded. "A condo in La Playa. I figured if I'm moving to a coastal city, I should live as close to the shore as possible."

"Can't argue with that. I'd love to be near the water.

Sacramento's land locked. It's flat and brown."

"Then come visit me. Get some sand between your toes."

"Not sure I can. Too much stuff going on at home."

"Good thing you can hop on a plane any time you want. Quick weekend getaway? No problem." Jason grinned. "It's nice to fly free."

"True."

"So, it's all set? You'll visit?" Jason set his glass down and leaned against the bathroom counter. Then he pulled her toward him, pressing their hips together. "You can meet my dog, Vella."

Lexi could see her reflection in the mirror behind him, auburn hair tumbling from her SkyLine ballcap. Ruffled white tank top tucked into khaki shorts. Blue scarf encompassing her collarbone. She looked like a softball player from the neck up and a librarian from the neck down.

Jason seemed unaware of her mismatched attire. He stared at her with hopeful eyes, his gaze warming every inch of her skin.

"No promises," Lexi said slowly. "My brother's struggling. I'll have to see how he's doing before I plan any trips."

"Of course. I hope he's okay, Lexi."

"Thank you. Me, too."

"Hey, what do you say we go get some food?"

"I need to change clothes. Meet me in the lobby in fifteen minutes." Lexi kissed Jason and headed out the door.

Lexi's dinner plans were met with suspicious glances. Tamika raised an eyebrow, looking especially smug.

Lexi rolled her eyes at her friends.

"Just you two? Venturing off-campus, huh?" Carrie asked. She reached across her empty plate, stealing a fry from Luis. He slapped her hand jokingly, missing by several inches.

"Yeah, just Jason and me." Lexi nodded toward the

elevators. "He'll be down in a minute. He said there are some good restaurants within walking distance."

"This is officially a date. You guys move fast," Tamika mused.

"Are you two, like, engaged?" Luis asked, lifting an eyebrow.

Lexi folded her arms across her chest. "I've known him twenty-four hours. We're hungry, that's all."

"I bet. By the way, where have you been the past hour?" Tamika asked, a smile tugging at her lips. "I messaged you around seven o'clock, but your GeoTrack showed you going into a room on the fourth floor."

"Yeah, back to my hotel room, obviously." Lexi tried, unsuccessfully, to conceal a grin.

"Except you're on floor six. Same as me," Brandon pointed out. "We walked back to our rooms together the first night. So, Miss Lexi, who were you visiting on the fourth floor? Big mystery."

"Um, the ice machine?" This time, Lexi didn't attempt to hide her smile.

"Right. Took you a full hour to get a couple ice cubes. So much for your no-SkyLine policy." Tamika chuckled.

"That's a dumb policy anyway. Glad you bent the rules," Luis teased, jabbing Lexi's ribcage.

"Lots of things got bent tonight," Brandon quipped.

"Well, there's my exit cue." Lexi nodded toward the hotel entrance. Jason had stepped off the elevator and was standing beside a coffee table, hands in his pockets. Lexi hurried toward the lobby without looking back.

Jason greeted her with a broad smile. "I was worried I'd get stood up."

"Not a chance, baby mechanic. I'm starving." They stepped through the double doors together, entering the humid Central Florida night.

"What are you in the mood for?" Jason asked. "There's a fusion pop-up across the street, a Mediterranean place, a Mexican restaurant, a steakhouse . . ."

"Mexican food sounds good."

"Perfect." Jason took her hand. As they advanced toward a small restaurant with pink shutters, he filled her in on his training. He described the instructor's comical, slightly indifferent attitude as well as the temperament of the other mechanics in his class.

Jason's story was punctuated by the occasional roar of an airplane overhead. Glancing up, Lexi spotted the distinct red-and-black belly of several SkyLine planes. The AirBirds descended in intricate patterns, performing a synchronized dance through Orlando's airspace.

"It's pretty," Lexi noted, jutting her chin toward the sky. "Poetic, right? The way the planes weave around each other?"

Jason smiled as they approached the restaurant. "Never thought of it that way, but yes, it's nice."

"Or I'm just tipsy."

"Or that. Let's get some food in you, Lexi."

Lexi drenched a tortilla chip in queso. A trail of cheese led from the center of the table directly to her plate. Laughing, she wiped the mess with a crumpled napkin.

"Might as well drink the bowl," Jason noted.

"Don't tempt me. I'm starving. Someone got me toasted before I had any food in my stomach."

"Really? He sounds like an ass."

Lexi nodded solemnly. "Now that you mention it, he *does* have a nice ass."

Their waiter dropped off two enchiladas and a platter of fajitas. Billows of steam rose from the cast-iron skillet. The scent was heavenly. Lexi eyed the food, contemplating which item to try first. Everything looked good.

"Let me help," Jason suggested as though reading her mind. He piled vegetables and beef on top of a wheat tortilla. "Here you go."

Lexi leaned back, sinking into the plush booth. She devoured her food like a starved animal. Jason ate slowly, she noticed. His thoughtful bites contrasted sharply with her ravenous ones. He appeared to be enjoying the scenery. Taking his time.

When the bill illuminated the center of the table, Jason extended his thumb.

"Let me pay," Lexi insisted, holding up her phone like a trophy. "You bought drinks last night. And a SkyLine baseball cap today. Plus a bottle of champagne. You've basically paid for everything since I arrived in Orlando."

Jason grinned. "Put that phone back in your pocket. Really, Lex, it's embarrassing."

"Your sexism is embarrassing," she shot back, chuckling.

Jason stuck his thumb in the center of the table and waited for the scanner to read its grooves. Then he returned his attention to Lexi. "This isn't because you're a woman. You've had a rough week, so I want to treat you."

He placed a hand on her knee. The restaurant grew dim and quiet, fading to oblivion until Jason's sculpted face was all she could see. His brown eyes cast a beam through the darkness.

"You probably do this with every flight attendant you meet," Lexi teased.

"I've been in a relationship with an emergency room nurse the entire time I've worked at SkyLine, so I can assure you that's false."

"Good thing Miss Talia hates your guts now, huh?"

"Yeah. Thank God. I got dumped just in time to connect with an incredible teacher stew."

"Incredible might be an overstatement. *Meh* is more my

specialty."

"I don't believe you. But okay," Jason said, shrugging. "Let's get out of here. I can message Renee to see where the pilots and dispatchers are. Want to meet them for drinks?"

"That sounds fun. Or we can finish the bottle of champagne in your room."

"I like that plan."

Hand in hand, they coasted through the night. Stars shimmered overhead. Jason's fingers kept Lexi anchored as a warm breeze whipped her hair across her face. Through unruly auburn tresses, she spotted the taillights of a SkyLine plane. Tiny white dots floated toward the runway, majestic in their return to solid ground.

Jason pulled Lexi close as they slid through the hotel's double doors, entering the hotel lobby. There were no airline employees in sight, just a receptionist with her eyes glued to a Holoscreen and an elderly couple holding long-stem wine glasses.

Jason held his thumb to the elevator sensor, setting off an array of lights and dings. Lexi sighed contentedly. As she exhaled, she realized she'd been holding her breath for quite some time. She'd gotten caught up in the moment, basking in her post-entanglement glow.

"I know this week has been intense," Jason murmured. "Wish I could help."

"Maybe you can," Lexi said.

"Good," Jason replied as they coasted upward, ascending to the fourth floor. "Whatever you need, just say the word."

"Champagne is a great start."

"Easy enough. You'll have a full glass soon."

Inside his hotel room, Jason poured two glasses, draining the bottle. They sat on the bed, cradling their cups like trophies. Jason's leg grazed hers. Lexi sipped her drink and pretended not to notice the spot where skin met skin.

"Stay here tonight," Jason suggested.

Lexi gulped down her champagne, placing the empty glass on the nightstand. "Maybe I'm not as old as I thought. Round two?"

Jason set his glass on the floor, a few inches from their feet. Lexi accidentally knocked it over when she leaned into him. She gasped as the cold liquid spilled over her toes. Champagne trickled onto the carpet, creating a fizzy lake that was absorbed by the plush fabric.

"It's okay," Jason said quickly. "Don't worry about it."

He wrapped an arm around her back, guiding her toward him. She kissed him passionately, a kiss that he returned with equal fervor.

Jason's hands migrated to her waist. They lingered there before inching toward her chest. Lexi pulled them up eagerly. She closed her eyes to savor the feeling. Without wasting any time, she hoisted herself onto Jason's lap.

In a flourish, she pulled her tank top over her head. Then she reached for Jason's shirt. Their clothes landed in a messy heap beside the bed, dangerously close to the champagne-soaked wet spot.

"These need to go," Lexi demanded, reaching for the waistband of his jeans. Jason rose to his feet. Lexi unbuttoned his pants and slid them off. Meanwhile, Jason caressed her cheek with his thumb.

Lexi's EarLink buzzed with an incoming call, startling her. An unfamiliar number with a 916-area code flashed across her cornea. GeoTrack traced the call to Midtown Sacramento.

"Shit," she muttered. "It's someone back home. I need to take this." She scooted to the edge of the bed, facing the door. Every hair on her neck was raised.

Lexi swallowed and tapped her ear. "Hello, this is Alexis."

"Hi, Lex."

"Colin!" she exclaimed. "Where are you?"

"Someone smuggled an old-ass phone into the hospital. It's from ten years ago, at least. Limited AutoScan functions. Sorry, I don't have much time." His speech was clipped. "There're after me, Lex. But I'm safe now. Sorry I ruined your week."

"My week isn't ruined, kid. Don't apologize."

"But this is your training session. It's a big moment for you."

"I don't care. I just want you to be okay."

Colin inhaled sharply. "They chased me down. Coming here was my only option. The pills were a ruse. Even though I'm low on the list, they caught up with me."

"What list? I don't understand." Lexi gnawed on her lip so Colin wouldn't hear her strained breathing. She was halfway between a scream and a sigh.

From behind her, Jason draped his t-shirt over her shoulders and chest. He wrapped an arm around her side, a much-welcomed sign of solidarity. She clutched the shirt to her body, suddenly cold wearing only a bra and panties. A chill traveled down her spine.

"It's a mess," Colin said.

"That's okay. I'm here for you, kid. You're going to be fine."

"You don't know that."

"We've had rough patches before, Colin. You've always pulled through. I'll help however I can."

"This is different. It's worse. I can't escape the consequences."

Lexi sucked in a breath of air. "Consequences?"

"Sometimes I can power through it, you know? Tuck aside the worry. Like, fuck them and fuck their list of targets." Colin continued, ignoring her question. "But then the pressure builds. It becomes too heavy. I'm a magnet for bad things, Lexi. Even when I'm trying to make a difference in the world.

They hunted me like a wild animal. They almost got me. They came so close."

"What do you mean, Colin? *Hunted?*"

"You wouldn't understand."

"Try me, kid." Lexi silently pleaded for her brother to open up. She begged him to disclose his paranoid delusions, as though saying them aloud could erase them from existence. Colin had been frantic before, so this wasn't an isolated incident. He'd dealt with hallucinations, which he called *visions*. Obsessive images of his own demise. This time felt worse, as though the illness had progressed. He'd been on medication. At least, that was what he'd told Lexi. He was showing up for work. For months at a time, things had felt promising.

"I can handle it," Lexi said quietly.

Colin's breathing was quick and shallow. "Too dangerous. I'll explain when I see you. Everything fell apart. This is how my life works. It always ends the same, Lex."

Lexi closed her eyes and steadied herself against Jason's embrace. "I know it hurts. Marco left a big hole in your heart. But there's something you're forgetting. What about all the folks who love you?" Her voice came out weak and wobbly, like a small animal attempting to stand for the first time.

AutoScan – Switch to transdermal scan mode for 916 number, she demanded. *I'm with you through it all, Colin. So are Mom and Dad. You have amazing friends. Things will get better. They always do. And we are with you whether it's a good day or a bad one or a mix of both.*

She sent the soliloquy with a double blink. A buzz echoed in her ear, reminding her Colin's smuggled phone predated AutoScan functions.

"This is different," Colin whispered. "It's not about Marco. Please believe me, Lex. This is bigger. Marco couldn't handle the pressure, so he left. It's for the best. There's too much at stake. He could have been killed. You and Mom and Dad, too. These people are ruthless."

"Your mind's tricking you," Lexi assured her brother. "Nobody's going to get hurt. This is like a bad dream. Fortunately, you're stronger than your nightmares. You are not alone, Colin. So many people care about you."

A door creaked in the background, leading to a flurry of indecipherable activity.

"Shit, I thought I disabled the microcameras. The staff must have seen something. Gotta go. Just wanted to say I'm sorry. And don't worry. They can't break into the hospital, not with the protocols these days. I'm safe here."

Lexi sighed. Was her brother ever safe, really? "I love you, Colin."

A dull thud sounded in Lexi's ear, signaling the call had ended.

Lexi sat still. She pressed one hand to her chest, clutching Jason's shirt like a blanket. The other hand trembled on her lap.

"It's okay," Jason said from behind her. "I'm here with you."

His arm gripped her tightly, a pillar keeping her upright.

Lexi turned to face him. He was sitting on the corner of the bed, still only wearing his boxers. "Sorry you had to hear all that drama."

Jason smiled, a sincere grin that dissolved some of the discomfort in Lexi's chest. "I have an ex-fiancée praying I get punched in the face. Drama is my specialty."

"Your drama sounds like the exciting kind," Lexi noted with a dry laugh. "As opposed to the paranoid delusional kind. Hallucinations. Erratic behavior. What did the therapist call it? Deteriorated functioning or something."

The t-shirt fell to the floor as she snuggled against Jason, burying her face in his neck.

Jason ran his hands along her arms. "You're cold, Lex. Goosebumps everywhere."

"Yeah."

"I'll get your shirt."

While Lexi watched, Jason grabbed her tank top from the floor.

She inched toward him and accepted the clothing in his arms. Once her shirt was over her head, she placed a hand on Jason's side, gratitude emanating from each fingertip. He turned to pick up her shorts, crumpled beside the patch of rug still damp with champagne. The ridges of Jason's back came into view. The man was impossibly toned. Lexi stared at the impressive contours, the perfect symmetry of his body.

She was about to open her mouth when a smudge on Jason's shoulder caught her eye.

No.

No, no, no.

She squinted, disbelief flooding her veins. Jason's back displayed two letters, more faded than most but every bit as ominous.

There was no way to reconcile the distinctive symbol with the man she had gotten to know the past few days. The man she'd climbed into bed with just a few hours earlier.

"Holy shit," she growled. "What is wrong with you?"

Jason looked up at her in surprise.

"Your tattoo," Lexi hissed. "Where's your mouthguard? Armband? *We had sex,* Jason. Are you insane?"

"Slow down. I can explain, Lexi."

"You made me responsible for your life. Not to mention tons of others. How dare you?"

"Please listen. It's not what you think."

"Is this a joke to you, asshole?"

"No, it's not." Jason's eyes filled with something Lexi couldn't distinguish. Regret, maybe? Disappointment over the fact that he'd been caught in a lie?

A familiar gnawing emanated from Lexi's core. She placed a hand on her chest. She could feel the uproar rising to the surface.

She bit the inside of her cheek. Hard. The last thing she wanted was to unleash any laughter. Jason might assume he was off the hook, forgiven for his heinous deception. She stabbed her nails into her thighs, releasing only when she was about to pierce the skin.

Lexi snatched her shorts from Jason's hand, pulling them so quickly that she scraped his skin in the process. Tiny white lines appeared on Jason's wrist. Lexi was an expert in skin depth and the possibility of drawing blood. The scrapes were just deep enough to slice the innermost layer of dermis, she knew.

In a few moments, Jason would bleed. Only a couple drops, Lexi guessed. But enough to cause increased exposure. Higher odds of transmission.

As Jason stepped toward Lexi, she lifted a shaky hand to stop him in his tracks. "How could you hide your AR status from me? How could you put that weight on my shoulders without my knowledge? You're disgusting."

She sprinted from the room, slamming the door behind her. The noise echoed down the hall like an explosion. Inside the elevator, she held her trembling hand above several buttons. She arrived on the first floor after a few unnecessary stops.

The lobby was empty. Lexi darted toward the double doors, uncertain what time it was or where she was going or what, if anything, could calm the angry tempest in her soul. She exited the hotel without looking back.

"Shit!" Jason exclaimed to nobody, tempted to punch a hole in the wall. His fingers shook at his side. He balled both hands into fists, then released them slowly.

He should have told her sooner.

He meant to say something to Lexi, but things had escalated quickly. He'd barely been able to catch his breath. He wasn't expecting the afternoon to unfold the way it did. It had been so long since Jason was intimate with anyone. Talia hadn't had sex with him for months before their split.

Lexi had caught him by surprise in the best possible way. Afterward, at dinner, he'd felt calm, almost peaceful. It was as though he'd found all the best emotions, the ones that had been ripped away by the meteor shower, then ContaCan.

Briefly, the hurt from the past year seemed a little less heavy. It was still there, sure, but it wasn't the unbearable burden it had been for so long. The bricks on his shoulders were lighter.

He'd floated back to the hotel, high on adrenaline and tequila. *What a rush.* Jason hadn't been thinking straight. His permanent battle wound hadn't crossed his mind. He was too focused on the moment, the sensation of Lexi's hand wrapped in his.

Jason exhaled loudly, racked with anger over his mistake.

He'd botched this. Badly. Lexi's forgiveness was unlikely, he knew. People weren't very kind when it came to ARs. There were no second chances.

He'd felt the wrath of the hotel's security guards on Monday, after removing his shirt in the sanitation room. He had anticipated their disapproving looks, their judgment. But tonight was so much worse. Lexi's opinion mattered to him. She wasn't just a faceless stranger. Not anymore.

And Jason had ruined everything. He should've told her the truth. Hours ago. Before they fell into bed together. He could have prevented a fallout like this by simply being honest.

Lexi felt betrayed, Jason knew. She'd said some terrible things, all of which were valid. In her eyes, he was a liar. Possibly a sociopath. Jason couldn't blame her for the accusations she'd hurled at him. He deserved them all.

A buzzing erupted from the dresser. When Jason turned toward the noise, he realized Lexi had left her phone in his room. He picked up the device. Apparently, she'd summoned AutoScan for a few searches. The app had a two-mile radius, which meant Lexi couldn't have gone very far. Her search results flashed across the screen. These lines of text would also skate across her cornea.

The search was deeply personal. Jason understood exactly what Lexi had been looking for. The internet was providing answers to questions she'd been scared to ask previously. Anger could make a person bold, Jason knew. Fury had prompted Lexi to investigate the matter.

Jason placed the phone back on the dresser, worried he'd invaded Lexi's privacy. She was searching for statistics, desperate to find the odds of transmitting something terrible to Jason. She wanted to know if his untimely death would be her fault. If an endless river of clotted blood would be on her hands.

The screen illuminated again. Even from a few feet away, Jason could see Lexi had summoned another list.

Curiosity chipped away at him.

He inhaled sharply, weighing his options. He'd already screwed up as much as possible, right? Glancing at her current AutoScan activity couldn't make things worse, he figured. Nothing could deepen the massive hole he'd dug for himself.

He reached for her phone again. This time, a new list of names filled the screen.

Why choose this database? What are you looking for, Lex?

And then he saw it.

The air whooshed from Jason's chest. He wished that he could hold Lexi in that very moment. This information would wreck her, he knew. She would crumble to the ground, and nobody would be there to break her fall.

Chapter Nine

Swarms of bugs surrounded Lexi as she marched to the main thoroughfare. A crescent moon peeked behind wispy white fingers. Lexi lowered her head and quickened her pace.

He could have died.

He probably will.

Painfully.

News clips flashed through her head. Spouses who unintentionally killed their partners before anyone understood that a gene mutation makes certain people resistant to the antidote. Mothers and fathers whose children perished in their arms. College kids who buried their roommates, then withdrew from society altogether. It wasn't easy to carry that weight. Human interactions made less sense after causing a friend's quick, gory demise.

Lexi retraced her steps that afternoon. She and Jason had used protection. Still, there was a ton of exposure. Lots of skin-to-skin contact. Various exchanges of bodily fluids. They'd kissed for a long time. They'd spent hours together in close quarters. The risk level was absurd.

Cracked sidewalk greeted Lexi as she approached Semoran Boulevard. She made a split-second decision to turn left. Patting the pocket of her shorts, she realized she'd left her phone in Jason's room.

With no access to money, she pressed on. A shopping plaza stretched before her. Cheerful storefronts sparkled beneath the raven sky.

AutoScan – Quick Search: odds of transmitting ContaCan to an antidote-resistant human. No mouth guard. Hours spent together in confined spaces. Secondary search: odds of antidote-compatible person contracting ContaCan.

She held her breath. A stream of beeps indicated an internet search was underway.

As soon as the articles floated across her cornea, Lexi closed out of the search. Her heart pounded in her ears, a violent and dizzying roar. Each article was too horrific. She wanted to know. Then again, she did *not* want to know.

Of all the terrible roles she'd played in her life, being a potential murderer was the worst. By a mile. This wasn't a romantic tryst gone bad, an ex-girlfriend with a vengeance. Lexi could laugh off those incidents. She was no angel, but everyone calmed down in the end. People moved on. Lexi chased the next cheap thrill, and the globe continued spinning.

This time, Jason would probably die.

And before that grisly moment, there could be other deaths triggered by exposure. It all traced back to Lexi. She'd been unknowingly placed at the top of a very macabre chain.

Lexi practiced deep breaths as she advanced toward twinkling storefronts. She sat down on a bench beside a bustling, ultra-modern coffee shop. A family gathered at a table in front of a retro red-and-white bakery next door. One kid, a little girl with her hair in a braid, licked an oversized ice cream cone. Drops of vanilla soft-serve tumbled to the ground as the dessert melted.

People milled around the trendy dive bar at the opposite end of the plaza. They shared antioxidant steam-vapes, laughs, and hugs. Lexi was mesmerized by these strangers. She wondered how anyone could possibly experience joy in that exact moment. She felt like an alien observing emotions she couldn't embody. Mirth was a foreign concept, something that belonged to a different species.

Laughter rumbled inside her core. It began as a persistent itch, an ongoing tension. A gnat she couldn't swat. Just when she thought it had fluttered away, the buzzing resumed.

Lexi sighed. If she could talk to someone, really dive headfirst into a conversation, the sensation would fade.

She considered dialing her mother. Since Lexi was within AutoScan radius, she could access all her contacts without her phone. She could chat with Erin Brennan and relay Colin's phone call. She could explain the desperation in his voice, his frantic pleas. The fierce belief that he was being targeted by ruthless and nameless strangers.

But Lexi knew her mother didn't need to hear all that shit. The woman had been through enough already.

Calling Katie wasn't an option, either. Lexi wasn't ready to inform her best friend that she'd become a murderer. Without her consent.

"Damn," Lexi murmured aloud. The word floated away like a tepid Florida breeze.

She thought back to her PersonableSpin session with Jorge. He was the only person she would have felt comfortable pouring her heart out to.

J.R. would understand. He'd always dropped everything to talk to Lexi during the worst moments. The ones where she thought she'd lost Colin for good.

Lexi had hit the best friend lottery with Jorge, she knew. He was one of a kind. He could never be replaced, and that was something she'd just have to live with. Her kindred spirit was gone forever.

Laughter got the best of Lexi. She buckled over, chuckling until she couldn't breathe. She was aware of strangers' eyes on her, yet nobody came close. Lexi howled until there was nothing left inside. By the end, she was dizzy from exertion. She hunched forward with her hands tucked behind her knees, her throat achy and tired. Only then did she realize she was crying.

She straightened herself. Rubbed her eyes. Reached for a

tissue to soak up the liquid. To her dismay, her pockets were empty. She needed Jorge. He would have mitigated the laughter as well as the tears.

In a flash, Lexi remembered his request from earlier in the evening. Rather, his avatar's request. The rest of the night had unfolded so quickly. In the blink of an eye, really. She hadn't had a chance to follow through with her promise.

AutoScan – Quick Search: Emergency Expulsion Registry. List of names, sorted by most recent.

Lexi had no clue what to look for. She started at the top of the list. None of the names looked familiar. She was baffled by how many US residents had been deported because of a genetic trait they couldn't control. One flipped chromosome, and they were sent back to countries they'd only seen as infants.

She sighed. "What am I supposed to find, J.R.?"

The database had a *friend-of-friend* option at the top right corner, which Lexi found extremely messed up. How many people had searched for once-removed contacts? Too many, apparently. Folks must have been curious to see if distant acquaintances or family members were on the list.

Lexi highlighted the link in one swift movement. She blinked twice to activate the filter.

And then she saw it.

Antonio Rodrigues, D.O.B. 10/07/2006. Resistant gene detected in blood sample on 05/22/2038. Forcibly expelled to Mexico City, MEX on 06/01/2038.

Lexi's AutoScan alerted her to an incoming call from Jason. She swiped it away with a flick of her eye. He followed up with a text.

You left your phone in my room. I'm sorry about tonight, Lex. I can explain.

Lexi contemplated drafting a response, but she couldn't make it past the first word. Frustration brewed in her chest.

Another text from Jason flashed across her cornea.

Are you safe? Your GeoTrack is off, but I'll come meet you anywhere. Please, Lexi.

She rose to her feet. Her legs were heavy. Two concrete pillars, nearly impossible to lift. She trudged along, compelling her body to move forward. As she approached the hotel, she dug her left hand into her thigh. The pain lifted her. She loosened her grip before her nails plunged too far. There was no need to draw blood tonight, especially with a known AR nearby.

The hotel's double doors slid open gracefully, welcoming her back to the building capable of doubling as a safe haven and torture chamber. All in one night.

Lexi composed the shortest text possible.

I'm back. Hotel lobby.

A receptionist sat behind the front desk with her long blonde hair swept over one shoulder. The lobby was otherwise vacant. Along the far wall, there were a few empty chairs arranged in a semi-circle. Marble coffee tables and leather couches had been positioned to face each other, forming a secluded cove in one corner of the room. Elevator music played quietly in the background. Everyone had either gone to the bar or gone to bed, Lexi guessed.

Jason's response cruised across Lexi's cornea.

On my way. I'll bring your phone.

Lexi marched toward the cluster of armchairs and selected the one that looked most comfortable. She sank into the plush fabric.

Seconds passed by in a flurry, as rapid as Lexi's heartbeat. When she looked up, Jason was walking her direction. He grabbed a seat beside her.

Lexi pointed to an armchair several feet away. "Over there."

Jason glanced at the chair, then looked back at Lexi with somber eyes. His forehead creased, delicate grooves emanating from a single hard line in the center. He opened his mouth to speak, then promptly closed it. Wordlessly, he placed the cell phone on her knee.

"Hear me out," Jason pleaded. "First of all, no more secrets. I saw the searches you ran. I wasn't spying on you. The buzzing caught my attention. And I was hoping for clues about where you went. It's late, you know? You were out there by yourself. No phone."

"Great. Then you saw that I was researching the odds of infecting an AR," she said, her voice pure ice.

"Yes, I saw that. I know you're worried."

She narrowed her eyes. "Not worried. Pissed."

Jason sighed. His shoulders slumped. "Listen, I screwed up. I should have warned you about my tattoo."

"You think?" Lexi scoffed. She folded her arms across her chest.

"It's just some ink on my shoulder. It means nothing. I went to the ER when I tore my Achilles in May. They ran a bunch of tests. All the usual stuff, X-rays, and bloodwork. Referred me to a specialist to schedule my surgery."

Lexi unfolded her arms. A kink had formed in her neck, a knot she hadn't noticed earlier in the evening. She tilted her head side to side, attempting to dissolve the tension.

"My fiancée worked at that emergency room." Jason continued. "*Ex*-fiancée, sorry. She walked me through the whole thing. Back then, the ContaCan blocker was brand-new. Most people didn't have access to the antidote. It was only available to certain folks, remember?"

Lexi nodded. She leaned back and listened.

"Before surgery, they needed to administer the antidote. It was a precautionary measure. In the early stages, doctors didn't run multiple tests. They didn't have much experience with false positives. One quick blood draw indicated I had resistant tendencies, so the medical staff assumed I was an AR. I got a tattoo that day. Talia insisted. She meant well. She'd seen the way ARs were treated in the beginning. They received the best care. It was beneficial to be resistant back then."

"I remember that phase," Lexi added quietly. "We got Colin tested for the gene."

"Yeah. That period didn't last long. Within days, ARs flooded every hospital in every major city. They died so fast. Their bodies couldn't process the antidote. This type of cure . . . it had never been tested before. The human race had never seen a space pathogen like ContaCan, so it was ground zero."

"It was a piecemeal fix," Lexi reflected. "Rushed and a little uncertain, but mostly effective. Except for ARs."

Jason nodded. "ContaCan needed to be contained. It was the best solution anyone could come up with. It's not perfect, though."

"They didn't have much time. Humans might have gone extinct if they'd waited," Lexi noted. "This space shit came out of left field. It didn't have the same chemical properties as stuff here on Earth, from what I read."

"Right. An unrecognizable space germ, not alive and not dead, with the potential to wipe out humanity. That's why some people speculated it was alien warfare." Jason let out a breath, low and slow.

Lexi's anger had begun to melt away. She was tired of pouring so much energy into loathing someone, even if the guy deserved it. She took a deep breath. "Do you think aliens sent ContaCan?"

Jason tilted his head to the side. "I wasn't sure at first. As things unfolded, I realized human beings are perfectly capable of destroying ourselves without any help. The hatred and malice, well, that comes from our species. It's easy to blame some outer-space creature we've never seen. The truth is, we tend to be our own worst enemy."

Lexi fell silent. She'd heard the insults hurled at Colin over the years, the bullying he endured for being sensitive and different. She'd also witnessed the impact of Jorge's family dysfunction. Everyone had abandoned him for being gay. None of it made sense. The hostility people were capable of exuding, it was unfathomable. Jason's logic seemed accurate. Aliens were the least of anyone's concerns, Lexi figured. There were enough villains already here on Earth, enough humans powered solely by disdain.

"So it was a series of unfortunate events, most likely," Lexi surmised. "No culprit. No alien warfare. Just bad luck."

"Extremely bad luck," Jason said. "I mean, didn't those giant-ass meteors cause enough damage? Fires, explosions, the whole nine yards? They took down a legend. They killed Captain Colleen. Then ContaCan intensified the nightmare."

"I thought the night the sky collapsed would be the worst fucking moment of my life. I was wrong," Lexi reflected.

Jason glanced at something Lexi couldn't see, a flicker of light near the front door. Or perhaps nothing at all. "It happened so fast. ContaCan wasn't even a threat before SkyLine's memorial service, the Celebration of Life. I mean, it *was* a threat. We just didn't know it yet."

"Until we got sent home. Ground transportation only. Contactless pods."

Jason nodded. "And then the world completely fell apart. The best cure they could find, a hormone-based immunomodulator, didn't work for people with a certain genetic code."

Against her will, Lexi cracked a half-smile. "Are you mansplaining the antidote to me, Jason?"

Jason hung his head. "Shit, sorry. Most people don't know the details. I nerd out when I talk about it. A lot of stuff went over my head until I turned up positive on the preliminary AR test. Then I couldn't afford to *not* pay attention. My life depended on it."

"I'm just being a dick," Lexi said, her smile fading as she met Jason's gaze. She couldn't justify what he'd done tonight. On the flip side, she knew he wasn't a malicious person. In his eyes, she saw care and concern. "Honestly, I only know the basics. Just enough info to keep me and my family safe. Everything beyond that is hazy. I only look things up when random incidents happen before my eyes."

Like when that chick collapsed in a bloody heap in front of my apartment.

She'd crumbled to the ground, convulsed, bled from very visible orifice. And then she was gone. Each millisecond felt like a year. Lexi had been truly powerless, staring in shock from two stories above. She saw the girl take a final, desperate gulp of air. Lexi couldn't remember the woman's name, but that image? It would stay with her forever, she knew. No matter how hard she tried to erase it.

Despite the pleasantly warm air in the hotel lobby, Lexi shivered.

"ContaCan is confusing as hell," Jason murmured, his voice low.

"Took me a few months to realize it isn't really cancer," Lexi noted.

"Most people aren't aware of that, even after all this time. It was named *Contagious Cancer* because it mimicked a fast-acting, communicable type of cancer. In truth, it's more of a flesh-eating disease." Jason scratched his head. "Am I still mansplaining?"

"Yeah. Boring as hell, but at least I'll sleep well tonight." Lexi faked a yawn.

"Well, that's a win. Maybe you'll hate me less if I'm responsible for the most satisfying sleep of your life," Jason commented, his eyes filling with something Lexi couldn't put her finger on. Hope, maybe. Or redemption.

"Don't get too excited. You're in the doghouse, baby mechanic. But I don't hate your guts anymore. I just dislike them."

"Sounds like progress."

Lexi resisted the urge to grin. The boulder in her stomach felt lighter. She could breathe again without choking. "You know, it seemed like a victory when the antidote was created. Like maybe things would finally improve. I never imagined a whole group of people would be unable to process the cure."

"Same. Once the shot came out, I thought we were safe."

"Buh-bye, miserable space pathogen."

"It was a celebration. Everyone got jabbed in a hurry. We thought we were in the clear, until some folks continued to catch the pathogen. They died so quickly," Jason reflected in one breath.

Lexi had read some of those articles. After a few days, she'd silenced the VirtuAlarms because they were too devastating. Only bad news. "Scary shit."

"Yeah. And really messed up," Jason said. "ARs were blamed for ContaCan mutations, even though half the country hadn't gotten the antidote yet. ARs became everyone's favorite scapegoat. Deportations. Apartment evictions. Job terminations. College admissions rescinded. They had nowhere to go. They were banned from most hospitals."

Lexi swallowed. "Did you see my second search tonight? Did you understand it?"

"I think so. That's the same last name as your best friend, right? His brother, I'm guessing?"

"Twin. Identical twin."

"Shit."

"Yeah." Lexi looked down at her hands. "They stopped talking when Jorge came out. That was a few years before he started flying for SkyLine. Jorge's relatives were very traditional and religious. They disowned him for being gay. Which still infuriates me."

"That's how you ended up with his cat, huh?"

Lexi nodded. "Jorge's family abandoned him years ago. Never thought I'd be a cat mom, but here we are."

"Here we are."

"Anyway, Antonio was an AR. He was forcibly sent back to Mexico in June," Lexi explained. "Jorge would've been one, since their DNA is identical. Never in a million years did I ever think I'd say this, but maybe it was for the best J.R. died in the meteor shower. I wouldn't want him to see what this world turned into. Other countries send all their ARs into abandoned buildings, right? Just round them up and leave them to die."

"Not just other countries, Lex," Jason said quietly. He reached across the chair, grabbing Lexi's hand.

Lexi tilted her chin up, allowing herself to look directly at him. He held her gaze.

"When I went in for my Achilles surgery, the doctors ran additional tests," Jason said. "Turns out I carry a similar AR gene. However, I'm not resistant to the antidote. The first test was a false positive. I was given the ContaCan antidote on the spot, and guess what? It worked. I survived. I'm not resistant. I tried removing the tattoo once ARs started getting backlash. I only completed two sessions."

"And that's when the government made tattoo removal illegal," Lexi murmured, filling in the blanks.

"Exactly. And then everything went downhill. Human rights organizations fought like mad, but they couldn't win that battle. The administration mandated all ARs get tattooed. They made it illegal to remove those tattoos. Politicians paved the way for systemic discrimination by forcing ARs to make themselves identifiable. They changed the laws. Rewrote the Constitution. Criminalized a genetic anomaly."

"Damn. I never met anyone who went through all this crap," Lexi reflected. "When the antidote was released, I had a lot on my mind. Between Colin's struggles and the recession and the possibility that SkyLine might go bankrupt, I was stressed to the max."

"Understandable."

"There was also the looming possibility I would catch ContaCan and die," Lexi continued. "Friends from college, teachers from high school, and neighbors in my apartment complex were killed by the pathogen. The truth is that AR issues hadn't stood out to me. I just saw it as another terrible event in a really terrible year."

"You're not alone. Most people looked the other way, which is why the AR situation got worse and worse." Jason stared at something in the distance, his expression grim. "Everyone was in survival mode. That can make people a little self-centered."

"Lame excuse," Lexi whispered, her comment aimed mostly at herself. "Jorge would've been among the folks deported. I didn't do anything when the government cracked down on ARs. No letters to my senators. No donations to the groups fighting for civil liberties. I didn't even try, Jason."

"You didn't know how bad it was."

"Because I didn't pay attention," Lexi clarified. "I saw some of the VirtuAlarms about ARs being harassed and assaulted. I wrote them off as isolated incidents. You know, a few bullies on a power trip. I'm glad J.R. wasn't around to see that godawful mess."

Jason nodded. "It's brutal. I keep VirtuDocs on me that explain I'm not actually an AR. My database profile contains a whole section describing my health status. Even after people see the medical records, they're still suspicious I'm hiding something. I'm treated like a serial killer."

"Can't DefenderTech fix your database profile? And what about that skin grafting thing, the three-dimensional organ printing?" Lexi said, her thoughts racing. "Is that an option? DefenderTech should be working on this."

"They're doing what they can, but my problems are small in comparison. People are hurt and killed every day. ARs are hunted like wild animals."

The word echoed in Lexi's mind. *Hunted.* It was the term Colin had tossed around during his phone call.

"For what it's worth, I wasn't mad that you were an AR," Lexi explained, suddenly desperate to justify her behavior. "I was angry that you lied to me. You made me responsible for your health and safety, without informing me of that risk. What if you'd caught ContaCan through me? I could've harmed you simply by being near you. I could have—"

"You didn't do any of those things," Jason interjected. "Because I'm not resistant, Lexi. I should have shown you my paperwork and warned you about my tattoo. I dropped the ball. I didn't put you in a dangerous situation, though. I wouldn't do that."

Lexi bit her lip, unable to form a coherent sentence.

"If I were a real AR, would I have tried to save that waiter on Monday night? Also, would SkyLine have sent me to a special training at Headquarters, in close quarters with tons of strangers?" he asked.

"No. That's a fair point. I'm still convinced I was chosen to teach because I was one of the first flight attendants to get the antidote. The doctors raved about my response. I felt superhuman when they ran my bloodwork."

"How many antidotes have you gotten?"

"Four rounds so far. I'll go in for a fifth next week. Originally, my plan was to go with Colin. Now I'll have to see how his schedule plays out. How many have you gotten?"

"I took my fifth dose a couple weeks ago," Jason said. "Look, if I were an AR, it would be damn near impossible to spend time at Headquarters. I'd have to wear a mouth guard and arm patch. Take a daily cocktail of preventative anti-viral meds and stick to a rigid diet. I'd never be able to eat at the

SkyLine cafeteria. The company would track all my interactions, which is difficult and costly in a setting like this."

Jason paused, then looked her straight in the eye. "But all that is beside the point. I would tell people, Lexi. I wouldn't hide my status from the folks I care about. The stakes are too high."

"People would have to live with the guilt of infecting you. Plus, they'd give ContaCan the chance to evolve again. Meaning we would all have to go in for another round of antidotes. And those who didn't get the newest one could get sick," Lexi said, playing out the scenario to its most violent end.

"Exactly. How could I put that much pressure on anyone? But this is all hypothetical since I'm not resistant to the antidote. I couldn't explain that because you ran off. Grabbed your clothes and left."

Lexi bit her lip. "I need to tell you something, Jason. Maybe it will clarify why I freaked out."

Lexi scrolled through her photos, searching for her favorite picture of Colin. It was taken during college, second semester of junior year. She'd almost failed that term. Half the semester was spent in Sacramento, begging her friends to send notes from the classes she'd missed. She cheated on a big exam. Her presence at home had been more important than cramming for an Advanced Educational Technology final.

She sent Jason the photo through AutoScan so he could view the picture in vivid detail.

In the photo, Colin's skinny arm was wrapped around Lexi. She was leaning into his shoulder, smiling like a fool. Their parents' dog, Monty, sat at their feet. Colin was squinting in the sunlight. It was the first day of a new treatment program. On that day, in that exact moment, the whole family clung to shreds of hope. They all believed maybe—just maybe—Colin's life would smooth out. Maybe his phobias would ease up.

"That was a really good day," Lexi said slowly. The words churned inside her, begging to be released into the atmosphere. She hadn't shared this with many people. Jorge had known, of course, but he was long gone. "Colin had an episode, so I left school and came back to Sacramento for a while. His doctor placed him on a groundbreaking new medication. I saw hope in my brother's eyes. His stare wasn't so empty that day."

Jason grew silent. He shut his eyes, and Lexi assumed he was observing the image reflected off his closed eyelids.

"Since high school, since the first time he tried to kill himself, I've been Colin's protector," Lexi continued, staring at a chandelier above her head. Delicate spider webs connected the bright fixture to the smooth, cream-colored ceiling. "I want to help my brother. Usually, I just end up feeling useless. Nothing ever changes. There's no such thing as improvement, just highs and lows. Moments of clarity followed by really bad episodes. I can't help Colin. I can't pull him back when he gets too close to the ledge."

"I'm so sorry," Jason murmured.

"I haven't slept through the night since high school. No matter what anyone tells me, I'll always feel responsible for my brother. When he's hurting, I'm hurting. When he's doing well, I can relax. Briefly."

"That's tough."

"It's all I've known since I was a teenager."

"You're a good sister. And a good person."

"Debatable. Sometimes I'm a shitty human." Lexi's mind reverted to blackout weekends, hazy motel rooms with strangers, her palpable disgust when they asked to meet up again. "My point is, there's so much pressure to keep Colin afloat. When I thought you'd put me in a position to harm someone or end a life, it was too much. I couldn't even look at you. The last eighteen years, I've tried to keep my brother safe. I failed but I sure as hell tried. And it felt like you'd reversed all that without my knowledge."

Jason inhaled sharply. "I would never do that to you, Lexi."

"I know. I was just caught off guard."

"Which is my fault. I'm sorry I made you feel like you failed to protect others."

"You don't understand. I *have* failed," Lexi whispered. "I couldn't save Jorge. I wasn't there when his plane blew up. And I've been fighting to save Colin, but it hasn't changed a damn thing. Tonight was different, though. This was a huge loss in a game I didn't even know I was playing."

"You deserved to know about my tattoo. You deserved a warning."

"A warning would've been nice."

"I fucked up."

"You fucked up, baby mechanic. We both did."

"Mostly me. Know something? You're fierce when you're angry. You said some mean stuff," Jason noted with a lopsided grin.

"I'd like to strike those comments from the record."

"Deal."

They sat for a moment in pensive silence. The lobby was still empty, a wide-open space occupied by exactly two hotel guests and one employee. Instrumental music floated over their heads, soft and sweet and unobtrusive.

Lexi yawned.

"It's been a hell of a day. Let me walk you back to your room," Jason suggested.

"I have a better idea," Lexi said. She stood up and headed toward the elevator, motioning for him to follow.

Chapter Ten: October 7, 2038

Lexi woke up with Jason's arm draped over her side. A vent near the window pumped frigid air through the room. She nestled into Jason's chest to retain some heat.

They'd fallen asleep around midnight, arms and legs intertwined. Each time they'd woken up, they'd shifted to a new position. There was never a moment when they weren't touching.

Jason opened his eyes and yawned. "Morning."

"Hi."

"Did you sleep okay?"

"Yeah." Lexi hoisted herself up and leaned against the headboard. "You know, I haven't done this in ages."

"Done what?"

"Slept through the night."

"Mission accomplished. You're welcome."

Lexi laughed. "I'm not saying you're the cure. Maybe I was so upset yesterday that I wore myself out."

"Which I also take credit for," Jason said with a contented sigh.

Snorting, Lexi hopped to her feet. She gathered her clothes off the floor and slipped into the outfit she'd been wearing the previous night.

"Want to meet in an hour for breakfast?" Jason asked, looking up at her with hopeful eyes.

"No time. Our van leaves for the training center at seven. When do you have to be there?"

"Not until nine. Grab a protein bar from my backpack, at

least. I'd hate to be the reason you skipped breakfast."

"Deal. I'm stealing the cookie dough one," she announced, tucking the snack in her pocket. "See you this afternoon?"

"Yes. Don't forget your bikini."

"Duh. And my brand-new SkyLine ballcap."

"This is huge. It's a milestone for SkyLine Airways. You're part of a movement. You're the face of the future," Reggie informed everyone from his perch at the front of the class. One elbow rested on the podium, an antique piece which deviated from the classroom's modern aesthetic. With a chartreuse front panel and brass accents, it looked like a relic from the 1960s. "As most of you know, the technology behind PersonableSpin has been available for years. SkyLine waited to purchase it because there were glitches initially. Then ContaCan hit. Training equipment was placed on hold."

Lexi sat up straighter. PersonableSpin would be a huge help during classes, she figured. After testing out the platform the night before, she knew it was compelling. It could be a powerful educational tool.

"In January, SkyLine slashed its budget in every department. We prepared for the worst," Reggie continued. "Once an antidote was released, the tide shifted. SkyLine rose to the top of the industry. Apparently, passengers trusted our airline. We got a lot of media attention in May and June. We grew immensely. While other airlines folded, we stayed strong. This underdog airline, founded by two starry-eyed daydreamers thirty-eight years ago, transformed into the golden child of air travel."

Reggie's expression, typically stoic, curved into a grin. After a period of doubt and anxiety, the industry's unsung hero had emerged victorious. His pride in the airline's eleventh-hour success was visceral.

We're on the upswing. Lexi couldn't help but smile. SkyLine had survived dark times. Against all odds, the company had emerged stronger than ever.

"Two months ago, we purchased PersonableSpin tutorials for this class," Reggie explained. "You're the first flight attendants to gain access. Pilot classes utilized the technology last month. Mechanics and dispatchers received the software around that time. This is the first flight attendant course with PersonableSpin capability. Moving forward, SkyLine will include PS in all classes. Soon we will give each employee a unique PersonableSpin code. Folks can take classes with real-time interaction and feedback from a hotel room, their homes, or anywhere else. No equipment required except AutoScan. No need for wi-fi, a tablet, solar power, or electricity. It's a sustainable service. The possibilities are endless."

Reggie cleared his throat before continuing. "Now, I'd like to share a message straight from the San Jose Special Projects Building. When you lead your own classroom in your respective bases, you will be able to access pre-recorded sessions. You'll also have the option to establish a live connection with the two flight attendants who designed this program. And with me, of course. We'll be there to resolve any issues that arise. You can turn on AutoScan now, just for this segment. Sync it to the SkyLine PS Instructor function."

Reggie dimmed the lights. From the back of the room, he pulled up a Holoscreen. Red lasers formed a translucent square above his tablet. He tapped the weightless screen. Lexi squinted through the darkness, observing each motion as he brought PersonableSpin to life.

There was a quick buzz, then a flash of light.

Two female flight attendants materialized in front of Lexi. Both stood within arm's reach. Their images were every bit as believable and compelling as Jorge had been the day before.

A breath of air got caught in Lexi's throat. Several years ago, before PersonableSpin was available to the public, Lexi wouldn't have believed the humans standing before her were an intricate hologram, a product of lasers transposed onto her cornea. The realism was baffling.

Lexi wished her brother could see this.

In 2037, her brother read a bunch of articles about PersonableSpin. He invited Lexi to his house to discuss PS over wings and pizza. Colin intended to purchase it, and he wanted Lexi to help him pick which model and add-on features to buy. She was clueless, unable to match her brother's lifelong obsession with brand-new apps. She suggested the most advanced one, knowing Colin would master it in minutes. And then the meteors hit. The pathogen ripped through humanity. Colin's employer, Sacramento's biggest digital marketing company, announced potential layoffs. There was no money to spend on fancy new gadgets.

It's as mind-blowing as you imagined, kid. Lexi silently conversed with her brother. *Wish you could see this.*

Directly in front of her, the women began to speak, their voices soothing and affable. Lexi spotted streaks of white in the blonde lady's hair. She could practically feel the air whoosh past her cheek when the woman laughed.

The flight attendant was extraordinarily pretty. Freckles formed a thin line over the bridge of her nose. The other flight attendant, a couple years younger, had smooth brown skin and the shiniest jet-black hair Lexi had ever seen. It seemed to glisten beneath the fluorescent lights overhead, which was literally impossible since the woman was standing in a room in Northern California, with rays of sunshine filtering through the window at different angles.

The women discussed the structure of the groundbreaking four-hour class. They reiterated the correct order for each topic. Lexi's mind kept drifting. She was captivated by PersonableSpin's uncanny ability to mimic reality.

The flight attendants breezed through the customer service

portion before describing SkyLine's new safety standards. They reiterated the need for revised medical procedures mid-flight. Their speech ended with a joke about the long work-days awaiting SkyLine's newest instructors.

They opened the floor for questions. Lexi could think of a dozen at least, yet she didn't speak. Neither did anyone else. From the back of the classroom, Reggie cleared his throat.

"Thank you, Meredith and Kamilla. We appreciate your time. We'll be seeing more of you in the upcoming months," he said.

Lexi swiveled around to watch Reggie wave to the air in front of him, which contained an image only he could see. Meredith and Kamilla twinkled in her peripheral vision.

Reggie pulled up a Holoscreen and pressed his thumbprint to the red square in the center. The PersonableSpin image dissipated.

"Okay, class. AutoScan off," he instructed.

Lexi faced forward. Her unobstructed line of sight bore no trace of the flight attendants who'd occupied the space five seconds earlier.

"What did you think?" Reggie asked, flipping the lights on.

"Holy shit," Luis said from the left side of the room. He gasped after the words escaped his lips.

Reggie chuckled at the outburst. "I get it, Luis. I felt the same way after my first PersonableSpin session."

"The accuracy is shocking," Lexi said. "It was hard to pay attention. I still can't wrap my head around the fact that these flight attendants weren't here in the room with us. It's incomprehensible that they're in San Jose right now."

"Do you think students will be distracted?" Reggie asked Lexi.

"At first, yes. Eventually, the astonishment will wear off, and they'll be able to learn a lot."

"Good. Did anything stand out to you from the speeches

Kamilla and Meredith gave?"

Lexi tilted her head to the side. "A couple things. They ran through the structure of the class, explaining the order we'll teach each topic. Customer service first, followed by SkyLine's revised policy for medically mandated seat upgrades. Then we transition into the health and safety portion."

"Can you deviate from that order?" Reggie quizzed.

"It's not necessary. The current order makes sense. We open with a lesson on approachability and basic hospitality. It's an icebreaker. Then we transition to new information, procedural stuff that's been updated to meet new guidelines. Life-or-death policies created in the aftermath of ContaCan."

Reggie meandered through tables, returning to the front of the room. "And what's your role as the instructor of the class?"

"We're facilitators more than teachers," Lexi quipped. "We guide the discussion. Since our students also happen to be our coworkers, they will determine the flow. Students steer this course. We just provide the framework."

Reggie nodded. "Couldn't have said it better. Are you willing to demonstrate for everyone?"

"Sure." The word came out as a question rather than a statement.

"Come on up." Reggie motioned for her to join him at the front of the classroom. "We'll skip the first two sections. Start with the health and safety portion, please. Are you comfortable teaching that part?"

Lexi shrugged. She hadn't reviewed that lesson even though it had been assigned as part of last night's homework.

"Excellent. Read the CDC Updates, then give a quick tutorial." Reggie handed her his tablet, Holoscreen hovering above it.

With a few ocular swipes, she found the section she'd been asked to read and cleared her throat. "*Previously, SkyLine flight attendants were provided with standard protective equipment.*

Regulations were loosely enforced. The goal was to assist passengers using any means possible. Protocols have changed, with mouth guards required post-emergency and seat reassignments mandated to keep an ill passenger as far from other travelers as possible. Crews perform CPR, utilize the defibrillator, contact FlyingMed, and follow the instructions. If communications fail, medical professions are paged for help as a last resort. All crew members have the option to quarantine for five days following the incident. It isn't mandatory if the individual has had a minimum of four rounds of the antidote."

"Excellent. Now make it your own," Reggie instructed.

Lexi set the tablet on the podium. She turned toward her mock students. "You might be wondering about a few details. We used to page for medical personnel first, right? Pre-ContaCan, it was the first thing we would do in a health-related emergency. We'd ask doctors and nurses to assist. Now, we must protect the other passengers on the plane. Since there could be undeclared ARs, we can't take chances. We have new measures in place to ensure our health and safety. Although we've received the antidote, we could still carry the pathogen. We might infect those who are susceptible. That's why we have to wear every piece of protective gear available. Preventative supplements and equipment are not enough. Not anymore."

She paused, trying to recall any major points she'd forgotten. "Another revision is that we don't use onboard medical personnel unless our FlyingMed connection fails or the passenger's condition deteriorates. By limiting the individuals involved, we reduce the risk of transmission. The more people hovering over an ill patient, the more opportunities for cross-contamination and exposure. It's only worth the risk if we're desperate and unable to assist the passenger by ourselves."

She glanced at Reggie, whose expression was inscrutable.

"Has anyone had a medical emergency over the past few weeks?" Lexi asked the class. "Anything requiring a call to FlyingMed, mid-flight?"

A few people nodded.

"Tell me what happened," Lexi said.

"A lady ran up to the forward galley. She said the woman in the window seat was slumped forward and unresponsive," Kenyatta, a Philadelphia-based flight attendant, called from the left side of the room. All heads turned toward her. "The lead flight attendant stayed up front to monitor the clear zone in case it was a ruse to breach the flight deck."

"Thanks for pointing that out, Kenyatta. With so much focus on ContaCan, we tend to forget the very real threat of terrorism," Lexi noted. "Kudos to your crew for keeping an eye on the flight deck door."

Kenyatta nodded. "The lead flight attendant stayed in the front galley. She called to the back to let the other girl know there was a medical emergency mid-cabin. Meanwhile, I followed the passenger back to her seat."

"Did you grab anything before heading into the aisle?" Lexi asked.

"CCK," Kenyatta responded without missing a beat.

Lexi immediately knew which kit she was talking about. The technical name was *ContaCan Protective Equipment Kit*, or CC-PEK, but most people used its shortened nickname. "Good. What happened when you found the unresponsive passenger?"

"Before I approached her, I used decontaminant eye drops. I put on a mask and an arm patch. Positioned the mouthguard in place and swallowed the immunity booster tucked inside. Then I stepped into the passenger's row," Kenyatta said. "Luckily, she was the only person sitting there. Since the middle seat was empty, I didn't have to crawl over people or ask folks to move. I stuck an armband on her. Checked for a pulse."

"Gloves on?"

"Yeah, I forgot to mention that. Sorry. Gloves on. I'd

applied CCK hand gel earlier. I use some before each individual flight. Force of habit," Kenyatta explained. "Turns out the woman had a pulse. She was breathing. She wouldn't respond, though. The flight attendant in the back galley ran to us in full gear. She connected her EarLink to FlyingMed as soon as the pilots patched us through to medical personnel."

"What did they tell you to do?"

"Since the passenger had a pulse and was breathing, we were told not to begin CPR. We cracked open the Medical Emergency Satchel, then grabbed the ammonia inhalants. The passenger regained consciousness and explained she had a medical condition which causes fainting."

"Did you divert?"

Kenyatta shook her head. "No. We were twenty minutes from our destination. We landed wearing our protective gear and waited for EMTs to take the woman. My crew was pulled from the trip. We all opted into the five-day quarantine period. We tested clean and returned to work."

Lexi nodded. "Thanks for that example, Kenyatta. These incidents happen frequently. With thousands of flights per day, medical emergencies are bound to occur. They can range from minor inconveniences to life-threatening illnesses. We must stay vigilant. We need to rely on our training and do our absolute best in unpredictable situations."

Lexi scanned the crowd. All eyes were fixed on her, a good sign. She hadn't lost anyone's attention. "It helps to have background knowledge. Muscle memory kicks in, and you do exactly what you need to do. That, my friends, is the point of this training. SkyLine has revised our standard procedures. I have no doubt you'll adapt to these new policies smoothly and easily."

Reggie reached over, giving Lexi a high-five. "Class, that's how it's done. You share info, ask for feedback, explain a specific concept to them, and let them present their stories or concerns. Nice work, Lex."

Lexi grinned, soaking up the first real compliment she'd received since training began. A final glance around the room proved that she hadn't lost her audience to fatigue or boredom.

Reggie announced a fifteen-minute break, and Lexi returned to her seat.

"My teaching partner is a rockstar," Tamika mused. "You nailed it."

Brandon hopped onto the edge of their table. His slim legs dangled off the side. "You're a natural. You didn't flinch. Too bad you can't teach at the Nashville base. We could use you, girlfriend."

"Nah. She's property of San Francisco International Airport, and I'm not sharing," Tamika said with a smile.

"I feel so loved," Lexi mused. "Something clicked for me when I got up there. All the pieces fell into place."

Tamika shrugged. "Because you're meant to do this."

Lexi rose from her chair and lifted an eyebrow. "I hope you're still saying that in three months."

"I will be."

"Good. Well, I need a bathroom break," Lexi said. "Be right back."

In the hallway, Renee flagged her down. She had a to-go bag of cafeteria food in one hand and a notebook in the other. Her black hair was pulled into a ponytail, accentuating high cheekbones and a youthful face.

"Lex," she said breathlessly, as though she'd been searching for Lexi all day.

"Renee, hi. What's up?"

"I saw Jason at lunch. He wanted me to relay a message if I ran into you. Everyone's meeting at the main entrance at three o'clock. Is that cool? Three?"

Lexi nodded. "Sure. I think we're dismissed at two-thirty

today. Why didn't Jason text me?"

"He did," Renee said with a shrug. "No response."

Lexi frowned. "Shoot. My AutoScan is off."

"They guy's obsessed." Renee smiled triumphantly.

"Huh?"

"He's a whole new person. A couple weeks ago, he was stressed about studying. Kinda quiet. He'd join us for dinner, then head to his room. Now he's doing beach trips and playing darts until last-call. You brought him back to life." Renee chuckled. "I gotta head to the simulators. See you this afternoon?"

"Yeah, for sure," Lexi said as Renee hurried up the winding staircase. Lexi activated AutoScan, allowing the messages to float past her eye. Sure enough, she'd missed several texts from Jason.

Hey, you. Tentative plan is three o'clock, at the main entrance.

Another text had come in ten minutes later.

Lexi, does that work? Hopefully you finish training by then. If not, I'll come up with some excuse to pull you out of class. I'll get creative.

A third text had been sent after that one.

You must be busy in class today. Hope it's going great.

Lexi grinned. She had to give the guy credit—he was definitely persistent.

"Sounds like a plan," she murmured aloud as she stepped into the bathroom.

"Be safe. Pace yourself with the drinking and reapply sunscreen every hour. A sunburn is the last thing you need," Tamika instructed, shaking her finger. "Full-body skin grafting is expensive as hell. We don't earn pilot salaries, Lex. Better protect yourself."

Lexi rolled her eyes. "Yes, Mom."

"Call if you need an escape or an alibi," Luis added with a sly smile.

"Go enjoy the pep rally, guys. I'll be fine," Lexi promised.

Jason was waiting in front of the building, a beach bag slung over one shoulder and aviators concealing his luscious brown eyes. Lexi advanced toward him, shedding her sweater in the process. The sun seared into her skin. It was a welcome contrast to the intense air-conditioning inside the building.

"Want to change before we head out?" Jason asked. "Ben's pulling the car around. We can wait."

"No need. I wore my bikini under my clothes."

"Smart." He flagged down Ben's blue SUV. They piled into the back seat beside Renee. A salt-and-pepper pilot named Daron sat in the passenger seat. Lexi greeted everyone and thanked them for letting her tag along.

"No problem. You can be our token stew," Ben said as he steered toward the Beeline Expressway.

"Token *teacher* stew," Jason corrected him. "Ben, does this thing have self-drive mode?"

"Of course," Ben replied. "But the electric charge is low. I'll let the solar power battery soak up the sunshine at the beach, then flip to self-drive on the way back."

"Yes. After we drink a bunch of beer," Jason said. Lexi leaned against his shoulder as they cruised onto the interstate.

Their gear was painfully mismatched. Gray hotel towels overlapped with vibrant Florida-themed ones they'd bought at a corner store. There were five people in their group but a dozen towels. They'd been arranged to form a patchwork quilt, an unsightly yet comfortable oasis among miles of sand.

Renee and Daron rose to their feet, advancing toward the rolling blue waves. Ben followed closely behind.

Lexi cracked open a beer and held the can against her forehead.

Jason's head rested on her lap. A hat shielded his face from the blazing sun. While Lexi watched, his chest rose and fell methodically. He'd been asleep for a while. The beach was quiet and empty. Perfect napping weather.

Ships drifted past, tiny figures dotting the horizon. They were too far away to make much noise. Jason's dreams wouldn't be pierced by the blaring horn of a tanker.

Carefully, Lexi poured her beer into a cup, then dropped the hemp can in their designated compost bag. She stared at the ocean while sipping her drink. Daron lingered near the shoreline while Renee and Ben ventured into the deep blue. With their arms and legs moving in unison, they looked like expert swimmers. Impressive endurance. Impeccable form.

Lexi activated AutoScan, composing a note she knew her brother wouldn't see. At least, not anytime soon.

It's a perfect beach day in Florida, kid.

You were always so obsessed with the waves. Remember when Mom and Dad finally caved, sending us to summer camp in San Diego? You tumbled a thousand times before successfully balancing yourself on that surfboard. The trip was awesome. You achieved your goal. You rose above the crest.

I love you. The ebb and flow is natural. The waves will continue to dance. And I'm with you for all of it, Colin.

With a blink, she deleted the whole thing. She sat still, absorbing the stunning scenery in which she was immersed.

Colin was fluid like the ocean pulsing before her. He rose and fell, ad infinitum. There was nothing calm or consistent about Lexi's brother. Yet, as a swirl of emotion, heartache, and loss, he was also his own unique masterpiece. Colin Brennan was continuously in motion, sometimes moving forward and sometimes backsliding. He possessed raw beauty despite the chaos. He was smart and wild and passionate, often too passionate for his own good. The guy was otherworldly. In many ways, he was so much better than the things of this world. For that, Lexi loved him fiercely.

She gasped.

At the sound of her cry, Jason stirred below her. He lifted the hat off his face and squinted in the bright sunshine.

"You okay, Lexi?"

"Just had an epiphany. I know what my tattoo will say."

Jason sat up. The towels shifted below him, revealing a square patch of sand. He yawned, then placed his aviators over his nose. "You're getting a tattoo.? When?"

"This weekend. I want something that honors my brother."

"That's cool. What's it going to say?"

"*I'll ride the wave with you.* Cheesy?"

Jason paused and took a drink from his tumbler. "He surfs?"

"He's not the best, but he loves it."

"I see. If it means something to him, it'll be perfect. Let's get your tattoo after class tomorrow."

"Nah, I can get it in Sacramento," Lexi said with a flick of her hand.

"Daron got all his tattoos in Orlando. He used to live here," Jason said, jutting his chin toward the water. Daron had a half-sleeve and an intricate watercolor design on his chest. "I'm sure he's got local connections. Do you have time tomorrow? We could go after class, before your flight home."

"Training's done at three. My Sacramento flight leaves around seven."

"Plenty of time." Jason sat up and kissed her forehead, still damp with perspiration. "It's a date."

Katie's message floated across Lexi's eye as she was stacking coolers in the trunk of Ben's rental car.

How's this? I can send more sketches. Let me know.

A dusky glow had descended upon them. In that twilit atmosphere, the image affixed to Lexi's cornea seemed especially striking. Katie's sketch contained a trail of words in the shape of a wave. It was small, a bite-sized tribute to Colin. But it packed a massive punch.

Lexi marveled at Katie's design, impressed by its ability to capture the endless stream of support she intended to offer her brother.

"You okay?" Jason whispered in her ear. Daron, Ben, and Renee had already hopped inside the vehicle.

Lexi nodded and forwarded the image to Jason. "My best friend's a graphic artist. She came up with this sketch."

"I like it. Where will you get the tattoo?"

"Not sure yet." Lexi pointed to her forearm, just below the crease of her elbow. "This spot, maybe? If it looks good on me."

"Everything looks good on you." Jason wrapped an arm around her shoulder. "Not to mention *off* you."

Lexi grinned. "Are you trying to win some points through flattery?"

Jason's eyes glinted in the milky twilight. "Just being honest."

Lexi chuckled. Before they climbed inside the vehicle, she shot a final glance at the beach. Dark water swirled all the way to an indistinguishable horizon. The sky was various shades of blue, as shadowy and alluring as the waves lapping the shore.

Lexi snapped a photo with her eye. She figured Colin would appreciate the scenery. Someday.

The car was searing hot after soaking up the sun all afternoon. With a wince, Lexi climbed onto the scorching faux leather. Cooling coils brought the material to a reasonable temperature. Mercifully.

Ben sat up front in the driver's seat. His hands stayed far from the steering wheel. The ride back to Orlando was quiet as the car drove itself down the Beeline Expressway.

Lexi drifted off and woke with her head on Jason's chest. Exit signs indicated they were approaching Orlando. The SUV autonomously edged its way across two lanes, coasting toward the ramp with the grace and skill of an expert motorist.

A few minutes later, the vehicle arrived at the crew hotel.

"How are you feeling?" Jason asked as he helped Lexi out of Ben's SUV.

"Good. I needed that catnap."

"Do you want to grab food downstairs? Or we could order room service."

"Room service, please." Lexi hugged Renee, then waved goodbye to Ben and Daron.

With hands clasped together, Lexi and Jason walked through the lobby. Inside the elevator, they used AutoScan to order their meals.

In Jason's hotel room, Lexi grabbed a seat on the edge of the bed. Jason stood above her, his left hand gliding through her hair. She was about to hoist herself up toward his face when someone knocked on the door. Jason reached into the hallway to grab their food.

Lexi stuffed a couple fries in her mouth, savoring each crispy bite. The salt awakened her tastebuds. It dawned on her that she hadn't eaten anything since lunch, which was about eight hours earlier.

"We should've brought snacks to the beach," Jason noted as though reading Lexi's mind. "I'm freaking starving."

Lexi licked a drop of ketchup off her lips. "I guess we were more concerned with beer and sunscreen. Which is good. My pale skin would've burned without it."

"I don't think your skin is pale."

Lexi lifted an eyebrow. "You know you're Black, right? I'm basically glow-in-the-dark compared to you."

Jason's jaw dropped. "I'm Black? Are you sure?"

"Smartass."

He finished his panini. "You slept here last night. To my knowledge, no glowing occurred. Except maybe if we'd shined a black light on the sheets."

Lexi chuckled. "Maybe we should sleep together again, just to be sure."

"Excellent plan." Jason lifted his t-shirt over his head. "Well, I've got sand everywhere. What do you say? Shower time?"

Lexi tilted her head to the side. "Together?"

"Sure. Conserve water. Save the planet."

Lexi placed Jason's hand under her tank top, just below the hem. Then she raised her arms into the air. Jason lifted the material over her shoulders. She stood before him in her bikini top and shorts.

Hand in hand, they walked to the bathroom. The shower was big enough for two people, with a ledge on one side and a rectangular shelf on the other. Keeping her focus on Jason, Lexi slid out of her shorts. When he pulled off his swimsuit, something brewed inside her chest. Her bones felt electric.

She wrestled out of her bikini at lightning speed. Lexi sensed Jason's eyes on her, admiring every inch of her body. She turned on the faucet and pulled him toward her. Warm droplets cascaded over their skin.

Lexi watched Jason lather up the soap. His hands navigated across her shoulders first, then down to her waist. Instinctively, she wrapped her arms around his neck and kissed him, pausing to look in his rich brown eyes.

Strands of hair clung to Lexi's chin. Jason swept the tresses from her face.

"Today was a good day," Lexi murmured, piling her hair into a messy bun. "The best, actually."

"Can I ask you something?"

"Go for it."

Jason paused. "It's kind of personal. But, because you're my first, um, non-straight partner . . . do you have a preference? Do you mostly date women?"

Lexi blinked. She knew exactly what she wanted to say. She felt it in her core—it was central to her being. She wasn't sure how to articulate it, though. People rarely inquired about her preferences. Mostly, they just made assumptions and placed her in a tiny box. One that they could wrap their heads around. One that was frequently lined with judgment or wildly inaccurate stereotypes.

"My brother came out in high school. I was proud of him, but I never had that same kind of conviction. I wasn't drawn to one specific type of person. Colin paved the way for me, though. It was easy to be my true self after he laid the groundwork." She reached over, wiping soap off Jason's arm. "As far back as I can remember, I was attracted to boys and girls. My first big crush was a volleyball player named Taryn. It was my sophomore year of high school. I went to all her games, cheered so loud I lost my voice. I loved those games, even though I didn't know anything about volleyball."

"Did she ask you out?"

Lexi shook her head. "We kissed behind the bleachers our junior year. She made me promise never to tell anyone. That was the last time we spoke. I wasn't about to be her dirty little secret." She finished rinsing soap and sand from her body, then turned off the faucet. Jason handed her a towel.

"Did you date men after that?"

"I dated a few guys in high school. Nothing serious. In college, mostly women. As an Education major, sixty percent of my peers were female. I hit it off with a couple of them. One girl, Blair Ferreira, was awesome. We really clicked. But I was taking care of stuff at home, so I spent most weekends in Sacramento. It never went anywhere. I was gone too much."

"Do you prefer one gender over the others?"

Lexi wrapped her hair in a towel and pulled Jason close. Their damp bodies pressed together like glue. "Not really. For me, it's about a connection more than anatomy. I like all parts.

Including yours. Definitely including yours. Have I demonstrated that?"

Jason laughed. "You've made it clear. But I won't say no to a reminder."

Lexi guided him back to the bedroom. As they reached the foot of the bed, Jason's EarLink buzzed loudly, surprising them both. Lexi scanned the dresser, nightstand, and comforter to help locate his phone. All surfaces appeared empty.

He tapped his ear to accept the call. "Hello?"

An oversized t-shirt rested on the corner of Jason's bed. Lexi pulled it over her head and burrowed into the soft fabric.

"Cool. Thanks, buddy," Jason said. He was facing the window. Damp skin showcased every toned muscle. "Shit, I can't believe I left it in Ben's car."

Jason reached up, clicking his EarLink off. Lexi handed him a pair of boxer-briefs. He slid into them and sat with his back against the headboard.

"That was Daron," Jason informed Lexi. "He booked an appointment for you tomorrow with his tattoo artist. This girl, Tatiana Somebody, is a big deal in Florida. I guess she accepted a last-minute appointment as a favor to Daron."

"That was nice."

"It's all set, Lexi. You're good to go. Well, after you forward Tatiana the image you want. Daron's sending her info via AutoScan because I left my phone in Ben's car," Jason said with a smile. "Like a dumbass."

"What's with us losing our phones this week?" Lexi shook her head.

"A little preoccupied, I guess."

"Should we go get your phone?"

"We can wait a few minutes." He motioned to his side. "Come here."

Lexi gladly fulfilled the request. She nestled into Jason's arms with ease. As his fingertips floated down her sun-streaked skin, she closed her eyes. "Mmm. This feels good."

"Funny, I was thinking the same thing. You're perfect."

"Nobody's ever accused me of being perfect." Lexi shrugged. "Flawlessness isn't my thing. Stick around long enough, and all my true colors will bleed out."

"I plan to stick around," Jason responded. "Can't wait to see the full spectrum, Lex."

Chapter Eleven: October 8, 2038

Jason lifted his head from the pillow, instructing AutoScan to pause the luminescent Soothe Alarm. Self-generating diode lights slowed their synchronized march across the ceiling. The polite vibrations pulsing in his ear weakened.

Beside him, Lexi yawned. Jason pulled her closer. He loved the way she curled into his neck, her button nose pressed against him.

He uttered a half-awake good morning while lacing his fingers through hers. He never ceased to be amazed by the softness of her skin.

"Time to get up," he heard himself murmur, despite the overpowering temptation to stay in bed a little longer. "We need you packed and ready to go."

"Today's the day, huh?"

Jason nodded. "Straight to the tattoo shop after class. Then the airport."

"Are we *Swyfting* everywhere?"

"Nope. I claimed Ben's rental car for the afternoon." Jason placed his thumb on the nightstand scanner, and golden light emanated from two lamps on opposite ends of the room. "Just have to bring it back to the airport by seven o'clock."

"That's when my flight leaves." Lexi yawned once more, then sat up and rubbed her eyes. "Last night was great."

"Off the charts."

"And now for the walk of shame . . ." She smiled. "Hey, you should go back to sleep. Doesn't your training start at nine? What time is it anyway?"

Jason tapped his wrist to activate the daily morning update. Red lights appeared on the ceiling, providing a brief overview of the day ahead. Numbers and letters glowed brightly against the white paint.

05:30 AM. October 8, 2038.

Forecast for Orlando, FL, partly cloudy, 89 degrees, 60% chance of afternoon thunderstorms.

Amway Field, Team Orlando v. D.C. Unity Corps, tickets available.

National News, Constitutional Amendment approved granting authority to the Executive Branch over all others. In historic measure, the Executive Branch bypassed the ratification process to pass amendments without approval from Congress or state legislatures.

Thirty-Fourth Amendment secures additional power for the Executive Branch, with US President now deemed High Moral Leader. Congressional approval no longer needed to pass laws or make constitutional modifications. In his first act as High Moral Leader, US President issued Executive Order 19424, which approved all AR mandates and regulations implemented across the nation.

"Ho . . . ly . . . fuck," Jason muttered. He zoomed in on the notification and blinked twice. The letters on the wall rearranged themselves to provide more information.

Per Executive Order – EO – 19424, forced AR registration and GeoLocation tracking by Patriotic Safety Teams – PSTs – legal within Texas, Florida, Georgia, Alabama, Oklahoma. Noncompliant ARs to be charged with treason. Those with falsified documents to be charged with treason. Thirty-Fourth Amendment ensures no state legislatures or members of Congress can interfere with Presidential authority.

Surgeon General to meet with Dept. of Health and Human Services at 14:00 to discuss novel strain of ContaCan discovered in Birmingham, Alabama. New CC Strain 5.2 believed to be caused and spread by undeclared ARs.

Jason froze, hardly breathing. Rage stirred inside him. It had happened. The president had achieved his horrific goal of securing uncontested, near-total power. The country had become a dictatorship, for the most part.

Texas had implemented an AR-tracking law a few weeks ago. Other southern states quickly issued mandates of their own, piggybacking off Texas' harsh policy. There was supposed to be a constitutional amendment at the end of October. Congress nearly had the votes to pass it, and state legislatures could be convinced by enough public pressure. Civil liberties unions had publicized the hypocrisy written into each mandate, drawing attention to the corrupt politicians who issued them and the harsh ramifications of the laws. DefenderTech was in their corner, Jason figured. DT had helped them dig up some dirt, and they'd subsequently published articles challenging the politicians' motives.

Jason had clung to the hope these egregious mandates would be reversed. Congress could codify human rights into law. ARs were people, just like all other people. A genetic glitch did not make them subhuman. Jason had kept hoping for justice.

Instead, President Dipshit found a way to sidestep the established process. He already had the Supreme Court in his pocket. Those bigoted assholes had been ruling against basic human rights ever since that *Kava – no, I'm not a sexual predator, I just like beer* guy joined their crew of sick sadists twenty years ago. He was a pathetic excuse for a man, a lumpy old misogynist with a grin as empty as his soul, but he refused to die. That vile jerk was determined to live to age three hundred, just so he could continue destroying the nation.

There was no hope for the judicial system. For two decades, Jason had known the Supreme Court was a lost cause.

But now, with Congress out of the picture, the president had secured nearly all the power in America.

"What does this mean for ARs?" Lexi asked beside him, her voice thick with sleep.

"That it's getting worse," Jason answered, unable to pry his gaze from the ominous warning embedded in bright red letters on the ceiling. "We're so screwed, Lexi."

"Why? What's going on?"

Jason scratched his head. "The president passed a constitutional amendment saying he can do anything he wants. He doesn't need Congressional approval anymore."

"What the actual hell?"

"And his first act as High Moral Leader, the name he gave himself, was to crack down on ARs. As if things weren't bad enough. We already have a national database. Now ARs will be forced to self-disclose and get a GeoTrack implant. Every movement, interaction, decision, and purchase will be monitored. ARs can't leave state lines. They've been killed while trying to flee to sanctuary states like California."

"They've been *killed*?"

"Yeah. Looks like people are using untraceable explosive devices that hover over someone and burrow under their skin with one quick command."

"I heard about the micro bombs. They're terrifying. And who the hell has the time to do all this? Track every movement and chase people down at the state border? Send deadly self-guided bombs to attack ARs?"

Jason shrugged. "That's what President Shithead's newest task force is for. It's a government-sanctioned militia. Eventually, they'll round up every AR. That's their goal. Hunt 'em down and toss them in abandoned buildings."

Lexi grimaced. "And leave them there to die, like the elementary school that was set on fire?"

"Yes. As always, they'll find a way to spin it. They'll claim they're protecting the public. This stuff has been going on for months, and nobody's been able to fight it. Not with any level of success. Now, Congress has been rendered useless. There's no way to push back." Jason exhaled slowly. "The Executive

Branch calls it a protective measure, a matter of national security or some nonsense. They're appealing to the extremists, and it's working. Check out the name of the group running this whole mess—Patriotic Safety Team. *Patriotic* strikes a chord with the America First crowd and *safety* pegs ARs as a threat to the public. The feds have rigged it so nobody can fight the system. ARs will lose everything they've ever had."

"That's what they did to Antonio, I guess? Found him through the database and sent him to die in another country," Lexi murmured. "I didn't even like the guy. He sucked. Still, he didn't deserve that."

"He abandoned his brother, right? Sounds like a real piece of work."

"He quit talking to Jorge years ago. How do you disown your identical twin? Jesus. When Colin came out, I was so happy for him. I was glad he could love whoever the hell he wanted. And we aren't even twins. Two years apart."

"Older or younger?"

"I'm the baby."

"Which means your brother's my age."

"Yeah. You'd like him, Jason."

He nodded. "I bet I would."

After timing out, the daily overview reverted to the homepage. A world clock flashed on the ceiling.

Lexi's eyes flicked toward the oversized numbers. "Shit, I need to go. What am I supposed to wear back to my room?"

She rose from the bed and gathered her clothing. Every item was covered with remnants from the beach. While Jason watched, grains of sand tumbled from the wrinkled shirt and shorts in Lexi's arms.

Jason turned toward his dresser and rifled through the top drawer. He handed Lexi the smallest t-shirt and basketball shorts he owned. The shirt had shrunk in the hotel dryer. It was tight on Jason, practically obscene.

"Perfect fit," Lexi commented after putting on his clothes. The shorts dangled past her knees.

Jason grinned. "Sorry that I'm six-foot-four. You should see how big my shoes are."

"Your shoe size is one of your best features."

"Oh? What are the other ones?"

"Wouldn't you like to know?" Lexi grinned and made her way to the door.

"I'll bring you coffee," Jason volunteered as she stepped into the bright hallway. He cradled her face in his hand for a moment.

"That would be nice."

"See you soon." Jason watched her walk toward the elevator in shorts that dwarfed her body and a shirt three times her size. To him, she looked absolutely perfect.

Lexi shoved the last few items in her suitcase and pressed down hard to zip it up. The shuttle would arrive to take her to Headquarters soon. Lexi and her coworkers wouldn't return to the hotel after training. They'd jet off to various corners of the country, settling back into their lives before teaching their first class.

A knock resonated from the hallway.

Lexi opened her door to find Jason holding a brown bag in one hand and a coffee cup in the other. His hair was wild and wonderful, a smattering of gray curls mixed in with black ones. The man was jarringly handsome, even at this ungodly hour.

"Good morning, part two," he said, handing her the bag of food. "Figured you could use a balanced breakfast."

She ushered him inside her room. They sat at the round table beside the sliding glass door. Directly before them, the sun crept up the horizon. Rays of light cascaded to the ground, bathing streets and buildings in a golden haze.

"Thanks for doing this," Lexi said.

"Waking up at the crack of dawn when I don't have to be at Headquarters until nine, you mean?" Jason smiled. "You're worth it, teacher stew."

He pulled a cardboard box of eggs, bacon, and biscuits from the bag, then fished around for two sets of biodegradable pseudo-plasticware.

Lexi grabbed a piece of bacon with her fingers and nibbled the end. "You're off this weekend, right? Are you flying home?"

"Nah. I have to be back Monday for the last four days of training." He sighed. "My ex is off the whole weekend. I don't really want to deal with that stress. I'll stay in Orlando and prep for the last few days of class."

"What about Vella?"

"My neighbor takes care of her when I'm gone. She's spoiled, trust me. Bacon for breakfast and endless belly rubs. I get routine pup-dates."

"Clever. Did you coin that term yourself?"

"Would it impress you if I had?"

"Obviously."

"In that case, yes."

"Great. So you'll get plenty of pup-dates from your neighbor while you're in Orlando this weekend. And then you're back to work?"

"Yep. One more week of training. After that, I pack up and move to San Diego. Not sure how Vella will do on the cross-country car ride."

"She'll love it. A new adventure, right? Lots of big changes ahead," Lexi noted as she stabbed her fork into a mound of fluffy eggs. "So much to look forward to."

"You, too, Lexi. In a couple weeks, you'll be teaching a class at the San Francisco base. You're gonna run the whole Inflight

Training Department someday."

"We shall see," she reflected with a frown.

Jason's EarLink buzzed. "Shoot, sorry," he murmured. "Forgot to silence my VirtuAlarms."

"What's the newest update?" Lexi asked as she popped half a biscuit in her mouth. "Do I even want to know?"

"It's not good," Jason admitted. "Vigilante justice in the southern states. More mandates and more bullshit. They've sent in the National Guard to suppress any resistance. That didn't take long."

Lexi toyed with her biscuit before taking a bite. "Is there ever an end to the bad news?"

"Doesn't seem like it. I wish we could do something."

Lexi swallowed. Her mind traveled back to the class she'd always wanted to design, the one that would teach coping skills to youth with mentally ill siblings. The one she hadn't received when she needed it most.

There was always a way to change things, she figured. Always a new path to help people evade the suffering of those who had gone before them. She'd never designed the class, but she'd come so close. And she still yearned do it, even if it took ten years to complete the project. Because people deserved better than a heaping pile of nothing. They deserved a lifeline during their toughest moments. Lexi had been alone, fumbling in the dark. Maybe it didn't have to be that way for others.

"Why can't we do something?" Lexi mused, not really expecting an answer.

"I have no clue where to start or how to make a difference. But if I come up with an idea, you'll be the first to know. Lord knows this country needs help. Badly."

Lexi nodded. She finished her biscuit and swept the crumbs into the empty bag. "Hey, switching gears, I want to thank you for not suggesting a threesome last night."

Jason stopped chewing. "Um, what?"

"When I tell a dude I swing both ways, that's usually the first thing that comes out of his mouth." Lexi rolled her eyes. "Listen, I'm not shy. I like a good threesome as much as anyone else, but on my own terms. Not so some misogynist can turn my sexuality into his new fetish."

Jason lifted an eyebrow playfully. "So you're saying you're into threesomes?"

Chuckling, Lexi balled up the paper bag and threw it at his head. "Shut up."

"Nah, I take it back. I don't want a threesome. Wouldn't be fair."

"Oh? How's that?"

Jason shrugged. "Well, with a dude, he'd see my junk and feel inferior."

"It's *not* small," Lexi agreed with a nod.

"And with a girl," Jason continued. "I'd ignore her the whole time. I'm only interested in you. She'd be bored on the sidelines."

Lexi tilted her head to the side. "Know something? That might be the sweetest threesome refusal I've ever heard. You're very romantic, baby mechanic."

"Select a corner of the room for your mock teaching session," Reggie instructed the class. "One person runs through seat reassignments and emergency procedures while the other person covers aircraft differences. Emergency equipment locations, too. You can address the health policy if there's time. Got it?"

They dispersed to various sections of the classroom. Tamika and Lexi picked a spot near a massive window. Sunlight warmed the left side of Lexi's face. Outside, on the grassy quad, bright red picnic tables glistened in the sun. She stared for a few seconds too long. She could practically feel the sunshine searing her skin, could nearly taste the hints of saltwater floating in the breeze.

She realized, in a flurry of emotion, that she would miss this place. As tough as the week had been, it had also been amazing. There were bursts of breathtaking radiance, like tiny fireworks transforming the muted gray backdrop of Lexi's life.

Clearing her throat, she turned her attention to her co-teacher. "Wanna go first?"

Tamika shook her head. "No, thanks. You can start. Aircraft equipment locations or revised seating? You could also do the nondiscrimination health clause."

"I'll go with seat assignments."

"Cool. Ready when you are."

"All right, class, everyone here is aware that several hundred aircraft are returning to our SkyLine fleet. We've also added brand-new planes," Lexi began. "As we continue to grow, we want this to be a smooth transition for everyone. My goal is for you to step onto an AirBird Premier model, or an AirBird Eco-Modern series for that matter, feeling confident and comfortable. No first-day jitters. No wondering where you're supposed to reseat main cabin passengers if they have unique needs. How does that sound? Any questions?"

Tamika flung her hand in the air. Lexi narrowed her eyes suspiciously.

"Look, I've been a SkyLine flight attendant for twenty-two years," Tamika hissed. "By this point, I know these airplanes like the back of my hand. I can adjust to a new AirBird model. Planes are planes, right? I'll figure it out. I'm not worried about that, but I have a problem with ARs."

"You've got an issue with folks who have a glycoprotein deficiency?"

"Of course." Tamika scoffed. "Their special treatment is unfair and counterproductive. I shouldn't have to relocate

ARs to a seat up front, which is permanently blocked off for them. That's prime real estate. We could charge crazy money for that seat. Also, I don't want someone susceptible sitting that close to my jumpseat. Don't I have rights, as someone with fully-functioning glycoproteins? ARs are incapable of self-protection, which forces the burden onto me."

Lexi's mind flashed to Jason's faded tattoo, to all the folks who silently or overtly judged him for a few lines of ink on his shoulder. "That's a lot to unpack. Thank you for your honesty. While I respect your opinion, I have to remind you that we signed up for a job where we interact with the public. Sure, life drastically changed when ContaCan arrived on the scene. Some employees have strong feelings about certain passengers, specifically ARs. However, we were hired to accommodate people and provide excellent service. We were also hired to ensure the safety of our travelers, regardless of their demographics or glycoproteins. So that part is non-negotiable. These recent changes comply with federal regulations as well as SkyLine policies. We can get fined if we neglect certain duties. We're also subject to disciplinary measures."

Tamika glared, but Lexi pressed on.

"That's the current situation," Lexi explained, surprised by her calm and even tone. "It's your choice whether you obey the rules or not. I'm here to show you standard procedures. I'll give you the tools to thrive. What you do with that information is entirely your decision."

Tamika rolled her eyes. "Okay, sure, fine. But can't I just read about the procedures on our internal employee site? Why do I have to be here? I'm wasting a whole day."

"This information is complex and relevant to things you'll see on the plane daily. I don't consider that a waste," Lexi said. "I'll do my best to make it fun. Plus, you're being paid for this training. Most of our competitors filed for bankruptcy. They don't have new trainings like this one because they don't have a future to prepare for. Right?"

"Whatever. I guess."

"Damn, girl," Lexi muttered, breaking her professional demeanor. "You're making me earn my paycheck."

"It's gonna be like this! Some stews are lunatics. You're doing great. Keep your cool. That's the only way to de-escalate the rage."

"Noted. Back to business. Let me start with a question for you, since there are updated procedures that accompany the new AirBird Premier model. This plane is bigger, and the seats have a different pitch. There are more rows, which means additional options to address some tough situations. How do we prioritize revised seat assignments on that plane?"

Tamika paused. "Families are at the bottom of the list. As long as a child sits with one parent, they'll be fine. Other family members can handle the minor inconvenience of sitting apart from each other."

"Which we address as amicably as possible," Lexi added.

"Yeah, obviously. Families are at the bottom, with service animals next on the list. You can't fit a hundred-pound seeing-eye-dog in a normal row, so they'd get reassigned to a bulkhead or the last row of business class."

"Correct. Any exceptions?"

"No."

"What about row twenty?"

"Oh, I forgot. The pitch of the seat is bigger. Large animals can fit there."

"Exactly. And if there are ARs?" Lexi pressed.

"They should've self-disclosed before stepping onto the aircraft."

"True, SkyLine offers a chance to provide that info. But passengers aren't legally required to divulge it, for a very important reason. ARs have faced a lot of prejudice. There have been documented cases of harassment, assault, and worse. Way worse."

"They're legally required to disclose it," Tamika pointed out. "And travel's restricted in some states, as of this morning."

"Oh, shoot," Lexi muttered. She used ocular swipes to rifle through the instructor manual on her tablet. "Looks like we haven't updated our procedures yet. It could take a month before it trickles down to the airline. So, at this moment, ARs are not required to disclose that info to SkyLine. If they become uncomfortable after takeoff, how do we handle it?"

Tamika grimaced. "They get the aisle seat in the first row. And I already expressed how I feel about that."

"Fair enough. What if it's occupied?"

"That's a one-in-a-million scenario. If that seat was occupied, we'd reshuffle other passengers."

"Correct. And SkyLine has authorized us to provide travel vouchers as an incentive. It's a new policy. We won't need to use it often, but it'll save us in a pinch."

"Really? That's generous of the company."

"Yes. We can accommodate people with special needs while compensating those who were inconvenienced. Everyone wins."

"Except for those of us who don't want ARs in our personal space." Tamika shifted her gaze to something over Lexi's shoulder. The corners of her mouth curved upward.

"Stay with me, class. We have a lot of material to cover today."

"Look behind you, Lex," Tamika whispered. "You've amassed a following."

"Huh?" Lexi whirled around to find Reggie and all her classmates staring at her. They had clustered together in a silent huddle. "How'd I do?"

Reggie answered first. "Great."

"You didn't hesitate," Vinh, a Pittsburgh-based flight attendant, mused. "You improvised on the spot."

"And made it interesting," Brandon chimed in.

"And tolerated the most obnoxious student," Carrie said, jutting her chin at Tamika.

Tamika curtsied, beaming at the compliment.

Lexi smiled. "Thanks. You're too kind."

"Keep going," Reggie suggested. "It's okay if we watch, right? You don't mind an audience?"

"Not at all," Lexi confirmed. "Okay, class, moving on . . ."

Tamika pulled a tissue from the box in the center of the table and dabbed her eyes.

"Who knew this would be so emotional?" Lexi whispered to Brandon, sitting on her right side.

He nodded. "It's nuts, right? After one week together, we've become family."

"Any last thoughts before we wrap up?" Reggie asked from his post at the front of the classroom.

Luis raised his hand. "Nobody imagined SkyLine would make it this far. First, the meteor shower where we lost eleven coworkers. Then ContaCan hit, and everyone stopped flying. We recovered from that, slowly, only to have an AR situation. Things got sticky again."

"It's been one challenge after the next," Reggie agreed. "Yet here you are, teaching a class that signals the return of several hundred parked aircraft and the delivery of brand-new airplanes."

"Exactly," Luis said. "We made it. We powered through the awful stuff."

Tamika scrawled a note on her tablet using ocular swipes. Then she turned the device toward Lexi.

This is it, girl. A new start.

Lexi smiled. Training week was officially complete.

Reggie thanked everyone for their time and effort. "I know

you have flights to catch this afternoon. Before we disperse, I want to say that you are trailblazers. This class you're about to teach represents growth at a critical time. Thanks for sharing that momentum with your fellow flight attendants. I appreciate each one of you. Go be great."

With that, everyone burst into applause. Luis came up behind Lexi, wrapping an arm around her neck in a cross between a headlock and a hug. Tamika gave Carrie a high-five, then turned to Lexi and did the same. Everybody laughed. They promised to stay in touch.

The chatter died down as people packed up their supplies. Within minutes, the room thinned out. An AutoBus was parked outside, soaking up solar rays while waiting to transport employees to Orlando International Airport.

"When do you fly home?" Tamika asked. She grabbed her suitcase from the storage closet.

"Seven o'clock flight to Sacramento," Lexi said. "How about you?"

"Five-thirty flight to San Francisco. Let's get drinks at the airport."

"Shoot, did I forget to tell you? I'm going downtown with Jason first."

Tamika nudged Lexi's shoulder. "Of course you are."

"We're on a mission. I'm getting inked tonight."

"First time?"

"Yep."

"Interesting. I'm guessing there's a really good story behind it. Send photos, Lexi. I'll see you next week when we set up our classroom." Tamika wrapped Lexi in a bear hug. "If there's any way I can help with your family stuff in the meantime, let me know."

"I appreciate that," Lexi murmured into her shoulder. "You're a good friend, Tamika."

"Friend and teaching partner and co-conspirator."

Lexi nodded in agreement. She grabbed her bags and darted into the hallway, veering the opposite direction from the other flight attendants. The elevators at the end of the hall beckoned to her. She shot up to the third floor. Dragging her suitcase behind her, she arrived at Jason's classroom to find it dark and empty. With a sigh, she activated AutoScan.

"I can take those," a familiar voice said.

She spun around to discover Jason standing behind her. He grabbed her suitcase and leaned in for a peck on the lips. "You're not supposed to drink before getting a tattoo, but the appointment isn't until four-thirty, and I know a place that makes badass cocktails. What do you say, maybe just one?"

"Sure," Lexi agreed as they made their way to the elevators. "My first tattoo, and we chug booze beforehand. What could possibly go wrong?"

"We'll pace ourselves. You won't even catch a buzz. I promise to take good care of you, Lexi."

"I'm trusting you, baby mechanic. My life is in your hands."

During the drive downtown, Jason told Lexi about his day. She shared tidbits of hers, too, mentioning the moment she discovered she was on display for the entire class.

Jason careened into a parking spot beside Lake Eola. "Are you excited to start classes?"

Lexi unbuckled her seatbelt and swung open her door. "I think it'll be cool to teach half the month and fly a little in between."

"Sounds like a good balance."

"Yes. I've always wanted to be an instructor. The timing and circumstances never worked out."

"Until now," Jason corrected her.

Lexi nodded. "Until now. Teaching is my zen. When I'm up there in front of students, all the chaos in my life becomes background noise. I love the flicker of understanding in someone's eyes when I explain a concept or a new idea. It's better than sex, almost."

"What? No way." Jason grabbed her hand.

"I said *almost,*" Lexi clarified with a laugh. They crossed the street together, approaching a bar with lights strung over the patio.

Chapter Twelve

"Funny how one drink always turns into two," Lexi noted as she finished a glass of cabernet.

Jason gestured toward the half-empty plates on the table. "Food cancels out the first glass."

Lexi nodded. "True. It's science."

"The laws of nature. You want the last bacon-wrapped fig?"

"Nah. Go for it."

Jason looked at his watch while he chewed. "Appointment's in twenty minutes. We might have time to walk around Lake Eola if you want."

"Sure." Lexi reached for her handbag, dangling from a hook beneath the table. Her EarLink buzzed with an incoming call, and a single word flashed across her cornea. "I need to take this. Meet me outside?"

Jason nodded. "I'll come find you."

Lexi darted through the restaurant's entrance. Waves of sunshine washed over her as she tapped her ear. "Mom? Everything okay?"

"Colin's staying longer, baby."

"Huh? Why?"

"He's been stockpiling his meds. Pretending to take them. The doctors caught him today."

"Why the hell isn't he on a slow-release pack? He should be a prime candidate, given his terrible history with pills."

"I agree. The doctors are concerned."

Lexi exhaled slowly. "Do they think he was going to hurt

himself?"

"Nobody really knows, Lex."

"How did he sneak this past everyone the last four days?"

"They have 'round-the-clock monitoring. Somehow, the microcameras were deactivated for a few seconds at a time. It was a quick blackout each day. Way too short for anyone to notice until they did some digging. The images were spliced together. I didn't understand the full description."

Lexi shook her head. "Of course Colin found a way to break into the system. He's too smart for his own good. He shut off the cameras just long enough to hide his meds somewhere. Even without access to AutoScan, he figured it out."

"He probably did," her mom agreed. "It looks like Colin's resisting treatment. Or maybe he doesn't believe in medication anymore. We might not be able to visit him tomorrow. I'm waiting for the hospital to call me back."

"Will they finally give him a slow-release pack?"

"They're planning to insert one soon. Maybe this will be the extra push they need."

Shielding her eyes from the sun, Lexi took a few steps forward. A white bench rested under a tree, partially covered by the shade. Lexi sat down on the weathered wooden surface. People strolled past, exchanging lighthearted banter. Their laughter felt distant and muffled. It was from the wrong universe, Lexi decided. That carefree place, full of easy chatter, was not Colin's world. It wasn't hers, either.

Lexi tilted her face toward the sky. Birds circled overhead as though everything was fine. A plane drifted past cartoonish white clouds.

Fierce longing stirred in Lexi's core. She ached to be on that airplane, headed anyplace other than Sacramento. Flying furiously toward the horizon, toward an existence drastically different from her own.

"I hope Colin can have visitors tomorrow," she said

weakly.

"I know, baby. We all do."

"I'd like to spend time with him even if he's in bad shape," Lexi continued, her voice cracking. "I need to show him I'm there for him no matter what. When he's in the dark place, he forgets."

"You're a good sister. I wish I had better news, Lex. We'll update you when we get more information from the doctors. Do you want to stay with us tonight when you fly back to town?"

"That's okay. It'll be late, Mama. I should go home and unpack my bags after being gone all week. Check on the apartment. Feed Cleo. I'll come over for dinner tomorrow."

"Sounds good."

"Love you, Mom." She ended the call.

"Lex," Jason said softly, approaching her from behind. He took a seat on the bench and turned to face Lexi. His right shoulder was drenched in brilliant sunshine, while his left shoulder was covered in shade.

The sun blocked Lexi's vision as she looked up at him. His face was a silhouette, sharp and distinct. "Hey."

"Bad news?"

Lexi nodded, unable to speak. Thoughts spun through her head, then vanished unceremoniously. Puffs of air with no clear direction or purpose.

"I'm sorry," Jason told her. "Wish I could make things better."

"Things don't get better," Lexi reflected. Her voice sounded robotic in her own ears. "It's a never-ending crash course. Highs and lows forever. Since the day I saw him dangling, the day I realized how complicated and delicate his brain was, there has never been freedom."

"No cure."

"None. You just sit and wait for the next disaster. Nobody

can predict when it will happen. Know the worst part?"

"Hmm?"

"That I fucking love him," Lexi spat out.

"I know you do." Jason wrapped an arm around her, pulling her toward him.

"He's brilliant. That kid hacks every tech system he's ever seen. You wouldn't believe it, Jason. When President Dipshit took office six years ago, Colin broke into the Alabama lottery system. He mailed the winning ticket to a family whose daughter had been attacked by the state's anti-abortion wackos. The family won four million bucks. Spent it on medical care for their daughter and used the rest to start a foundation. The girl recovered just fine, thankfully."

"Okay, I like your brother already."

"He's sensitive and fragile sometimes. He's also really amazing," Lexi whispered, burrowing into Jason's neck. She refused to let the levee break. She'd already cried enough. It was boring. Lexi did not want her tears to define her, to mark the days of the week like yellow tape on a hiking trail.

"You're okay," Jason murmured. His voice echoed in his ribcage, pulsing against Lexi's ear. "You're doing great, Lex. This world needs people like Colin. He's a force for good. Everything will turn out fine, even if it doesn't feel that way."

Lexi paused, wishing Jason's sentiments were true. They were half accurate, half daydreams, as far as she could tell. "Do you have brothers and sisters?"

He paused. "Yeah. My sister and I don't talk anymore."

"How long has it been?"

"Since May. We got in a big fight."

Lexi pried herself from Jason's chest and rose to her feet. "Not to boss you around, but you might want to reconcile. Don't do it for my sake. Do it for yours. Life is too short to let some heated argument get between you and the people you love."

Jason nodded. Agony registered in his irises, a deep-seated anguish as potent as Lexi's inner tempest.

He blinked, and the sadness dissipated. There was no trace of remorse in Jason's deep brown eyes, just the usual flicker of compassion. Lexi wondered if perhaps she'd been imagining things.

They walked to Ben's rental car wordlessly. Jason opened the passenger door for Lexi, then climbed behind the wheel. Instead of starting the engine, he turned to face her.

"I'll fly to Sacramento with you, Lexi," he announced.

"It's five hours to Sac, maybe longer with a headwind," Lexi pointed out. "It's far. Stay in Orlando and enjoy your days off."

"Weekends are quiet around here. I'd rather be with you. You shouldn't be alone. Not in this shitty moment."

Lexi bit her lip. *Nobody stays during the shitty moments.* She recalled Colin's glassy stare the night Marco left him. *People leave. In the end, they always leave.*

Jason reached over the console, pulling her close until she forgot what she'd been protesting in the first place.

Intricate tattoo designs covered the entrance to the shop.

Lexi marveled at the artistry etched into every image. The tattoos looked three-dimensional, as though Lexi could reach forward and run a finger across each contour. These drawings were incredible. Her tattoo would come to life here, she knew. It would be flawless and stunning. Exactly as it was meant to be.

Lexi approached a receptionist. Beyond his desk, plastic screens separated each chair, vestiges of a scarier time. Ominous digital signs flashed across a nanoscreen at the back of the room, shouting warnings to clients before dissolving into thin air. Grave risks and responsibilities were presented in neon letters.

The man at the front desk rose from his swivel chair. He

was nearly as tall as Jason, and his hair was gelled into a purple mohawk.

He tapped his tablet twice, initiating a Holoscreen. A transparent rectangle materialized in front of Lexi, the words flipping themselves horizontally.

The first form asked how many times she'd received the antidote. Her antibody levels were requested. The document demanded that she prove which glycoproteins were floating through her bloodstream. Lastly, she had to authorize the tattoo parlor to look her up in the National Antidote-Compliant—AC—Database.

Yes, she scrawled in messy letters. She thought of Jorge. His twin brother. All the others who were singled out over a minor genetic anomaly, ostracized, excluded, and regarded as subhuman. *AC authorized, reference number 3610.55.*

Lexi sighed.

The next form issued a warning that falsifying AC/AR status was punishable by steep fines and jail time.

A chill ran down Lexi's spine as she skimmed the paragraph.

She glanced at Jason, wondering how often he'd been forced to answer degrading questions like these. He was sitting in a chair near the entrance, thumbing through a glossy magazine. His t-shirt covered his tattoo. Lexi could imagine the uproar that would ensue if his shoulder was exposed. Most of society had deemed him a criminal. A pariah.

Shaking her head, Lexi scribbled her name across the holographic signature box. Then she lifted her thumb. Tiny lasers scanned every curve and wrinkle embedded in her skin.

The transparent screen shrank to a red dot. Two seconds later, the image disappeared, uploading itself onto the display in front of the spiky-haired receptionist. Lexi watched the man's eyes skirt across the transparent screen. She imagined he was silently ticking the boxes, ensuring her responses were satisfactory.

"Alexis?" a dark-haired girl called from the far corner of the room, pulling Lexi's attention in that direction. The woman smiled warmly, then slipped a mouth guard between her teeth.

Jason hopped to his feet and headed toward Lexi. He grabbed her hand in one swift motion. Together, they approached the tattoo artist.

"Nice to meet you. I'm Tati. Don't mind the mouth guard. It's a precaution in case anyone forges the paperwork," she said. Black hair tumbled over her shoulders in symmetrical waves. One arm was bare, a blank slate. The other was covered with ink from her clavicle down to her wrist. "Daron called yesterday. I couldn't turn down a request from an old friend. He's a good guy. One of my first clients when I moved to Orlando six years ago."

Lexi swallowed. "Thanks for making time for me, Tati. It's my first tattoo."

"A virgin! How exciting." She gestured toward the black chair.

Jason grabbed a seat on a crimson bar stool beside Lexi. He leaned toward her, mere inches from her face. "You ready?"

"Yes," Lexi breathed. "I've wanted to do this for years."

"It'll look amazing," Jason promised.

Lexi nodded. Tears welled in her eyes. She bit her lip, urging the waterfall to retreat.

She grasped one leg, determined to thrust her nails into her thigh. As though reading her mind, Jason reached over. He placed his hand in hers. Their intertwined fingers created a sensation far more powerful than anything Lexi could have orchestrated on her own. Her tears retreated.

Tatiana rearranged the vials of ink on the wall. She pulled several tools from a cylindrical machine that was whirring around like a carousel. She inspected each item while Lexi watched in wonder.

"Lex," Jason said gently, pulling her from her thoughts.

She blinked. Jason and Tati were staring at her inquisitively.

"Sorry, can you repeat that?" she murmured.

"I was just asking the tattoo's location and color," Tati said. She held up a piece of paper with Katie's design etched into it in bold strokes. "I'll put a stencil on your skin to make sure you like the placement."

"Sounds great. Okay, I had a couple ideas in mind," Lexi began. "But I narrowed it down to one spot."

"Where's that?"

"Left shoulder."

Tati's eyes widened. She appeared to stop breathing for a moment. As Lexi searched her eyes, she noticed the woman was truly striking, a work of art. With her bold body inscriptions and dark features, she looked like a model.

"You're sure?" Tati asked.

"One hundred percent."

"Listen, babe, I just need confirmation this is what you want," Tatiana murmured. Her voice rose at the end. "You know the current laws, right? And with the shit that just happened today, they might get even stricter."

Lexi nodded. "Illegal to have a shoulder tattoo removed. I know."

"There are other rules." Tati's eyes widened, two saucers of disbelief. "I'll pull up the forms on my Holoscreen."

She tapped her tablet, head tilted downward. Shiny black bangs fell over her eyes as she stared at the device. Lexi shifted in her chair. A rectangle materialized in front of her, red letters glowing brightly.

Lexi skimmed through the document, written in legal jargon. Her eyes flitted across terms like *irrevocable* and *punitive*. Over the years, she'd heard enough threats aimed at Colin to recognize intimidation and bullying. Especially when it was right in front of her face.

Lexi turned to Jason. She attempted, unsuccessfully, to form a coherent question. His eyes latched onto hers. Waves of support flowed from his irises.

"If you want this, a few politicians with self-serving agendas can't stop you," Jason assured her. His voice was confident and steady. "You have every right to put this ink wherever you choose."

"Maybe it's absurd. Maybe I'll regret this someday, but my shoulder feels symbolic. It has the most meaning."

"Then go for it."

Lexi swiped her finger across the Holoscreen, placing her initials beside every disclaimer. When she added her signature to the bottom of the page, the screen collapsed into a miniscule red oval. With a flash of light, it evaporated.

Tati set her tablet on the counter. She clasped her hands together. Unclasped them. Took a deep breath. She smiled at Lexi. The grin didn't quite reach her eyes. "You're the only person who's come in here and willingly gotten a shoulder tattoo since, well, pre-ContaCan times. You're sure this is what you want, right?"

Lexi swallowed. "I am."

"Okay. Here we go."

The needle carved back and forth at an angle, digging deeper into the same patch of skin. Based on the sweep of Tati's hand, Lexi assumed this was the wave's crest.

With her stomach and chest pressed into the chair, Lexi imagined the bird's eye view of her in-progress body art. It was an easy image to conjure. Before filling her needle with ink, Tati had rubbed a stencil on Lexi's skin. AutoScan, sensing the marking, was able to project the image onto Lexi's iris.

And now, twenty minutes later, the drawing was nearly

complete. Tati's needle traced its route like an expert swimmer carving a lane in an infinity pool.

Lexi visualized her skin cells shifting and expanding to welcome the black ink.

Tati lifted her needle. The buzzing ceased. Lexi opened her eyes to find Jason standing before her, patience and care written on his face.

We have this much in common, Jason. We're permanently marked in a controversial spot.

Jason helped her sit upright. Tatiana snapped a photograph of Lexi's shoulder, then placed tattoo butter on the spot and covered it in dissolvable plastic film. With a few clicks of her tablet, Tati projected the photo onto a Holoscreen for Lexi to observe.

Lexi expanded the image with two fingers, zooming in on the wave's ripple. It was shockingly intricate, even more remarkable than the stencil had been. Lexi almost expected the water to shimmer and flow.

"Do you add these photos to your website?" Jason asked, peering over Lexi's head to view the Holoscreen.

Tati paused. "Ordinarily, yes."

"But not this one," Lexi supplied. The dollar sign icon flashed in the corner of the screen. She sent the invoice to her phone with a couple ocular swipes, then added a massive tip. This was, after all, a strange experience for Tati. Lexi knew the tattoo artist had taken a big risk.

Tati offered an apologetic smile. "It's a bold move. Brave as hell. But not everyone is so understanding, know what I mean? These are weird times."

After thanking Tati, Lexi rose from her chair. People gawked as she marched toward the exit. She felt a dozen strangers' eyes affixed to her tattoo, visible through the sheer eco-friendly covering.

Before Lexi could register what was happening, Jason

pulled his t-shirt over his head and covered her shoulders with it. He grinned, ivory teeth sparkling beneath the fluorescent lights. His undershirt revealed his faded AR tattoo. The writing was plain as day.

"There. Now they *really* have something to stare at," he told Lexi with a wink.

The door jingled cheerfully as they stepped outside.

AutoScan – Katie Hoffmeyer, you're amazing. Thank you for making this whole thing possible. We just left the tattoo shop.

Lexi sent the message with a double blink. Katie responded instantly.

We? And you're so welcome! Happy to help.

Lexi bit her lip. Had she forgotten to tell Katie about Jason? *AutoScan – Katie Hoffmeyer, I went with a new friend. Nice guy, mechanic for SkyLine.*

Big green signs pointed to the airport exit. Jason steered right, then merged onto the ramp. Once they were on elevated turf, the airport's control tower came into view. It was a structure Lexi had seen dozens of times, yet it had never shined quite this brightly. She peered up at the sky, searching for the distinct red-and-black fuselage that had been her soul's refuge since 2034. Clouds stared back at her. An endless blue and white canvas stretched all the way to the horizon.

The Sacramento flight would depart in exactly one hour. Lexi guessed the plane was parked at the gate, getting thoroughly disinfected before welcoming another round of passengers. She felt a sudden urge to head back to the crew hotel. Skip the flight home and spend the weekend here with Jason.

Jason's EarLink buzzed with an alert. "What the—"

"Travel advisory? Canceled flights?" Lexi asked, surprised by the eagerness in her voice. She pulled out her phone and authorized VirtuAlarms with a single stroke of her eye. A cryptic article scrolled in front of her cornea. The directives didn't make sense. "I don't understand, Jason."

Jason pulled his eyes from the road for a fleeting second. "It's a new requirement for transportation workers. We have to validate passenger documents before anyone rides on a plane or bullet train or even a bus. The government is issuing updating facial recognition scanners. New devices can recognize faces even after surgery, using algorithms."

"Skin grafting will be useless?"

"Doesn't seem like it's an option anymore. They're also revamping GeoTrack hubs at the city limits in Birmingham, Dallas, Atlanta."

"Why?"

"Someone scrambled the national database, one of the tech groups with a conscience. ARs' personal data was changed so they could escape before things spiraled out of control." Jason cruised into the right-hand lane as airline signs came into view. "Of course, the president wasn't happy about that. He called it a security breach. He accused ARs of treason and espionage. So now the transportation industry is required to stop anyone from traveling until their identity has been double, triple, quadruple checked."

"So we have to enforce the laws passed in Texas and Florida?"

"And Georgia, Alabama, Oklahoma," Jason added. "The administration is cracking down. Transportation workers are now cops, for the most part. After a few failed attempts to sequester all the ARs in the nation, the feds have gotten desperate."

"How did ARs change their documents? Is it that easy to mess with the national database?" Lexi asked.

"It's almost impossible. This is the work of DefenderTech, for sure. Good thing they stepped in. Six more states are jumping on the bandwagon. ARs are going to be attacked on the streets or sent to containment centers." Jason sighed as he cruised to a stop in front of the SkyLine ticket counter. "It's so twisted."

Defeat echoed in his voice.

He parked the car, grabbed Lexi's suitcases from the trunk, and rigged them together with the heavy-duty strap dangling from Lexi's roller-board.

"I hate this." Lexi sank into Jason's arms, her voice muffled by his t-shirt. "Jorge would've been deported. That waiter you tried to save at the hotel would've been sent somewhere remote, someplace nobody could contact him. Left to die."

"If someone hadn't sent a self-guided explosive to detonate in him." Jason exhaled, his ribcage rattling against Lexi's cheek. "It's awful."

Lexi nodded. "We have to figure something out, Jason. This is madness."

"I know."

She inhaled sharply and reached for her suitcase. "Are you parking at the airport?"

"I'll grab my bag from the hotel, then head back here. See you on the plane."

"Okay. I'll understand if you change your mind."

"Not a chance." Jason shook his head. "You're stuck with me, sorry."

He returned to the driver seat, started the engine, and merged into outbound traffic. Lexi watched the SUV disappear around a corner. Then she wheeled her bags inside the airport.

On the plane, she greeted the flight attendants. None of them looked familiar. With a polite smile, she navigated toward her seat, located a few rows in front of the aft galley. After sending a text to her mom and Katie, she leaned back. The seat frame dug into her flesh, still tender from the fresh new carving on her shoulder.

She winced. The thin sweater covering her back provided

very little padding. Gritting her teeth, Lexi sat upright.

The lead flight attendant began her opening announcement. Lexi glanced at the dwindling line of passengers entering the plane. Jason was not among them.

Her phone screen remained blank and lifeless. AutoScan was quiet. A flicker of disappointment pulsed in her core.

Lexi focused her attention on the petite flight attendant standing near the forward galley. The woman wrapped up her opening announcement with a reminder to disable AutoScan for takeoff.

After the flight attendant ended her speech, she poked her head inside the cockpit. When she reemerged, she offered passengers an apologetic smile.

"Sorry for the delay. We'll depart momentarily. First, we're handling a quick issue for everyone's safety," the flight attendant announced. "Shouldn't be too long, then we'll be on our way to Sacramento."

A thud echoed from the front of the plane, as though someone had slammed a suitcase against the bulkhead.

Lexi dug her nails into her thighs. She craned her neck to spot a scuffle between a thin teenager and several airport employees. The adolescent was outnumbered at least three to one, but Lexi couldn't be sure. There was too much commotion. Items were tossed around like confetti, landing in various spots among the first few rows. A backpack, a micro laptop, even a shoe.

Yelling ensued, followed by a sharp crack. Shivers traveled down Lexi's spine. It sounded like a fractured bone or maybe a smashed tablet. Lexi hoped it was the latter.

While she watched, a man in an EMT uniform tossed the tiny girl over his shoulder. The kid clawed at the air, her face contorted in panic. Long brown hair swung wildly, obscuring her eyes for a moment.

Lexi had never seen airport medical staff pull a person off

the plane like that. The girl was so small. She must've weighed ninety pounds or less. For Chrissake, she was just a child. Lexi couldn't imagine it would take multiple adults to drag her off.

Lexi turned toward the back galley. The flight attendant sitting on the aft jumspeat stared blankly ahead as though bored to tears by the scene unfolding up front.

"Hey, what's going on?" Lexi asked her. "I'm a crew member, just heading home. Everything okay up there?"

The flight attendant sauntered over, her blonde hair sashaying with each step. She picked a piece of lint off her dress before answering Lexi. "I guess the girl was an AR? Just another thug trying to evade the law. She came close, but the gate agent got suspicious. He found her in the database."

"Didn't the travel laws just get approved today? SkyLine already expects us to comply? I thought we needed new devices and a written procedure."

The flight attendant shrugged. "My crew isn't taking any risks. I think they'll find a camp in the countryside where this kid can't hurt anyone else. It's for the best. I'm so tired of all this. If people followed the rules, life would be way easier. It isn't hard."

Unless you're an AR. Lexi scratched her head and faced forward. A tall woman hurried onto the plane, holding a designer purse in one hand and a dog carrier in the other. She slid into the seat which had been previously occupied by the teenager.

Lexi grimaced as a burst of pain radiated from her shoulder.

Despite Tati's instructions not to mess with her tattoo, she rubbed the sore spot. The ridges of the tattoo were raised. Strips of elevated flesh outlined the design, creating a roadmap for Lexi's fingers. Through the dissolvable plastic wrap and thin sweater, she could feel the permanence of her new shoulder ink. Her body was no longer a blank portrait, miles and miles of unmarked canvas.

The lead flight attendant reached for the forward galley door. Lexi braced herself for the click of the latch, a sound nearly inaudible to the average traveler but quite familiar to those who worked in aviation.

Lexi wanted to text Jason about the incident during boarding. He would feel the same way she did—uncomfortable. And angry. Where would they send the teenager? What awaited her there? She was just a kid. She was so young.

Changes were coming, Lexi knew. Each update was more ominous than the last one. Apparently, President Bonehead had rigged the system to grant himself full authority. Bad things lingered on the horizon. Lexi hadn't imagined this type of persecution would happen so quickly, though. She thought there would be time to prepare. A delay before delving into the worst of the worst.

SkyLine had made a ton of public statements about equality, yet the airline was authorizing hardcore assault. Lexi shook her head. How could this flight crew decide to actively ruin a teenager's life before the proper tracking tools had even been installed? It didn't make any sense.

Lexi wanted to talk to Jason, but he wasn't there. The seat beside hers remained empty. Jason had missed the flight. Lexi figured he'd changed his mind. Maybe at the last minute he decided he didn't want to fly to Sacramento and get sucked into her family's sad dynamics. He probably had better things to do. Lexi couldn't blame him, not really.

So she messaged Katie instead. *AutoScan – Katie Hoffmeyer, Leaving Orlando now. Love you, see you soon.*

Katie's response arrived instantaneously. She sent warm wishes for a safe flight and told Lexi to come visit once she returned to town.

As the forward door closed, Lexi toyed with the idea of

texting Jason.

She gave in, sending a short message. *AutoScan – Jason Mechanic, Taking off. Guess you didn't make it.*

Then she disabled AutoScan and closed her eyes. Sleep washed over her easily, pulling her beneath its gentle lull.

Wheels smacked against solid ground, stirring Lexi from her nap. It was by no means a graceful landing. Rather, it was an abrasive touchdown, similar to Key West's abrupt landings on a condensed runway.

Lexi yawned and rubbed her eyes.

The seatbelt dug into her hips as forceful brakes curbed the plane's momentum. She checked her phone. Although they'd left Orlando on time, the plane had arrived in Sacramento forty minutes late. Lexi glanced at the SkyLine flight navigation app, a small square on the corner of her watch. Their route looked like something a toddler had scribbled in crayon. Apparently, the plane had flown in a series of jagged semicircles to get to California. Lexi guessed they'd dodged some huge storm cells.

When she activated AutoScan, a flurry of texts and VirtuAlarms floated past her eyelids. There were too many to keep track of. As the plane cruised to a stop in front of gate D4, Lexi tapped her EarLink to hear the highlight reel in chronological order.

9:52 P.M. Mom texted – No updates on Colin. Would be nice to visit him tomorrow. We will keep you posted. Fly safe. Love you.

Lexi sighed. She needed to find a way to see her brother tomorrow whether the hospital approved or not. She couldn't wait an extra day. Even an extra hour would be brutal.

8:44 P.M. Katie Hoffmeyer texted – I bet your tattoo is amazing. Please send pics! Or you can surprise me when we hang out this weekend. Thanks for letting me be a part of this, Lex.

Katie's sincerity wrapped itself around Lexi, seeping into her bones with fervor. She made a mental note to buy some wine as a thank-you for Katie's illustration, now permanently engraved on Lexi's back. A nice bottle of chardonnay. Katie's favorite.

Lexi's row was about to deplane, so she grabbed her bags. Across the aisle, two women spoke in hushed tones, comparing notes on a VirtuAlarm they'd received. The lady in the window seat, probably in her mid-sixties, had tears in her eyes. She mumbled something and tapped her ear, presumably to usher in more news.

AutoScan – Skip to VirtuAlarms. Lexi commanded. *Filter by most recent.*

While trekking up the aisle and the jetbridge, Lexi's vision flooded with a series of heartbreaking stories. Parents of a three-year-old AR tried to cross the Alabama border by vehicle, only to be stopped before entering Tennessee. Their hopes of escaping to a sanctuary state had been dashed in one fell swoop. Their documents were not falsified, which meant they wouldn't be charged with a federal offense, thankfully. No jail time. No treason charges. The government snatched their child, though. Lexi couldn't imagine anything worse than having your baby ripped from your arms. And what would anyone want with a toddler who had a genetic anomaly, anyway?

The VirtuAlarms continued flashing before her eyes.

Civil liberties groups had gone the record to express outrage. They'd filed a series of high-profile lawsuits. Unfortunately, with the Supreme Court run by Christian terrorists and sexual predators, Lexi doubted the lawsuits would amount to much.

Other VirtuAlarms discussed growing concerns from transportation unions refusing to enforce the required restrictions. Strikes and protests loomed on the horizon, assuming the unions had enough courage to follow through with their claims.

Lexi continued reading in the hopes that SkyLine would be

mentioned among the corporations opposing the new legislation. The airline was not listed, as far as she could tell. She disabled AutoScan. It was too demoralizing. Besides, what could she do? The cruel plan was already in motion. The nightmare was well underway.

Lexi reached the top of the jetbridge and emerged onto Terminal D. She was greeted by an abundance of lively décor. Sacramento had won the annual SkyLine Beautification Award earlier that year. Twinkling amber lanterns dotted the walkway, a welcomed contrast to the dismal VirtuAlarms echoing in Lexi's mind.

Lexi's gaze flitted to a shimmery lantern with vines etched on the glass. This one had been her own personal contribution to SkyLine's unexpected post-apocalyptic comeback. She'd spent entirely too much time on that thing, recruiting Colin to help her. He'd chosen the colors and patterns. He was no artist, but he'd worked diligently to make sure the lantern looked good. Lexi smiled at the memory.

"World's best smile," someone bellowed from her left side.

She turned toward the familiar voice. Jason strolled beside her, casually, hands tucked in his pockets. A messenger bag was strapped over one shoulder.

Lexi's jaw dropped. She stopped cold, forcing passengers to weave around her. They groaned, whipped their suitcases in a semi-circle, and shook their heads disapprovingly.

"What the . . ." Lexi sputtered.

Jason shot her a sly grin. "Didn't you see my text? I missed the SkyLine flight by thirty seconds."

"I was listening to VirtuAlarms. There were a lot of morbid ones," Lexi noted. "How'd you get here?"

"After I missed the SkyLine flight, I sprinted to the Bright Coast terminal. I was sweating like crazy. The gate agent probably felt bad for me. She listed me on the flight even though it was already closed out. I think we broke a hundred inter-airline nonrevenue travel rules."

"She probably wanted to bang you."

"The woman was pushing seventy-five years old."

"Age is just a number," Lexi responded with a chuckle. She shook her head, impressed by Jason's tenacity.

His airline ID was tucked inside an arm band, the barcode visible through a square plastic covering. Lexi's eyes swept across the badge.

It dawned on her that she'd never bothered to ask his last name. After a week together, she only knew him as Jason or, more often, baby mechanic.

"Jason Bresline, huh? Your last name's so close to mine," she mused.

"Yeah, when Tati used your full name at the tattoo shop, I almost did a double-take. To tell you the truth, I thought she was messing with me," Jason admitted. "Putting some kind of spin on our names."

"I'm sure no one at the shop had a clue about your full name or profile info. No way they would've let you stay—" Lexi bit her lip as she realized the implications of her comment.

Jason nudged her shoulder. "It's okay, Lex. I've gotten used to being kicked out of places because of my AR records. Nobody believes the tattoo was done in error, even though I have a billion documents to prove it."

"I'm sorry."

He shook his head. "Makes me miss the days when people only got harassed and accosted due to old-fashioned racism."

Lexi's eyes widened.

"Relax. I'm just kidding." Jason tilted his head to the side. "Sort of."

"Are you, though? I bet you've experienced some shit."

"It's okay. I mean, it's not okay," he clarified. "But I'm trying to stay optimistic that things will change for the better. I hope this whole AR situation teaches everyone that people are people, period. No exceptions. No asterisks."

"Me, too. About damn time, huh?" Lexi glanced around. The stream of passengers had dwindled away, leaving the terminal quiet and empty. It was just the two of them, and the award-winning SkyLine employee decorations, and the majestic night sky pouring in through floor-to-ceiling windows on either side of the concourse.

Jason grabbed Lexi's suitcase and wheeled it down the terminal. They burst through the exit doors, greeted by warm autumn air. The van to the employee lot was waiting in its usual spot at the second curb.

Instead of advancing toward the van, Jason paused. He turned to Lexi. "How are you?"

"Good."

"No, how are you really?"

Lexi looked up at him. When she tried to breathe, her lungs faltered. There was so much care in his eyes. It was unlike anything Lexi had witnessed before. This wasn't raw yearning, the aggressive kind that spilled from every orifice. Jason's brown eyes contained no trace of self-serving indulgence, satisfaction, hunger. None of the usual tasty thrills, the ones Lexi chased and emulated. Flawlessly.

With Jason, there was no need to evade reality or summon her favorite magic tricks.

The employee shuttle departed while Lexi remained keenly focused on Jason. In her peripheral view, neon taillights wobbled toward the parking lot. The next shuttle wouldn't arrive for twenty minutes. This felt unimportant, a minor inconvenience compared to the human-sized mystery standing before her.

"I'm wrecked," Lexi finally stammered. "My brother is sick. He'll always be sick, probably. He either takes too much medication or skips it entirely."

Jason nodded without speaking.

"Meanwhile, there's a human rights meltdown in progress," Lexi continued. "I'm worried about Colin while the whole world goes up in flames. Is America even a democracy anymore? It seems doubtful. Sometimes I'm thankful Jorge isn't around to see this. I never imagined this kind of genocide would happen. Not here. Not during my lifetime."

"Things have always been bad, Lexi," Jason said quietly. "They're just more visible now. The attacks are out in the open for everyone to see, and the rules are getting crazier."

Lexi blinked. Her whole life had been confined to her little California bubble, she knew, and Jason's experience was vastly different from hers. She'd been judged and stereotyped, sure. But she'd never faced outright persecution. California never revoked LGBT or women's rights when the southern states did so in the 2020s. Throughout her entire existence, Lexi had remained mostly protected. A few blows to her confidence. Nothing that would leave a permanent scar.

Jason, on the other hand, had seen the ugly truth of discrimination. He'd been on the receiving end of blame and loathing. His life decisions had been dramatically affected by the wrath of others. For no reason except demographics. He'd been imprisoned by rules he never agreed to, all because some folks disliked the perfect color of his perfect skin.

The war on ARs might be new, but the fight for equality was not. That much, Lexi was certain of. Her brother's battle for validity in a heteronormative world was not lost on her. Jorge's estrangement from his family, birthed from archaic traditions and religious dogma, had been painfully real.

This tension, this fucked-up power grab at the expense of ARs who were perceived as *different*, was as old as time. Jason had battled injustice long before this specific issue came to light.

"I'm so sorry," Lexi told him. She meant it. "I'm sorry for

what you went through. I'm sorry that racism is rampant in this nation and people are too stupid or sheltered to admit it. And I'm sorry for what innocent people are enduring right now. For the crimes that will continue to be committed against folks who happen to have a random genetic glitch. What can we do? Is it hopeless?"

Jason pulled her in for a hug. She folded into his body like a collapsible doll.

"We'll figure out a way to help, Lex. But not tonight," he whispered into Lexi's hair. "Tonight, you just need to breathe. No stress. We can come up with a plan later. Tomorrow will feel much brighter."

Lexi melted into his welcoming arms. *It already feels a little brighter.*

"Where do you live?" Jason asked as he fastened his seatbelt. "Does this thing have self-driving mode?"

"Victory Eaves Apartments. My car's not automated. I paid for the solar-power upgrade. That was the only add-on I got." While she watched, Jason swiped a finger across his tablet. He pulled up a Holoscreen, used a few ocular swipes to issue a command, then tapped his ear.

There was a flash of light at the bottom of Lexi's dashboard. The entire windshield transformed into a roadmap. Red lines covered the glassy surface, creating a sophisticated network of streets and landmarks. The solid yellow arrow in the center of the screen indicated the quickest route to her apartment.

"My car has a HoloRoute display?" Lexi mused.

"You never tried it?"

Lexi shook her head. "Colin mentioned something. I never took the time to look into it. I already know these streets inside-out."

"In that case, you're the perfect tour guide for my first trip to Sac."

"Are you interested in the touristy stuff?"

"Sure. What's on the list?" Jason asked, his gaze fixed on the illuminated windshield grid.

"The Capitol Building's cool. You might enjoy the auto museum. Not sure you'd be interested in the art museums with your mechanical brain and all."

"I like lots of things, Lex," Jason responded with a chuckle. "I appreciate more than just fixing airplanes."

"Is that so? What are you into, baby mechanic?"

"I took an acting class in college. And I played baseball my first two years, until I wrecked my knee," he said. "Let's see, I almost went to culinary school. I decided against it at the last minute."

"You like cooking, huh? That's convenient because I like eating. Maybe you can cook for me sometime?"

"Absolutely."

The yellow arrow on the HoloRoute flashed, indicating their exit was quickly approaching. "I love this thing," Lexi noted, admiring the spectacle on her windshield. "Hey, I want to hear more about your culinary background."

"Nah, HoloRoutes are more interesting than my chef skills. I get it." Jason chuckled. "The technology comes pre-installed on your work tablet. You can use it when you drive to the Bay Area. Or anywhere else."

"It's like the world's been laid out for us," Lexi mused.

"Exactly. The grid tells you everything you'll ever need to know."

"Much easier to navigate than real life."

They drove down N Street, past the twinkling bars and restaurants where Lexi had found, on more than one occasion, the quickest way to erase herself. Her magic tricks had not originated in this part of town, but they'd been refined and perfected here.

"I've taken this route a billion times," Lexi said.

"Everything feels different with the streets illuminated like this."

"Yeah. What will they come up with next? Maybe a HoloRoute display for major life decisions."

"That would be convenient. What about a HoloCareer app?" Lexi shook her head. "And then maybe HoloFamily, although they'd have to find a new name for it."

Jason snickered.

"Why stop there?" Lexi continued. "HoloTimeTravel. I really thought teleporting would be a thing by now."

"Same here. ContaCan was a major setback for the chrono-tech industry. Big companies lost their grants. Emergency funds were redirected to biomedical groups racing to find a cure."

"I heard about delays. I didn't realize the companies lost their grants, though."

Jason shrugged. "I followed it closely. Actually, I kept up with almost all VirtuAlarms. Once I had a literal target on my back, I paid attention to the news. Suddenly, new laws mattered to me. You'd be surprised what goes through your head when you're placed in a bad position. You start to care about shit you didn't notice before."

"I bet."

"If the world hadn't come to a screeching halt for months and the chrono-tech companies had actually created a time machine, would you use it?" Jason asked. "Is there anything you'd do differently?"

"Absolutely. The more fitting question is whether I'd do anything the same," Lexi reflected. "How about you? Would you go to culinary school?"

"Nah. I'm happy with the way things turned out. I like being a SkyLine mechanic."

"SkyLine *baby* mechanic," she corrected him.

The HoloRoute arrow prompted them to turn left. They

cruised into the parking lot of Lexi's apartment complex. Jason pulled into her designated spot and killed the engine. There was a flash in the center of her windshield, a sliver of white. Then the display disappeared. Lexi stared through the glass at the concrete wall lining the periphery of the parking lot.

She climbed out of the passenger seat and led Jason to her apartment.

Awakening with a jolt, Lexi reached for her phone. The screen illuminated her bedroom, casting a blue haze across the empty walls. No missed texts from her mom or dad. No messages from a random number with a Sacramento area code.

She placed the phone back on her nightstand. Remnants of a dream lingered in her mind. Colin was screaming. Or maybe she was screaming.

It was me. Lexi burrowed into her pillow. *Definitely me.*

She'd yelled and yelled. Colin was too far away to hear. He was sprinting toward the Consumnes River, and Lexi couldn't catch up. He'd always been faster than her. For decades, Colin had been one step ahead, moving toward the darkness like he owned the night.

The dream faded to a foggy memory.

Lexi rolled over and glanced at the man beside her. His shoulder blades were sleek and toned. Muscles bulged from smooth, dark skin. The sheets were pooled around his waist, folds of soft fabric overlapping at his body's narrowest point. Lexi was tempted to reach out and place her hand on his side, just to feel something solid beneath her fingertips. Something real. Something full of life.

Instead, she leaned forward to pet Cleo. The cat was positioned at her feet, a half-moon of white fur with two reflective green eyes. Cleo purred as Lexi rubbed her cheek. She stretched, her tiny paws tapping Lexi's toes in the process. With a yawn, the cat closed her eyes and went back to sleep. Her tail fluttered peacefully.

Lexi sank back into the pillows. Beside her, Jason rolled over. With great care, he pulled Lexi toward his chest. His arms gripped her waist, shifting her tank top so it stretched across her midsection. Their bodies merged into a pile of tangled limbs.

Lexi had always imagined that being woven together, being spiritually and physically intertwined, would feel like prison. Like a pair of steel hands squeezing her neck. She'd assumed that a deep and lasting connection, the vulnerability which had reduced her life to chaos, would be suffocating.

Instead, it felt like freedom. Lexi nestled into Jason and fell back asleep.

Chapter Thirteen: October 9, 2038

"Are you sure you're ready?" Jason asked gently.

Lexi nodded. The building stretched before them, its auburn façade ominous and imposing against a cloudless sky. The monochromatic backdrop made the hospital's red bricks appear black. Devoid of all color. Threatening in their calm, quiet lack of vibrance.

Lexi had been inside the hospital too many times to count. But it had never looked quite this sinister.

Her sneakers slapped the pavement as she neared the building's entrance. Blood swooshed in her ears, creating a thunderous roar. Nothing made sense. Noises were inverted. Twisted. Upside-down.

Glass doors swung open, leading to the registration desk. A man sat behind it, scrolling through his tablet.

Lexi glanced at the cameras overhead, hovering black dots no larger than a housefly. They were propelled by tiny motors instead of fluttering wings. While Lexi watched, the cameras weaved around each other, arranging themselves to get the best view of her and Jason.

A nanoscreen on the wall informed her that Lutheran Midtown was doing everything possible to ensure the health and safety of all patients. Letters flashed across the smooth surface. The font was buoyant. The message was not.

The last time Lexi had set foot in this place, a camera with a heat sensor floated over her head while she peed. After ContaCan, privacy laws were rewritten. Invasive regulations, disguised as protective measures, were implemented. Peeing in private was no longer a right. It was a privilege that could be rescinded at any moment. According to the federal government, the Fourth Amendment had run its course.

"Hello," the man at the front desk said. His steely voice matched his expression. "Here to visit a patient?"

"Yes. Colin Brennan, Behavioral Health Unit. His visitation privileges were approved this morning," Lexi supplied. "I have the eleven o'clock slot."

"Name and relationship to the patient?"

"Alexis Brennan. I'm his sister."

"You'll need to declare your AR status or sign a waiver indicating you choose not to disclose the info," the receptionist told me. "I recommend self-identifying. It reduces risk and allows us to better serve our patients. Failure to provide the information jeopardizes everyone's safety. It's also incredibly irresponsible. Most states require it. Once again, California's slow to crack down."

And thank God for that. Lexi cleared her throat. "Antidote-compatible. It's all in my profile. I've gotten four rounds."

The man nodded. A blue square materialized above his tablet, ready to accept Lexi's thumbprint. She held her hand above the scanner until the grooves on her finger had been identified. Her photo appeared on the screen along with all data the government had accumulated over the past few years. There were lots of details. Pages' worth, in tiny font, certain phrases highlighted for the benefit of anyone sorting through her information in a hurry.

"You're all set." The man turned to Jason. "Family only, sorry. You can wait in our containment room. Sanitation procedures are in full effect."

Lexi's hands trembled. She shoved them in her pockets. She'd been there before, in that exact spot, with those same cameras tracing the room to capture her from every angle. She'd seen Colin at his worst. Over and over. This was nothing new, she reminded herself.

She swallowed a mouthful of dread.

The visitation room was just down the hall, but her feet refused to step forward.

This time, she didn't want to do it alone. She didn't want to walk down that corridor and face her brother by herself. She was tired of that lonesome struggle. For every victory, there were a million failures. Tiny slivers of sadness sliced through her bones. Jorge helped ease the pain. He'd been a powerful, compassionate ally on the battlefield of Lexi's life. Until Jorge died and the hurt intensified.

"Jason *is* family," Lexi blurted out. The words echoed in her ears, as though they had been uttered by someone else. "My husband. Quick civil ceremony because of the, um, lockdowns and all. We eloped. Jason Brennan."

She spotted Jason in her peripheral vision. If he was surprised, the shock didn't register on his face. He nodded swiftly, easing Lexi's frayed nerves.

"I took my wife's last name," Jason added. "Jason Brennan, thirty-six years old."

"Thumb, please, unless you want to sign the nondisclosure form," the receptionist said, his speech clipped. "As a reminder, that would risk everyone's wellbeing."

"No, it's fine. You can access my records," Jason said. He held his thumb to the device. A faint beep indicated his information had been uploaded.

"Here, we have to show you the tricky part," Lexi said hurriedly, leaning over the counter to scroll through Jason's information. She slid down to the medical records, hoping the receptionist didn't spot the small differences between Jason's surname and her own. "His preliminary results were inaccurate. Turns out he isn't an AR. He just carries the gene. It's all listed right here, below this line. See that red sentence? He received the antidote in May. Then several additional rounds.

No complications."

The man frowned as he reviewed Jason's profile. "You know there have been issues with ARs falsifying documents, right?"

"It's all over the news," Jason conceded. "But I have proof on my phone, verifiable with the database. There should be a local order as well. I'll pull up the Tennessee records. You can check my thumbprint and biometrics."

The man narrowed his eyes at Jason. "Just remember you're liable for any pathogen you spread if these documents are illicit. Jail time with a life sentence or worse."

Lexi shuddered.

The receptionist gave her an access code for the visitation room. She and Jason hurried down the long, winding hallway. For the first few steps, Lexi held her breath. She inhaled sharply as they approached a windowless metal door. Stale air rattled through her nostrils.

"Global health emergencies are the shittiest time to get married," she murmured to Jason, noting the cameras buzzing overhead. "But I'm glad we did. It would suck going into this by myself."

Jason cracked a smile. "Never imagined marrying into a leprechaun family, if I'm being honest."

"Just so you know, all that stuff about the luck of the Irish? Pure fiction." Lexi said with a shrug. "Bald-faced lies."

Using ocular swipes, Lexi entered her access pin into a scanner. The door creaked open like the entrance to a crypt. Colin sat in a metal chair facing them. He glanced up at Lexi with hollow eyes.

Behind her back, the door swung shut. A resounding click indicated the bolt had slid into place.

Lexi was frozen in place. She wanted to wrap him in a hug and protect him from the chill in this room and the sterile gray walls. That wouldn't do any good, Lexi knew. She couldn't shield her brother from the elements. God, how she'd tried over the years.

Colin's cheeks were sunken in. Leaden rings circled his eyelids like smeared eyeliner from three days before. His frame, which had always been lean, now appeared emaciated.

Lexi swallowed. It seemed her brother's exterior was competing to become as cavernous as his insides.

She stepped forward and swept him into a gentle hug. Even without applying much force, she felt his sharp bones through his standard-issue white t-shirt. When Lexi pulled away, Colin rubbed his shoulder.

"Sorry," Lexi apologized. "Didn't mean to squeeze so tight."

"Not your fault. I'm sore from the hospital bed. It's like sleeping on a slab of concrete." He smiled at Jason. The grin fell short of his eyes. "Hey, man."

Lexi sat down in one of the metal chairs. "I asked Jason to come with me today. Is that okay? I should've checked with you first, kid."

"It's fine. I'm happy to see you two, just surprised. They usually restrict visitors to—"

"Oh, we let the receptionist know it was a last-minute civil ceremony. ContaCan really changed things. It made more sense to head to the courthouse," Lexi said with a flick of her wrist. Cameras fluttered above her head, recording every move. "Anyway, Jason has to return to Orlando for training soon. He's just here for the weekend."

"Nice to meet you, Colin," Jason said as he slid into the seat beside Lexi.

Colin nodded. "You, too. Sorry it's in this dungeon."

Lexi cleared her throat. "How's everything? How are you holding up?

"I'm okay." His eyes were dull and unconvincing. "Ready to go home. When are they going to release me?"

"The latest update was sometime this week," Lexi said, tilting her head to the side. "Everyone wants you safe and healthy. Maybe this is the best place for you right now, Colin."

He shook his head. "It was the safest place when I checked myself in. But not anymore."

Lexi swallowed. "How's therapy going?"

"They put me on all the standard treatment plans. CBT, electroshock, eye movement desensitization. Same stuff as before. You'd be surprised how little has changed in the psychotherapy realm over the past twenty years." Colin shrugged. "In terms of mental health, everyone is stuck in the past."

"Sorry it feels stagnant." Lexi paused. "Before I forget, Katie said hi. There are so many people who care about you, kid."

Colin unfolded and refolded his arms across his chest. Lexi blinked, waiting for him to speak.

"Look, I'm okay," he finally said. "They were after me, so I needed to take cover. Things are calming down. I'm not in danger anymore, and I want to go home."

Lexi bit her lip. She'd been hoping medicine would minimize Colin's delusions. "I know you do."

"Then help me get out of here. Please, Lex."

"I wish I could. Everyone thinks this is the safest spot for you right now."

"Everyone except me," Colin pointed out.

Lexi paused. "I heard you made some progress with one of the social workers."

Colin nodded. "A little, yeah. Listen, not to be rude, but I've spent all week analyzing my brain with nurses and psychiatrists. Let's talk about you, Lex. I want to hear about training."

Lexi glanced at Jason. He offered a warm smile.

"I met some amazing people," she told Colin. "I'll set up my classroom next week, then start teaching the week after that. This class is all about updated health and service procedures. Protocols for the new delivery of planes we'll receive soon. Pathogen preventative measures mid-flight."

"Things to protect ARs?" Colin asked. A flicker of interest sparked in his eyes. "Any word on the transportation mandates? I've been following it as much as I can with the limited communications in here. Has SkyLine revised its policies?"

"We haven't gotten an official update from airline management yet," Lexi said. "It's still unfolding. The class I'm teaching was designed to help flight attendants protect ARs. Meanwhile, the feds are telling us to persecute them. It makes no sense."

"So you don't know which rules apply or how they're enforced? Maybe there's some latitude," Colin said.

Lexi lifted an eyebrow. "Latitude?"

"Leeway. Wiggle room," Colin clarified. "I've been looking into this stuff. It's hard to keep up since they took my phone and disabled AutoScan. But there's a room here with nanoscreens."

"What kind of stuff do they show?" Jason asked.

"No social media access. No news updates because they think it's too triggering. Mostly cartoons and sitcoms from before I was born," Colin said with a nonchalant shrug. "And we have access to a Holoscreen on a shared tablet. VirtuAlarms are disabled."

"Doesn't mean you haven't seen them," Lexi whispered, her voice just low enough to evade the hovering cameras.

A smile crept across her brother's lips.

"What's that old saying about rules?" he murmured.

Lexi chuckled. Her brother couldn't pass up an opportunity to hack into systems, no matter how tricky or complicated. If anything, that made him more determined to gain access. Encryption never stood a chance against Colin Brennan.

"Listen, shit's spiraled out of control," Colin said. "Did you know in thirty-two states, it's legal to deny prenatal care to women if they're ARs? Even before the mandates were approved yesterday, hospitals could turn away expectant mothers. Refusal to disclose their status meant they were treated like ARs. It's draconian."

"It's way worse than people realize," Jason agreed.

Lexi turned toward him. She placed a hand on his arm while he continued.

"Tennessee law allows landlords to evict people from an apartment complex if they have the tattoo. The state justifies it by saying it poses a risk to the other tenants in the building. In reality, it's just another bullshit law intended to exclude people. It's no different than the racist housing policies that kept minorities out of certain neighborhoods for decades."

Anguish echoed in Jason's voice. Lexi slid her hand down his arm until their fingers locked. She felt the urge to defend him from painful battles he never should've had to fight. Of course, there wasn't much she could do except remind him, in every possible way, that she was on his side. And that she would do her part to dismantle the oppressive systems which had failed him.

"How is this happening?" Lexi murmured. "As a society, how are we moving backward so fast?"

"We've always been backward, Lex. At least, for the past ten to twenty years. But now we're just shifting the hatred. These days, ARs are everyone's favorite scapegoat." Colin shook his head. "Did you know it's almost impossible for an AR to infect someone who's had the antidote? The far more likely scenario is that an antidote-compliant person will have remnants of ContaCan in their bloodstream and pass it on to the AR with fatal results."

Jason nodded. "I did CPR on an AR this week, trying to save the guy. People were shocked by it, but he had a much higher risk than I did. It's all scare tactics, you know? It's easy to generate fear. Convince folks every problem in the world can be traced to one group of people. It's a tired old strategy. Unoriginal."

"But effective," Colin quipped. "Man, we need to pull our heads out of our asses. Think of all the amazing things humanity could accomplish if we weren't so focused on annihilating one another."

Silence descended on the room.

"I really want to get out of here," Colin said, slicing through the quiet.

"I know. The doctors need to see progress, though," Lexi explained. "When you stop taking your meds, it causes a delay."

He frowned. When he spoke, his voice was hushed. "Turn on AutoScan."

Lexi blinked. "Huh?"

"Trust me. Activate it," he said, his voice still quiet. "I need your phone for two seconds."

Lexi pulled her phone from her pocket, holding it at her side. With a flick of her eye, she activated AutoScan. She handed the phone to her brother under the table, hoping the cameras didn't capture her gesture.

Colin's arms moved slightly, nothing more than a twitch. Lexi could tell he was messing with her phone beneath the stark white table. His gaze remained fixed straight ahead. He was navigating by memory.

A beep echoed in Lexi's ear. The sound was followed by a notification of a change to her settings.

Encryption mode on. Auto-erase will refresh every ten seconds. Action cannot be undone. Firewall secure, self-notes enabled.

Lexi swallowed.

She glanced at Jason. She wasn't sure she should have brought him here, to this room filled with despair and tough topics. And a man who was equal parts brilliance and unrest.

As she offered Jason a wordless apology, a message zipped past Lexi's cornea, catching her off guard.

Lexi Brennan, self-note – unknown location, GPS disabled – I was worried the doctors would sedate me, and I couldn't risk falling asleep. You've seen what's happening in Florida, Georgia, and Alabama?

Lexi gasped. Colin had synced his AutoScan electrodes with hers, a feat all the tech companies had claimed was impossible when they released the prototype. CEOs, experts, and billionaire investors had sworn up and down that there was absolutely no way anyone could infiltrate someone's personal thoughts. They promised it was impossible to manipulate the electric vibrations pulsing across another human being's cranium.

Those experts never met my brother. Lexi smiled. Despite everything, the melancholy hospital room, Colin's gaunt face, and her own gnawing sense of helplessness, pride swelled in Lexi's chest.

AutoScan, Lexi Brennan – self-note – Lexi thought, composing a response to herself and, simultaneously, her brother. *What's the connection, kid? I'm lost. You stayed awake to follow the news about the AR laws?*

His reply came immediately. *There's something you don't know about me. Are you familiar with DefenderTech?*

Lexi's breath got caught in her throat.

Of course her brother would be part of the world's largest group of ethical hackers. DefenderTech initiated the massive security breach of 2036. They released private documents about an Eastern European crime ring. Those high-profile murderers had covered up scandal after scandal for half a century. Everyone knew about their transgressions, but there was no concrete proof. Until DefenderTech found a way to release hundreds of hidden documents and videos.

Colin was still with Marco at the time. Although they'd gone through a rough patch, they managed to pull through.

Lexi was heartbroken when their relationship crumbled a year later.

You're with DT? Lexi asked, already knowing the answer. She'd assumed her brother's lottery hack several years ago was an isolated incident, but maybe it was part of a bigger mission. One with a goal of protecting the most vulnerable people in society. *Is your involvement new, or does it trace back a while?*

His response floated past her eyes.

Not new. Last week we programmed the collapse of the national database. Ten of us worked together to scramble the info for most ARs. We set it on a time delay so it would happen this week if the laws were authorized by the Prez. And you know how that turned out.

Lexi nodded. *President Vampire has almost all the power in this country. That monster launched a full-on war against ARs,* she commented, guessing her brother had already discovered that information.

Right. I had to be sure DT's resistance efforts went off without a hitch. I checked myself in last week because I was in danger. Once I was here, I needed to stay alert. I couldn't fall asleep for days on end. I had to see this through. I had to keep ARs safe and healthy.

"But what about your health and safety?" Lexi asked aloud before she could stop herself. The corners of her eyes filled with moisture, which she blinked away furiously. "I need you, too. Alive. You have so much work left to do, kid. That goes away if you don't take care of yourself. You gotta take your meds."

"Does it really make a difference when I try? Maybe I'm just crazy either way," he noted with a frown.

"I'm out of the loop here, but I'd like to say that your sister's been bragging about you all week," Jason chimed in. "You've got so much talent."

"Exactly. You can change the world, Colin. You're already doing it. Tell me more," Lexi pleaded.

"That's all for right now. I'll fill you in when I'm released," Colin said.

"Well, I'm proud of you."

"Thanks, Lexi." Colin's green eyes glimmered beneath the self-generating diode lights. His stare was less vacant than it had been when Lexi arrived.

For a second, Lexi could imagine her brother recovering from all this. The tan wristband on his arm, proof of his mandated stay in a behavioral health facility, was no match for the resilience in his eyes. Despite Colin's best attempts to starve and abuse and destroy himself, he still had a lot of life tucked inside. Lexi was sure of it.

Colin cleared his throat. "Why were you in Orlando, Jason? What kind of training was it?"

"SkyLine wants me to fix all those airplanes parked in California. They've been grounded since the start of ContaCan."

"He's a mechanic," Lexi supplied.

"Yep. I'm learning to prep the planes for their return to service," Jason explained. "After training, SkyLine will send me to San Diego."

"San Diego," Colin echoed. "It'll take a few months to get all the planes back in working order, huh?"

"Three months is the estimate. SkyLine wants them ready by January of next year, which means I'll need to complete my repairs quickly. Then I'll transfer to San Diego for good," Jason explained. "It's one of our biggest bases."

"It's also a fun one," Lexi reflected. "Crews there seem chill. Easygoing."

Jason nodded. "I've been in Nashville the last four years. I'm ready for a change."

Colin tilted his head to the side. "Did Lex tell you San Diego's my favorite city?"

Lexi cleared her throat. "I mentioned it holds a lot of significance. And that I went to college there."

A loud buzz made them all jump. Numbers materialized on the wall, massive red lights indicating the visit would end shortly.

"Three minutes left," Lexi reflected. "Colin, there's something you need to see. I did this for you. For both of us, actually."

She turned around and tugged at her shirt, pulling the neckline to reveal her tattoo.

"Holy shit!" Colin exclaimed. He leapt to his feet, the metal chair clattering to the floor behind him. "That's real? Even after the government's latest fiasco?"

"Shh," Lexi urged, jutting her chin toward the mobile cameras circling their heads. "It's henna, can't you tell? But if it were real, it would be a symbol of solidarity. It would be my way of saying I'm permanently on this journey with you, kid."

Colin walked to Lexi, tracing the outline of her tattoo. His fingers swept across the ridges where the needle had pierced flesh.

"I'm honored . . . and also confused," Colin said. "What were you thinking?"

"I should've stopped her," Jason admitted sheepishly. "She was determined, though. Your sister's stubborn as hell."

Colin snorted. "No kidding. I can't wait for Mom and Dad to see this."

"I bet they won't care. You know them. They're the most accepting people in the world," Lexi assured her brother.

He nodded. "True. Still, they'll be surprised. Nobody saw this coming."

"That's okay. Sometimes you gotta live your truth. Others will come around," Lexi mused. "I've wanted to do this for years. You're my brother and my best friend. I chose this spot for a thousand reasons."

"I love you, Lexi."

"Ditto. The wave felt right, you know? It's how life works . . . the crest rises and falls. And whatever point you're at on your journey, that's where I am, too."

Colin nodded. Glowing red numbers behind his head indicated there was less than a minute left in their visit.

Lexi scooped him up in a bear hug. "I know your back hurts, old man. Sorry."

"Don't crack a rib," he groaned. "You might be scrawny, but I'm a freaking skeleton these days."

"We'll work on that once you're home," Lexi promised. "Donuts for breakfast, chips and candy between meals."

"Fast food dinners. Extra-crispy fries."

"Obviously." Lexi inhaled sharply. "Never, ever forget how much I love you. A couple more days here, just to get on the right track, then you'll be home. I'll show you all the cutting-edge apps SkyLine uploaded on my tablet. All the info for this new class I'm teaching. Good plan?"

"Sure," he said into her auburn hair.

"In the meantime, go easy on yourself. You're the inspiration behind my new tattoo, which, I think you know, is most definitely *not* henna," Lexi whispered. "Things will get better, Colin. It might not feel like it, but things always get better. You're helping people. Making this world a better place. Saving lives, one scrambled AR database profile at a time."

"Sometimes it feels like a lost cause. But I sure as hell tried." He sighed. "Thanks for coming to see me, Lex, and for doing something so bold and stupid in my honor. I love it. You're the world's biggest idiot for getting inked. Complete dumbass."

"You're welcome, kid," Lexi responded with a chuckle.

"Also, your friend's cool. I'm glad you brought him."

"He's great, right? I'll see you in a couple days. Take care of yourself, Colin. Just ride the wave."

CHAPTER FOURTEEN

A dry breeze swept Lexi's hair across her face as she trekked through the hospital parking lot. Briefly, her line of sight was blocked. She reached up to sift through the stray tendrils. Jason beat her to the chase. He gathered the loose strands floating at various angles.

Lexi smiled and tied her hair in a bun, then called her mother via AutoScan.

"How is he?" Erin Brennan breathed into Lexi's ear. "Your dad and I stopped to get food for Colin. The hospital delayed our visit to one o'clock. Something about a deep cleaning of the visitation room because of a non-resident with a questionable AR status."

Lexi bit her lip. She guessed the receptionist didn't trust Jason's medical records. Or perhaps the microcameras had spotted her tattoo. Maybe the android monitoring the video feed had concluded that the body ink absolutely *wasn't* etched in henna.

"Colin's doing okay," Lexi said. She spotted her hybrid amid rows of automated vehicles. "He could use twenty extra pounds and a week's worth of sleep. But he seemed better than I expected. There were flashes of excitement."

"Wow," her mom murmured. "Maybe the meds are working."

"Assuming he's taking them."

"Yes. We'll see you for dinner, right?"

Lexi glanced at Jason, leaning against her car. "Can I bring someone?"

"Sure. Katie?"

"No, a new friend," Lexi said. "See you tonight, Mom."

Lexi ended the call and collapsed into Jason's arms. Goosebumps traveled down her spine. She wasn't sure if they were caused by the wind or Jason's welcoming embrace.

"It was nice to meet your brother," Jason said, resting his chin on top of her head. "He seems great."

"It's not what you'd imagine, right? The psych ward?" Lexi asked into Jason's chest. "The first time I visited Colin in the Behavioral Health Unit, I pictured something out of a horror movie."

"I thought the same thing."

"That's the stereotype. I hope it's changing. These things take time, I guess."

"Yeah. Your brother's cool. Smart as hell."

"Colin's the most intelligent person I've ever met." Lexi pulled back just far enough to look at Jason's soulful brown eyes.

"*Ever* ever?"

Lexi laughed. "You're smart and all, but Colin could reprogram your company-issued arm band remotely and fuck up your entire mechanic shift. You'd be taping planes together with bubblegum."

"That's what we already use," Jason said, a playful edge to his voice.

"Right. Safety first."

"Always."

Lexi paused. "Listen, I gotta tell you something. What Colin messaged me about, inside that visitation room, it's important. But I need to check with him before sharing. I also need to verify it's real."

"Understood. You're a good sister."

"He's a good brother," Lexi countered. "The kid has a heart of gold. He's compassionate beyond belief, just an overall good dude."

AutoScan – Lexi Brennan – self-note – you still there, kid? Can I tell Jason about DefenderTech? I think he can help. He's got a mechanical brain like yours.

Lexi waited for her brother's response, unsure whether her signal would penetrate the soundproof hospital walls, and also whether Colin's AutoScan syncing capabilities had been deactivated by this point.

She bit her lip and waited. Silence persisted.

"Maybe it's genetic."

Lexi blinked. "Huh?"

"The whole thing about being a decent person. Maybe it runs in your family."

"Somehow, the trait skipped me," Lexi scoffed.

"You've got a rescue cat at home who would argue otherwise," Jason points out.

"That hardly makes me a saint," Lexi said, cracking a smile. "I'm no angel. Just a teacher stew who felt bad for her friend's orphaned kitty."

Lexi raised her hand to the scanner on her parents' front door. Just before the laser identified the grooves on her finger, she lowered her arm and turned toward Jason. "You sure you want to do this? You could drive around instead. Ditch this place and explore town. I won't be offended."

"Stop. I want to be here," Jason assured her with a smile. His bright white teeth glimmered in the afternoon sun. "Plus, I was told there would be alcohol."

"Duh. We're Irish."

"Fantastic. How about you, are you worried? Am I the tallest dude you've ever introduced to your folks?" Jason tilted his head to the side. "The Blackest?"

Lexi snorted. "Try the *only*."

"Oh. You've only brought home girls?"

"Not exactly," Lexi reflected. "Believe it or not, I've never introduced my parents to *anyone* I banged. Ever."

Jason narrowed his eyes as though convinced she was messing with him.

"Weird, huh? Thirty-something years old, and I've never brought anyone home to meet my parents." Lexi shrugged. "Long story. Super boring. Anyway, feel free to blow this joint."

"I'm not leaving."

"This is your chance, baby mechanic. Clean break."

"The last time I included Talia in family festivities, my sister and I got into the worst fight of our lives. My sister, Jen, threw her glass at the wall. Talia was pissed, so we spent the whole night screaming at each other. Pretty sure she told me to *just go die* at some point." Jason shrugged. "Whatever your family dynamic is, whatever shit you've got tucked in your closet, I've seen worse."

"Challenge accepted," Lexi told him with a playful jab to the stomach. "To clarify, we aren't dysfunctional in the traditional sense. Things are complicated, though."

"Fine by me."

Lexi paused. "Just so you know, I'm going to need details later. I'm curious about this botched Bresline family party. Sounds fascinating."

"Not the term I'd choose, but sure." Jason jutted his chin toward the door. "Let's do this."

Lexi lifted her thumb once again. The door swung open, welcoming them into her parents' home. Hardwood floors and light gray walls offered a subtle greeting. There was an oval window to the right, unique enough to pass for vintage. On the left, a winding staircase led to three modest bedrooms.

"This is where I grew up," she told Jason as they hung their jackets on the coat rack in the foyer. "My parents moved here when I was three and Colin was five."

Jason followed her down the hall, past the living room and

kitchen. Her parents' Chihuahua, Monty, rounded a corner and sprinted toward them. Lexi hunched over to pet his head. He lifted his hind leg, scratching a nonexistent itch with delight.

Jason chuckled at Monty's enthusiastic response. The dog flopped onto his back, exposing his round belly.

"Do I smell like Lexi's cat?" Jason asked while rubbing Monty's tummy. "There you go. Good puppy."

"No puppies here. This guy is a straight-up senior citizen," Lexi pointed out with a laugh. "My parents adopted him when I was a sophomore in college."

"Which makes him, what, fourteen years old?"

Lexi shrugged. "At least. He was full-grown when they rescued him."

Through the sliding glass doors, they spotted her parents in the backyard. Sean Brennan was carrying a tray of food while Erin monitored the grill. Lexi inhaled sharply, then led Jason outside. Monty followed them, circling their feet excitedly.

"Hey, guys," Lexi said. "This is Jason, a SkyLine mechanic. He's visiting for the weekend. First time in Sacramento."

"Nice to meet you, Jason," Sean said.

"Thanks for having me over. It smells great out here," Jason responded.

Erin Brennan beamed at him. Her hair, which had faded from copper to marigold in recent years, tumbled in loose waves from beneath a floppy black hat. "We grilled too much, as always. Hope you two are hungry."

Sean headed inside to fix everyone a drink while Erin asked Jason how he liked Sacramento so far. The atmosphere felt casual and calm. For a moment, Lexi could hardly remember the sadness from earlier in the day. In fact, it was difficult to feel anything but gratitude.

"You've got a lot of exciting stuff ahead," Sean Brennan noted, helping himself to another serving of potato salad. "Getting all those planes back in working order."

Jason and Lexi were seated across from her parents at the picnic table. Pearly twilight had begun to descend upon the back yard.

"Jason's really good at what he does," Lexi said, pride echoing in her voice. "SkyLine only selected a couple mechanics for this specific project. Five, right?"

Jason finished his burger, then chased it with a swig of beer. "There are six of us. I'm eager to fix those AirBirds. Honestly, I enjoy taking things apart and rebuilding them. I like learning how they work, right down to the smallest detail."

"Funny, Colin would say the same thing," Erin Brennan mused. "He's a programmer for a digital marketing company. He's always cracking codes and building new ones."

"Yeah, Colin seems brilliant." Jason wiped his face with a napkin.

Lexi cleared her throat. "I might've snuck Jason into Colin's visitation room today. Sorry, we should have told you."

"Colin mentioned it. He was glad to see you both," Sean assured them. "It made his day. He asked us to tell you he wants some pictures of the planes in San Diego, the ones that are grounded. If possible."

Erin nodded. "Yes. He also talked about new software on the planes with, what's it called? That heat sensor, to track movements and read national database profiles."

"The government hasn't issued clear directives yet." Jason turned to Lexi. "It's still unfolding, but I would imagine they'll give front-line workers, like gate agents and flight attendants, a device to scan each passenger."

"Just awful," Sean Brennan noted, shaking his head. "The president's not going to stop until he's destroyed everything good in this country. He's on a mission to ruin lives with all the new laws against ARs. I never thought we'd get to the point where people were rounded up and sent to abandoned buildings against their will."

"Colin hates it, too. He's sensitive to this stuff," Lexi noted, wishing she could share more information about her brother's heroic initiatives. "He's got the biggest heart."

"He sure does," Erin Brennan agreed.

"That kid's an empath. To the max," Lexi said. *If only he could extend some of that compassion to himself.*

"What did you think of Sean and Erin Brennan?" Lexi asked Jason while brushing her teeth. A drop of toothpaste landed on her shirt, leaving a chalky smudge on the blue fabric. She rubbed the stain with her thumb until it faded. "Feel free to be brutally honest."

"I have nothing bad to say about your folks, Lex. They're easy to talk to."

"Yeah, they're super mellow. By this point, they've been through so much with Colin's illness, nothing surprises them. You could probably even show your AR tattoo, no explanation or anything, and they wouldn't freak out," Lexi reflected. "They'd just ask what extra measures they could take to make you more comfortable."

"That's how the whole world should react," Jason noted.

Lexi spat the last bit of toothpaste in the sink and rinsed off her brush. "True."

Jason pulled her toward him. "I bet most parents would lose their shit if they knew their daughter was dating an AR."

"Who says we're dating?" Lexi lifted an eyebrow. "And, technically, you're not an AR."

"Just a regular guy with an unfortunate tattoo."

"As of yesterday, I have an unfortunate tattoo, too." Lexi stared deep into Jason's eyes, letting herself get lost in them.

"Even if you were an AR, I'd take all the extra steps to protect you."

"Yeah?"

"Sure. Well, maybe. What does that include these days? Weekly shots in your butt, right? And a regimen of pills. Arm band. Mouth guard. Routine doctor's visits and bloodwork, plus daily metabolic checks."

"Yeah. Talia did all that back when we thought I might be an AR," Jason explained. "Painful shots and a cocktail of pills every morning. We took blood scanner readings five times a day. I had to carry the device around with me and take samples at midnight to verify my white blood cells were normal. Oh, and we both used a daytime mouthguard as well as a flexible nighttime one. There's nothing worse than sleeping with the daytime version. It feels like someone's wired your mouth shut. Trust me, that's a mistake you only make once."

Lexi nestled her head into his shoulder. "Sounds intense. Is the blood scanner thing painful?"

"Ever had a super-thin laser slice into your bone marrow? It's not pleasant." Jason shuddered. "The beam is supposedly thinner than a strand of hair, but I swear you can feel that thing poking straight down. Imagine a papercut that goes five inches deep. Trust me, ARs go through hell to stay safe."

Lexi shuddered. "My parents took Colin to get tested as soon as the AR tests were released. Did I tell you that? Back then, the resistant gene had a rumored link to mental illness, specifically bipolar and generalized anxiety disorder. Something about the thirteenth chromosome, I think. My folks weren't taking any chances. They brought Colin to a clinic right away."

Jason ran a hand through her hair, pausing to tuck a few strands behind her ear. "Were you scared?"

"More like shell-shocked. It was a confusing time. The results didn't come in for an entire week. Colin's sample was misplaced. Took a while for the medical company to sort everything out."

"I remember how chaotic it was in the beginning. People rushed to get tested. They had no idea the results would be used against them."

Lexi nodded. "Since Colin's results took so long, we had extra time to watch things unravel. Within a few days, the government mandated tattoos for everyone who tested positive. There were outcries from civil rights groups. The administration silenced the opposition. They accused them of being un-American. Called them biological terrorists."

Jason cradled her head in his hands. "Crazy how fast things spiraled."

"Yeah, and I looked the other way. Didn't lift a finger."

Jason turned out the light in the bathroom. They slid into Lexi's bed, and Cleo hopped up as soon as they'd nestled under the comforter.

Lexi curled her legs to give Cleo plenty of space. Then she tucked her arms beneath Jason's, clasping her fingers behind his back. Slivers of moonlight outlined his face. "You know, when Colin's results finally came in, I celebrated. Isn't that twisted? I rejoiced that Colin wasn't like *those people*."

"You didn't know any better," Jason murmured.

"But I should have. And I do now."

"Well, good. Now that you've learned more, you can do better."

"Yeah, I want to make it right. Let's fix things," Lexi suggested as they drifted off to sleep.

Chapter Fifteen: October 10, 2038

"Tell me about the Bresline party debacle," Lexi suggested, raising a spoon to her lips.

Jason chewed his cereal thoughtfully. "One word—shit-show."

"Those are always the best stories," Lexi quipped. She placed her wet spoon on a napkin. "I'm curious what caused a rift between you and your sister. If you're willing to share."

Jason shrugged. "Sure. But it's pretty dark."

"Story of my life. Go for it."

"In May, my parents hosted a PersonableSpin party. My sister, Jen, lives in Colorado Springs with her husband. I was in Nashville with Talia and my parents live in Denver. Our cousins were invited. There were about twenty people transposed into three-dimensional models. A few cousins didn't have the technology, so they joined as audio guests. They could still hold a conversation."

"I'm impressed your parents knew how to use PersonableSpin so early on. They're light years ahead of my folks," Lexi reflected. "My mom still refers to *Swyft* as a *lonely Uber,* since there's no driver."

"I mean, Erin has a sense of humor."

"She's mostly just clueless."

"Well, my parents have always been ahead of the curve." Jason slid his empty cereal bowl toward the center of the kitchen table and scratched his chin. "Mom was an engineer for AirBird. She retired a couple years ago. My folks live five miles from the aircraft manufacturing plant."

"Wow. I'm guessing you inherited your mechanical brain from your mother. She sounds awesome."

"She's the best," Jason said with a quick nod. "I'm not close with my sister, though. Sometimes she's a huge pain in the ass."

"Sorry to hear that." Lexi carried their bowls to the sink, then sat on Jason's lap. She placed a hand on his shoulder. "Don't let me interrupt anymore."

"Okay, so it's a big party. We're eating and drinking. Making long-distance toasts. We needed some stress relief, you know? Everyone just wanted to forget the world was crumbling around us. ContaCan took out so many of my old college buddies, I couldn't keep track." Jason sighed. "It was depressing as hell. Everybody wanted a fun night. *Needed* a fun night."

Lexi bit her lip. She could relate, perhaps too well. She'd spent years exploring the link between terrifying, outlandish circumstances and the desire to connect. Play pretend. Escape.

"It was a couple days after my Achilles surgery," Jason continued. "I was zipping around on my scooter, drinking scotch. Talia was chilling on the couch, talking with my cousins. Next thing I know, Jen's hovering over me, breathing down my neck."

"Figure of speech," Lexi murmured. "Since she wasn't physically there."

"True. Her *avatar* was hovering over me, angry as hell. She went off, screaming uncontrollably. She asked what the hell was wrong with me. Called me self-centered for getting an AR tattoo in today's political climate. She lost it. Threw her glass at the wall."

"Whoa. Complete meltdown?"

"Worse. It was like someone had set off a bomb. In the middle of a party, she's shouting about how disgusting I am. She said my genealogy would be traced. She said the government would use the carrier gene to ruin our family."

"Damn. I'm sorry, Jason."

"She told me everyone in the family would be targeted because of my selfishness." Jason shrugged.

Sunlight streamed in from the rectangular kitchen window. Half his body was illuminated in filmy golden hues. Lexi placed a hand on the left side of his face, the side still immersed in shadows. His skin was cool to the touch. Cleopatra strutted into the room, a wisp of fur in Lexi's peripheral vision. The cat meandered toward her food and water bowls. She sipped water from her paw, then glanced up at Lexi, curiosity emanating from her green eyes.

"Did anyone stand up for you?" Lexi asked.

"Mom defended me, saying my decision was nobody else's business. That made Jen angrier. She always needs to be right. She cut me out of her life on the spot. Told me I was dead to her, which was a terrible thing to say, considering how much *actual* death was swirling around in our lives."

"So much death. Way too much." Lexi swallowed. Her favorite high school teacher died from ContaCan. Lexi found out through a friend who worked at the school. Ms. Rossi had been one of the good ones. She'd encouraged Lexi to pursue an education degree despite missing half her sophomore year after Colin's first suicide attempt.

Lexi's mind also traveled to the college romance that had meant the most to her. The one that almost transformed into a real relationship, until Lexi spent a few weeks back home taking care of Colin. Things crumbled eventually. As always.

Blair passed away in April of 2038. She'd been so close to the finish line, just inches from surviving ContaCan. She died ten days before the antidote was released. Blair had been so complimentary, always showering Lexi with unearned praise. She'd made Lexi feel like a bona fide hero. A warrior who had overcome unspeakable trauma.

Blair's older sister called Lexi in May and left a voicemail. Poof, just like that. Blair had bled from her eyes and ears. And then she was gone.

ContaCan erased Blair Ferrera. When the pathogen took her life, all her encouraging sentiments turned to dust.

She was wrong anyway. Lexi sighed and placed one hand on Jason's chest. *Nothing heroic here. Sometimes I can barely make it through the day.*

A few of Colin's buddies in San Diego had lost their spouses and partners. Other friends had buried their children.

Lexi cleared her throat. "Before the antidote, everyone lived with one foot in the grave. We had to acknowledge our mortality on an hourly basis. Nobody was safe."

"Exactly. Everyone was waiting to see who'd be next." Jason leaned back in his chair and wrapped one arm around Lexi. "Anyway, that's the story of the botched family party. Right before she left the PersonableSpin session, Jen screamed that I was a self-centered motherfucker who'd put our entire family at risk. Then she vanished."

"Did you try contacting her after?"

"I wanted to. She's still my sister, even if she's got one hell of a mean streak. I thought about calling and trying to patch things up. Jen's a biomedical researcher. She played a role in the antidote development. I could've asked her advice. As a carrier for the resistant glycoprotein, I didn't know if I needed to do anything differently than other folks. Jen's a difficult person. Still, I wanted to fix things between us. Or at least try."

Lexi kissed Jason's arm, then removed herself from his lap. She walked to the corner of the kitchen, topping off Cleo's bowl with grain-free food stored in an airtight container to keep Jorge's ghost happy. "Why didn't you contact Jen?"

"Talia gave me an ultimatum. She was offended by my sister's outburst because it involved a decision Talia had encouraged. My fiancée never liked Jen, but this was the final straw. She demanded I cut my sister out of my life, which seemed easy enough. I mean, Jen had disowned me anyway." Jason rose to his feet and checked his watch. "I gotta get to the airport. Sorry to end our weekend with that terrible story."

Lexi shook her head. "Don't apologize. Look, if you want my opinion, which you probably don't, Talia had no business getting between you and your sister. I'd imagine Jen freaked out because she saw the tattoo as a personal betrayal. But she might have listened to you once she cooled down."

"Jen's always had a temper. You're probably right. After a few days, she would've been willing to hear my side of the story. Maybe." Jason planted a kiss on Lexi's forehead and grabbed his backpack off the kitchen counter.

"I wonder if Antonio would've reunited with Jorge," Lexi mused as they put on their shoes. "It's probably idealistic to think that. Naïve as hell. But they both would've been ARs, you know? Maybe something like that brings people together. Jorge would've been on the deportation list right alongside his twin brother."

"Yikes."

Lexi shuddered. "I would've hidden J.R. someplace safe, maybe gotten Colin to hack the system and alter his records. No idea if any of that would've worked. Guess I'll never know."

"I wish I could've met Jorge."

"You would've liked him. He was phenomenal, the funniest and coolest guy. Nice to everyone. Way nicer than me. I miss him every day." Lexi frowned. "I know I'm meddling, but it's not too late. You can still find a way to smooth things over with Jen. Trust me, regret is a hell of a thing to live with."

"I hear you, Lex. I really do."

During the drive to the airport, a sense of dread stirred in

Lexi's core. The sun glistened overhead, claiming a large chunk of the sapphire sky. The roads were calm and empty. Despite the buoyant atmosphere, Lexi's gnawing internal ache persisted.

Jason interrupted her thoughts with a question. Mercifully. "So, you've never introduced anyone to your parents before yesterday? Ever?"

Lexi glanced at him. He occupied the driver seat of her car like he belonged there. One hand was guiding the steering wheel and the other rested on Lexi's knee.

Lexi felt her anxiety dissipate as she channeled her energy into a coherent response. "You're the first person I've known in a remotely romantic context and introduced to my parents."

"Were you distant from your folks in the past or something?"

"We've always been super close-knit. It's not that." Lexi bit her lip. "It's a long story. You really want to know?"

"Yes. I'm curious."

"All right, I'll give you the condensed version."

"According to the HoloRoute your favorite baby mechanic installed in your windshield, we have eighteen minutes left," Jason said. "Take your time."

"Okay, then. I'll be thirty-five next month. Almost everyone my age is married. In fact, some of my friends are on their second marriage by now," Lexi explained. "That feels like a different universe. I've dated here and there, but long-term relationships never made sense. There was too much going on."

"Didn't you ever want to get close to someone? I thought everyone wanted that deep down. It's half the reason I tried to make things work with Talia even though we weren't a good match."

"I have lots of friends, but romantic relationships weren't

a realistic option."

"Why?"

Lexi frowned. "Sometimes I think I'll always be sixteen. That's when my life basically stopped."

"That's when Colin first tried to hurt himself?"

"Yeah. I failed him. How did I miss the signs? Why didn't he confide in me? I had so many questions. I still don't know the answers. Maybe they don't exist."

Jason grew quiet. His silence was oddly reassuring. It wrapped itself around Lexi like a warm breeze, giving her enough space to express herself.

"Colin went to college locally, and I left for UCSD two years later. I spent my entire college career shuffling back and forth to Sacramento. Mom and Dad tried to keep an eye on him, but they were tired. They couldn't do it alone."

"You gave up most of your college career to take care of your brother. That says a lot, Lex."

"I couldn't abandon Colin. He was my priority. I almost failed my classes. I managed to earn a degree, just barely. There was no time to build something meaningful with anyone. Plus, I didn't care about relationships. Too much on my plate."

Jason steered onto the airport exit. "What happened after you graduated?"

"I moved home. Accepted a job designing a new curriculum. It was a leadership course at Sac State. Had to quit within a year. Colin had a bad episode. After that, I took freelance jobs here and there, mostly in secondary education. Then I started at the airline. Didn't want to mix work and play, so I gave myself a strict no-SkyLine policy."

"Until you met me."

"Yep. You're my rule-breaker."

"Was it worth it?"

"I guess so," Lexi responded with a half-smile. "I've had

worse."

"Oh, really? Good thing I'm not last place." Jason pulled up to the curb in front of the SkyLine ticketing counter. He turned off the engine and hopped out of the driver's seat. Lexi joined him.

Jason placed one hand on the side of Lexi's face. "You've given so much to Colin. After meeting him, I understand why. He's a great person."

"He is."

"You didn't run from his challenges. You ran toward them," Jason continued. "And maybe you didn't have a long-term relationship. Who cares? That's nobody's business but your own."

"Even though you made it your business to know my back-story."

Jason grinned, his teeth glistening in the vibrant California sunshine. "It seemed fair after I poured out my guts about the embarrassing Bresline party. Look, you made big sacrifices to protect your brother. That's really selfless."

"I don't want you to go." Lexi's plea hung thick in the air.

"Same here."

She expelled a breath of air laced with vulnerability. More than she cared to admit. "I've never asked anyone to stay before, but I would like you to stay. Please."

"If I could get SkyLine to approve that request, I'd pull a U-turn and speed back to your apartment," Jason promised. "But I have to go. Training ends soon. Five days, then I'm free. I'm not leaving you."

Lexi stared at her shoes, unable to find any words.

Jason wrapped his arms around her. "You're tougher than you think, Lexi Brennan. Don't forget that."

Lexi kissed him. She tried her best to memorize the feel of his arms and the taste of his tongue. She knew Jason would stroll through the airport's double doors soon. And then Lexi would be on her own. She would have no lifeline in this tragic city full of doomed endeavors.

"I set up a recurring PersonableSpin mini-conference every day this week. Ten at night, which is seven your time. It'll be like I never left," Jason promised. He squeezed her hand, then turned toward the airport entrance.

Lexi blinked furiously, trying to organize her rapid-fire thoughts.

"Jason," she called out just before he reached the doors. He turned around, meeting her gaze. "Maybe you can call your sister sometime. If you want. Just a thought."

He nodded. "I will, Lexi."

Katie's expression was inscrutable. Aside from the rising and falling of her chest, she was completely still. Two wine glasses rested on the table. They'd been sitting there, untouched and filled to the brim with chardonnay, for fifteen minutes.

Lexi reached forward and took a swig of the pale liquid. Then another. "So, what do you think?"

"I'm still processing it."

"Which part?"

Katie lifted an eyebrow. "All of it. In five days, you met a dude, learned he has an AR tattoo, discovered it isn't real, brought him home to meet your brother and your parents. It's wild. A superhot mechanic with a fake tattoo. Also, you got inked. It looks amazing, by the way. But it's in an unexpected spot."

"Jason's tattoo is real," Lexi corrected her. "Just inaccurate. And my wave tattoo is exactly where it should be. It's a statement."

Katie nodded.

"How can we stand by and watch this happen?" Lexi pressed. "Colin easily could have been an AR. At first, doctors thought it was tied to the thirteenth chromosome."

"I remember those days."

"And Jorge was an AR for sure," Lexi continued. "He would've been deported. Sent away to die."

Katie's eyes widened. "J.R. had the gene, huh?"

"Yeah. I found out from his avatar during a Predictive PersonableSpin session earlier this week. I can't stop thinking about the laws in Florida, Texas, Alabama. Other states are joining that list. Travel's been restricted, and airline employees are required to monitor ARs."

"Shit."

"It's so bad, Katie. Cryptic as hell. Will California eventually do the same thing? Will the state force ARs to self-identify, then banish them to an undisclosed location? We can't let this continue."

"It's horrible," Katie agreed. She tilted back her head, downing half the wine glass.

"That's why I'm going to do something."

Katie lifted an eyebrow. "What can you do without getting caught?" She tapped her ear, then took her phone from her pocket and slid it on the floor, toward the couch. It wedged itself into the edge of the carpet.

"Good thinking," Lexi said. Using ocular swipes, she disabled all microphones and sensory apps on her phone. Then she commanded AutoScan to retroactively summon auto-erase mode. For the past twenty-four hours. Colin would've been able to ensure more privacy, she knew, but this was her best effort. "Look, I don't have it all figured out yet. The mandates will affect transportation workers. They're making me turn in ARs who try to fly. It'll be part of my job, moving forward."

Katie shook her head. "I can't believe this is real life."

"Me neither. My best friend would have been persecuted, Katie. He would've died in an abandoned building with his twin brother and lots of other people." Lexi sighed. "It's not like I have a ton of power. I'm just a flight attendant. I hand out sodas and snacks for a living. But I know folks in the training department. And I'm dating a mechanic now."

"Dating, huh?" Katie asked, her lips curving upward.

"Correction . . . repeatedly hooking up with," Lexi said, rolling her eyes. "Whatever. Close enough."

"They're very different."

"Depends who you ask."

"Maybe we should ask Jason."

Lexi laughed. "Please don't do that."

"Only if you promise to keep me updated on everything that happens between you two. I have a good feeling about this guy. Keep me in the loop, okay?"

"Deal. Listen, I gotta find a way to make a difference. I'm hatching a plan. The government said we're responsible for verifying credentials, but they haven't provided information about the devices we're supposed to use. Or how they'll hold us accountable to the new rules. Guessing they might issue something similar to Holoscreen thumb readers, but for facial recognition?"

Katie shrugged. "Who knows. Heat-sensor technology would work on the plane. They could install a box up front and let it scan each passenger so you don't accidentally miss one."

"That would actually be the easiest to work with," Lexi mused. "God, I hope that's what they use. Jason would be one of the mechanics installing it, and he'd know exactly which errors could cause a malfunction. Piece of cake. Colin could hack into the device as a backup."

"No government-issued tracking device would stand a chance against Colin. He's the best programmer at the office. Everyone knows it. We were all surprised when he turned down the San Diego offer. They hand-picked him out of hundreds of coders. I thought he'd go for it."

"Wait, what? When was this?"

Katie frowned. "You didn't know, Lex? It was last week. They're expanding the offices in San Diego, and they needed their top programmers down there. Quickly. I'm jealous they aren't looking for any graphic designers. The S.D. office is badass."

"Holy hell. Colin loves San Diego. Why would he refuse that offer?"

"He turned it down really fast, and he acted fine afterward," Katie said. "Nothing seemed off when we grabbed coffee in the breakroom on Friday."

Lexi wrapped her fingers around her ribcage, barely keeping her composure. "It doesn't make sense. To Colin, San Diego is the promised land."

"But it would've meant moving within a month. Maybe he wasn't ready?"

"Maybe," Lexi murmured. Her mind traveled to Colin's revelation from the day before. He had his hands full with DefenderTech's humanitarian projects. Still, Lexi couldn't imagine a world where Colin would turn down an opportunity to relocate to his favorite city.

"I'm sorry I mentioned it," Katie said.

"No, I'm glad you did. I didn't realize what Colin was going through and all the big decisions he faced. Gosh, now I'm about to pull him into another big project. One that could easily sink us all."

"But hopefully not. Will you go to jail over this, Lex?" Katie asked quietly. "You think anyone will catch on?"

"We'll be as careful as possible. Colin and Jason are experts. If anyone can make this thing untraceable, it's those guys."

"Understood. I'm not saying you shouldn't do it, by the way. I think it's really important. I just want you to protect yourself."

An idea struck Lexi. "Reggie, the training director, knows my background. He knows I've designed classes before. I could create a new one, possibly. Put on a good show for the government inspectors. Play by their rules. I'd go over every detail with SkyLine's lawyers to make sure the class was acceptable. I wouldn't explicitly tell people to defy any laws. I'd just show them the errors that *could* screw up the system. Ultimately, they would choose if they wanted to be part of the resistance."

Katie nodded. "You think they'd make the right choice?"

"Only one way to find out."

"Hey, can I ask you something? In the off chance you get caught, if anything happens to you, am I supposed to take care of Cleo permanently?"

"Of course, duh."

"I'm not really a cat person."

Lexi smiled. "I said the same thing, and look at me now."

Chapter Sixteen: October 12, 2038

Can't make our PersonableSpin session tonight. Sorry! Colin was released from the hospital. I'm picking him up soon.

Lexi sent the message with a quick ocular swipe. The Holoscreen in front of her flashed green, indicating Jason had received the note as an array of floating neon letters. She could've easily conveyed this information through AutoScan. The animated Holoscreen app was more fun, though.

Jason's response arrived instantly, complete with a realistic three-dimensional attachment. The celebratory dancing dog, with big round eyes and floppy ears, was smaller than Lexi's thumb. Yet it was bright enough to illuminate her entire apartment, which had grown dim with the setting sun.

Nice! That's great news, teacher stew. Let me know how it goes, the animated dog announced through a dialogue bubble.

"Updates to follow," Lexi responded, affixing her gaze to the *record* icon. She noticed a flashing yellow button on one side of the transparent display screen. Curious, she selected it with two rapid blinks.

Her sentence popped up as a series of words floating by on a virtual conveyor belt. The font had red polka-dots embedded in each letter. Lexi swiped left to see what other options were available.

A beach scene materialized, convincing enough to make Lexi believe a microscopic coastline had taken up residence in her apartment. Her sentence appeared in the sand, written by an invisible tree branch.

She swiped left again.

This time, her words were affixed to a rectangular banner fluttering behind a puddle-jumper airplane. The turboprop sputtered toward an unknown destination, towing her message behind it.

If she'd had more time, she would've scrolled through all the animated templates. But Colin was waiting for her. Lexi's brother was coming home.

Selecting the turboprop display, she sent the message to Jason. Then she tucked her tablet inside her backpack, grabbed a jacket, and left the apartment.

Streets passed by as a blur of color in her peripheral vision. Ever since Jason installed a HoloRoute on her windshield, the outside scenery had changed. It had become a watercolor painting, a luminous backdrop punctuated by bold red lines. Neon indicators pointed the way to the hospital. Lexi had memorized the path years ago, but it felt brand-new, thanks to the vibrant grid on her dashboard.

Colin was waiting in front of the hospital, sitting on a bench with his hands folded neatly in his lap. He smiled at her. Through the window, Lexi couldn't tell if the grin was genuine. She hoped so.

Colin jumped to his feet. His toothpick legs moved rhythmically as he approached the passenger door.

"Lexi," he breathed, fastening his seatbelt. "First of all, hi. Second, I see you finally installed HoloRoute."

"Yep," Lexi said, steering the vehicle away from the hospital. "Jason did it for me last weekend."

"Next best thing to a self-driving ride."

"Agreed. How are you feeling? How were the last few days?"

"Draining. The doctor grilled me for skipping my meds. Everyone thinks I'm screwing up just to be an ass. I have my reasons, though."

"We just worry, kid."

"I know. And I appreciate that, I really do. But it also gets frustrating sometimes." He paused. "God, I can't wait to get home. Freedom feels so good. I've missed the sunshine, the wind, and the little things like riding in cars. Inside the hospital, everything's so monotonous. But real life is colorful and constantly changing."

Colin's voice was thick with relief and something Lexi couldn't identify. Determination, perhaps. He rolled down the window and thrust one hand outside.

Lexi was relieved by the tone of her brother's voice. On his worst days, Colin was a blank slate. A sense of resolve was an improvement, as far as Lexi was concerned. "I'm glad you're coming home. Do you feel okay?"

"Yeah," he said. "They inserted a slow-release pill pack this morning. It's supposed to last six months."

"That's great, Colin. Where'd they place it?"

"Left shoulder, one-and-a-half inches deep. I'm hoping it leaves a scar so you and I can be matching freaks."

Without turning toward him, Lexi could tell he was grinning. Her own lips curved upward in response to Colin's jab. "Thanks, kid. You could join the club with me and Jason."

"Jason has a shoulder tattoo?"

"Yeah, he got the AR tattoo early on, before they could distinguish those who were resistant from the people who carried the gene. He received the antidote in May. He's doing fine, obviously."

"That's what the cryptic shit in his database profile meant," Colin murmured. "It makes sense now."

"Of course you found a way to rifle through his profile. Even inside a hospital with airtight restrictions," Lexi reflected, shaking her head.

"Duh. I'm not going to let just anyone date my sister."

"I wouldn't exactly call it dating."

"That's because you're a commitment-phobe," Colin

teased.

Lexi rolled her eyes as the HoloRoute directed her to steer left. "I prefer the term *free spirit*. I'm untamed."

"Yes. My feral sister. At any rate, I'm sorry Jason has to live with an AR tattoo. He must've taken a lot of crap for it."

"He's been through hell. It changed his perspective on things. It's changing mine, too."

"I bet."

"Jorge was an AR, you know," Lexi added. They paused at a red light, giving her just enough time to crack her knuckles against the steering wheel. "I found his twin, Antonio, on Emergency Expulsion Registry."

"Holy shit."

"Yeah. I'm so thankful you're working with, you know . . ."

Colin nodded. Lexi could practically hear the wheels in his head turning. "Hang on a second. Where's your phone?"

Without peeling her eyes from the road, Lexi reached into the center console and grabbed her phone from her handbag. She handed Colin the device. He tapped the screen a few times and dropped the phone back in her bag.

"Almost done. I just need the access code for your HoloRoute."

"Sure," Lexi said. She summoned AutoScan and sent him the pin.

"All good now. Everything's secure." Colin blew out a loud breath. "Lexi, it's been insane. The feds are pissed, but they can't trace anything back to DefenderTech. We covered our tracks. We're five years ahead of the government's tech team. Luckily for us, they're terrible."

"Seriously? The feds cheaped out on hackers?"

"They offered crazy amounts of money, but nobody with a conscience will work for them. Probably because the Executive Branch is a bunch of sick fucks," Colin mused.

"Scrambling the database was risky as hell. I was so scared they'd find each one of us, but as things continued to unfold, I realized we were in the clear. They can't tie us to anything. There's no evidence. We made sure of it."

"No chance they'll uncover anything?"

"Super small. You wouldn't believe the measures we had to take," Colin reflected. "And it was time-sensitive, which was why we barely slept. We rushed so hard. There was no time to spare since ARs are being slaughtered, and it's getting worse every day."

"Because of the transportation mandates?"

"Even more sinister than that. DefenderTech uncovered secure memos. Stuff circulating among the President's Cabinet and the Department of Justice. They're launching a full-fledged attack that might turn into a civil war. The goal is extermination."

"Shit."

"Self-identification and vigilante militias are just the start of the madness. The President's Cabinet plans to send micro bombs to known white supremacists and religious extremists. They've selected older folks who were part of the insurrection in twenty-twenty-one and similar events. They have a list of the psychopaths with a history of violence, and they're going to intentionally arm them with weapons to take out ARs, one by one."

Lexi shook her head. "How is this real life?"

"This nation has lost its mind, Lex. Somebody needs to intervene. Altering the national database bought us time, but the government is determined to achieve its goal. We have to act fast."

"I'm proud of you," Lexi said, her voice barely above a whisper. She reached over the seat and squeezed her brother's shoulder. "This fucked-up world needs a hero. Badly. You're doing so much good."

"We still have a long way to go."

"Well, if you're not too overwhelmed, I'd like to add another task to your plate," Lexi mused. "I have a new project that could really shake things up. I could use your expertise, though. If you approve, we can loop Jason in."

"Sounds interesting."

"Yes. And a bit reckless. My favorite combo."

"What do you need me to do?"

"Work your magic. You're the best programmer I know, so this should be an easy task for you," Lexi reflected. "Has DT ever launched a project in the transportation industry?"

"I'm in," Colin said as they cruised to a stop in front of their parents' home. "We can work out the details once I sift through memos and learn how the aircraft devices work."

"Thanks, Colin. I bet the info you find will be way more detailed than what the government shares with flight attendants." Lexi turned off the car, and the HoloRoute shrank to a grain of rice. Her windshield returned to normal, offering an unobstructed view of the twilit horizon. "Hey, on an unrelated note, I need to chat with you about something."

"Sure, after dinner? They're probably waiting on us." Colin jutted his head toward their childhood home.

"It'll only take a minute. Katie told me about the job offer in San Diego. You know you can tell me anything, right? Why didn't mention it?"

"There was nothing to say." Colin's voice was flat and detached, leaving Lexi to regret broaching the subject.

"Okay. I didn't mean to upset you. We can drop it."

Colin sighed. "Marco lives in Hillcrest now. He moved there a few months ago, right after the antidote was released."

"Whoa. I had no idea."

"He's doing well," Colin added. "I love San Diego, but I've never lived outside of Sac. And I have no desire to leave. Not long-term. Plus, it makes more sense to work with Defender-Tech from here. They already have enough folks in big cities. Sacramento is smaller, so I can take on extra projects here. I can also be more discreet."

"Were you afraid people would, um, stalk you in San Diego?" Lexi asked, tiptoeing around her brother's worries. Colin's involvement in the humanitarian group was dangerous. The risk level was extreme. But Lexi also knew Colin's history, his tendency to spin reality into a distressing, absurd nightmare.

"In a big city, there are tons of folks infiltrating personal networks and sharing connectivity. I'm better off here. Last week, my imagination got carried away, and I freaked out. Sometimes it's hard to keep sight of what's real, you know? But the truth is, I'm safer in Sac. Plus, I can make a bigger impact up here. I can also be more covert. You have to believe me, Lexi. San Diego is my favorite place to visit, but I have no business moving there."

"Was it tough to turn down the promotion?"

"No, it was simple." Colin paused. "But I felt weird after. It seemed like Marco had won. Which is hella dumb. There was never a competition. Nobody won or lost."

"You felt like he got everything?"

"Mm-hmm. It's ironic, right? Marco ended things. Then, a few months later, he packed up and moved to the one place that was *mine*. I don't know, Lex. It sounds childish when I say it out loud."

"It's not childish. The breakup sucked, and that's okay. There's nothing fair about a breakup. Ever," Lexi noted. She'd never officially had one, but she remembered the pain of discovering Blair had died. There would always be a million what-ifs, a stream of endless questions without answers. Severed ties were not fun. They evoked a torrent of remorse and insecurity.

"I get it. San Diego is sentimental, so it hurts knowing Marco gets to enjoy it without you," Lexi continued softly. "Awesome city. When you're there, you feel like you can be yourself, really connect with your roots and tap into your best parts."

"But I don't need to live in S.D., Lex. I was jealous over something I don't even want."

"Yeah. That's how I feel about San Francisco," Lexi reflected. "A move isn't feasible, plus I don't want to settle down there. It's more of a distant fantasy than a life goal. You're not alone, kid. I can relate. I would've listened and supported you. But you gotta let me in. That's the only way I can help."

"How could I burden you with this?" Colin rubbed his temple. "You think I don't know the only reason you've stayed in Sacramento all these years is because you have a crazy brother? Or that you're trapped here, anchored to the ground because of me?"

Lexi recoiled, sinking into the seat cushion as though she'd been slapped.

"That's not true," she argued, her voice a wisp of air floating through the dark. "You aren't weighing me down. You're my big brother, Colin. I *want* to be in the same city as you."

"I'm literally the only reason you haven't left. You might tell yourself you don't want to live in San Francisco, but we both know you do."

"I'm okay in Sacramento."

"Okay isn't good enough, Lexi. You weren't meant to coast through life or be average. Just admit it. You stayed close to home because I'm a disaster."

"How can you say that? Look at all the good you've done. You're risking everything to collaborate with the most effective humanitarian group on the planet. You're saving so many lives, Colin. Even with your own personal struggles, you're changing this world for the better. I'll be lucky if I can figure out how to sabotage one single government device. Meanwhile, you've already scrambled a database and given thousands of folks a new identity. A shot at a life worth living."

"President Shithead might still find a way to track them down."

"And when he does, you'll be there to create another diversion," Lexi pointed out. "You're giving ARs a fighting chance. You're keeping people safe, Colin. That's what you do, and it's who you are. You're a protector."

"Not to myself."

Lexi couldn't argue with that. "I hope that changes. You're making progress. You just got a pill pack, kid. You're doing great so far. Look, I stayed close because I care. I want to be here."

"You stayed close to babysit me." It was not an accusation or an insult. Rather, it came across as an apology. Colin's voice was laden with regret. "How could I talk to you about San Diego when I'm the reason you're stuck in Sacramento? How would that be fair? I didn't really want to move to S.D. Meanwhile, you actually *want* to leave. You've wanted to get the hell outta dodge since we were kids. When you left for college, I found a way to mess that up. You came home every weekend."

"That's not how it was," Lexi insisted. "I got through college just fine, right? I wouldn't change anything about the way it played out. I want to be here in Sacramento. You're heaping this guilt on yourself, but it's unwarranted. You didn't hold me back."

"I did, Lex."

"You did not. Yes, you're a big part of my reason for staying in Sacramento. But nobody forced me. I would choose this city again and again."

Colin turned toward the window.

Over his shoulder, Lexi spotted the Brennans' house illuminated against a rapidly-darkening sky. Bronze lanterns flanked the front door. Upstairs, a lamp had been turned on in Colin's old room. This would be his home for the next few weeks while he completed the outpatient program at the hospital. Lexi was relieved her brother would be monitored for the foreseeable future. She wanted him surrounded by family until he regained his footing. Became a little more stable and consistent.

"For what it's worth, I think you should chase everything you want," Colin said. "You've got this great plan, this strategy to make sure flight attendants aren't used as puppets for President Asswaffle. You're taking action, Lexi. I'm proud to be part of that, and I sincerely want you to move to Palo Alto or wherever the airline runs its special projects."

"San Jose, mostly. Sometimes San Diego."

"Right. Well, this is an important endeavor, Lex. And wherever it takes you, that's where you should go." Colin turned to face her. "I'm not meant to be in San Diego, not long-term. I love the atmosphere, and some of my best memories took place there. But Sacramento will always be my home. It's my domicile for life."

The aviation term made Lexi smile. "I don't even know if SkyLine will approve my new class, Colin. We're getting ahead of ourselves."

"Are you kidding? I heard all the public statements SkyLine made when the government first started targeting ARs. Your airline will get behind this project. They're a corporation, but they have a heart. More than most businesses, that's for sure. Soon they'll be begging you to run the whole educational department."

"We'll see about that. First, I need to survive the next few weeks," Lexi said. "One day at a time."

Colin tilted his head to the side. "Funny enough, that's my mantra, too."

Chapter Seventeen: October 15, 2038

"It's noon in Orlando, right? Is training officially over?" Lexi leaned against her parents' kitchen counter and grabbed her coffee mug. The last few ounces of liquid lingered at the bottom of the ceramic cup. She gulped them down, then smiled at Jason. He looked every bit as tangible as her brother, who was seated at the kitchen table.

"Training ends at three. We're on lunch break right now. I stumbled across an empty conference room, which happens to be the perfect spot for a PersonableSpin session," Jason noted. "Zero distractions."

"How's training?" Colin asked. "You're almost done, man."

Jason turned around to face Colin. "Yeah, we wrap up this afternoon. I'll catch the late flight to Nashville. Next week, I pack up and move to California. SkyLine wants me out there fixing the planes as soon as possible."

"Exciting," Colin said. "We should fly down and help you unpack."

Lexi meandered toward the kitchen table so Jason could see both siblings without swiveling back and forth. "We're inviting ourselves to your place, Jason."

"Fantastic," Jason said with a smile. "I'll be there next Friday."

"That's the day my intensive outpatient program ends. Perfect timing," Colin mused. "I don't go back to work until Monday."

Lexi tilted her head to the side. "Looks like it's meant to

be."

"On an unrelated note, have you thought about Lexi's idea?" Colin asked. "Just checking, you're in auto-erase mode, yeah? System-wide encryption with a modified key?"

Jason scratched his chin. "I think so. Let me forward my AutoScan settings."

Colin went silent for a moment. Lexi watched his eyes flick left to right while analyzing the image transposed on his eyelid.

"Send me your access code to make an adjustment," Colin said. "Got it. Yep, there you go."

"All good now?" Lexi asked.

Colin nodded.

"It was an easy choice. I'm in," Jason said without a trace of hesitation. "Lexi's plan is brilliant. Should be simple to cut wires or install the device with one corner detached from the base. It malfunctions if it's not flush, from what I understand. The device seems incredibly primitive. It's like a relic from fifteen years ago. A joke."

"The feds really blew it," Colin agreed. "For all the money they've poured into their Patriotic Safety Teams, you'd think they would've forked over some cash for modern tracking devices. But this thing's garbage. They bought the cheapest one they could."

"Which works in our favor," Lexi noted, lifting an eyebrow. "Why would they skimp? Was this entire initiative just for show, you think?"

"Probably. They're flexing their muscles," Colin said. "Bullies love attention. They need to feel powerful."

"Small-dick syndrome," Lexi reflected.

Jason shook his head. "Idiots. Can't they get an implant instead of destroying the world?"

"Fun fact. The press secretary *did* get an implant two years ago." Colin grinned. "The fancy kind. He bought the model that gets hard on command and takes on whatever girth, length, texture, and even flavor you program it for."

"Oh, Lord," Lexi said, cracking a smile. "I'm guessing you know this because you altered it."

"Let's just say he had to have the thing removed after two consecutive days with a fourteen-inch hard-on. It was red, then purple, then rainbow-colored. Just to add insult to injury." Colin chuckled. "That wasn't a DefenderTech hack. That one was all me. Best solo project of my life."

"Thank you for your service," Lexi told her brother, wrapping him in a side hug. She loved seeing that goofy grin of his. She loved that he'd used humor to fuck with a real-life supervillain, and that he could recall the memory with mischief in his eyes. "You're a true American hero, kid. Switching gears, today's the day Tamika and I decorate our classroom."

"Lexi, when are you presenting the new curriculum to Reggie?" Jason asked. "The devices are supposed to be installed on all planes by mid-March, right? I think system-wide activation is scheduled for April first."

"I'll talk to him today after I set up the classroom for the health and safety class." Lexi glanced at the local daily report displayed on the nanoscreen behind her brother. Traffic looked intimidating, and she was due in San Francisco in a few hours. "Shoot, I need to leave soon."

"What's your syllabus going to include?" Jason asked.

"Still hashing out the details, but I'll present it as a technology tutorial. The safety class I'm teaching with Tamika was designed long before this federal mandate. It's limited to health procedures. I want my new class to focus on SkyLine's tech systems. That includes the apps available on our tablet, the way they sync to new devices on the plane—"

"Installed improperly by the *worst* mechanic at SkyLine," Jason interjected.

"Yep. Who hired that dummy, anyway? Can't trust a baby

mechanic to do anything right," Lexi teased. "If the boxes happen to be working, flight attendants can crash the signal by keeping the ARtrack app running the night before their trip. Colin's busy learning all the other ways to derail this stupid device."

"I've got five methods so far," Colin explained. "Guessing I can find a few more."

"You'll present each one, Lex?" Jason asked.

"Yeah, after explaining the recent struggles ARs have faced. I'll open my class with some examples of repressive new laws and their real-life implications. I plan to spin it so I can get government approval. As long as I sound like I'm pointing out AR deficiencies or blaming them, the feds will allow it. I'll team up with SkyLine's lawyers to cover my ass. It should work, right?" Lexi tilted her head to the side.

"Absolutely," Jason said. "It makes sense. You show how bad the situation has become for ARs through some thinly-veiled conspiracy theories. Basically, you reverse-psychology the shit outta the government."

"Those narcissists will eat it up. The president and his loyal team of assholes love to be praised," Colin reflected. "Lexi will design the class to look like she's vilifying ARs and highlighting the importance of tracking them down. All the while, she's showing the hypocrisy that went into this initiative."

"I can speak in hyperboles and absolutes. It'll help to toss around terms like *freedom* and *Christian values*. The government will buy it. They've been masking bigotry as patriotism for ages." Lexi shrugged. "Some employees might miss the point. We have a couple extremists at the airline, die-hard nationalists with archaic religious views. But I believe most flight attendants will understand. Most employees will do the right thing. The ones with souls and even a tiny shred of compassion will join our movement to protect ARs.

"SkyLine took a hard stance against injustice in the

spring," Lexi continued. "Remember that, Jason? It was a big deal. Back in May, after the Women's March and the healthcare riots, SkyLine released a public statement. The company promised to promote justice. They were all about equality. They supported human rights and revised company policies to reflect that."

"I remember," Jason said. "SkyLine's public statements rattled some people. Controversial stuff. The airline made it clear they didn't support the government's drastic measures."

"That was a sad and embarrassing moment for America." Colin shook his head.

Lexi swallowed. "Yeah. I was proud of SkyLine's response, though."

"Same here," Jason said. "I wonder if it's part of the reason we survived this crisis while other airlines folded."

"When things took a turn for the worst, SkyLine endorsed acceptance," Lexi reflected. "Lots of people chose hatred instead. It's easier, and it requires less thought. But then there are the folks who truly care. Deep down, they know when something's just plain wrong. Those people were drawn to SkyLine. That's my theory, anyway."

"And now it's time to make good on those promises," Jason reflected. "Talk only goes so far. SkyLine needs to prove what it really stands for."

"And we will help with that." Lexi's confidence surged at the possibility of doing something big. Her brother had been involved in humanitarian efforts for years. He'd been making a difference, one person at a time. And now Lexi was going to join that quest. She marveled at the thought of launching a movement to change lives for the better.

"Reggie's going to love this idea," Jason predicted. "He'll iron out the kinks, smooth the rough edges. It's a done deal."

Jason's eyes shined through the pale mid-morning light flooding Lexi's childhood home. He was standing in a conference room in Florida, yet his face seemed to reflect the sunshine permeating the Brennans' sun-streaked California windows.

"Shoot, it's already nine o'clock," Colin gawked. "I'm gonna be late."

"Jason, good luck with your last few hours of training." Lexi lifted a hand to wave at him.

Jason pressed his fingers to hers. Lexi watched his skin turn to static as it grazed her flesh. Although his image was an optical illusion, Lexi could imagine the heat radiating from his body, the smooth texture of his skin. She missed everything about him. He felt close, thanks to PersonableSpin, but not close enough.

"Have fun setting up the classroom with Tamika," Jason said. "Send photos."

"I will. Bye for now, baby mechanic." With that, Lexi closed out the PersonableSpin session.

Colin grabbed his backpack off the kitchen counter, and Lexi followed her brother into the hallway. The front door made a clicking noise as it unlocked. Sean and Erin Brennan strolled through the door with Monty at their side.

"It's nice out today. You're leaving for the hospital?" Erin asked, shifting her sunglasses to the top of her head. "Got your autowallet for lunch, right?"

"Autowallets are *so* five years ago, Mom," Colin quipped. He held up his thumb like a trophy.

"I'll drive him to Midtown," Lexi offered. "Then I'll head to SF and set up my classroom with Tamika."

"Okay, kid, see you at six," Sean told Colin. He ruffled his hair, then marched toward the kitchen.

"Will you be here for dinner, Lex?" Erin asked, pausing at the end of the hallway.

"Yeah. Should be back by six-thirty, latest." Lexi grabbed a jacket from the coat rack.

For a moment, Lexi was fourteen again, getting ready to ride to school with her big brother. They were just a couple teenagers with Bohemian but amazing parents, in an unimpressive house that suited them just fine. They had a hyper dog and a backyard that was ideal for big parties. Colin's illness hadn't yet reared its head.

Colin and Lexi were just a couple kids with a long school day ahead. They were best friends, and they were all right.

On the drive to Lutheran Midtown Hospital, Lexi asked Colin if he'd noticed any changes since the slow-release pack was inserted. He reached for her phone and reset a few privacy settings before answering the question.

"I'm not as shaky. The past few days have felt smoother."

"That's great, kid."

"Last week was jarring. The work I'm doing is high-stakes, so I got carried away. I was sure I was being followed. The thought still occurs to me, but I don't obsess over it like I used to. I can quiet that fear before it takes over my life."

"That's amazing. I'm proud of you," Lexi said. The hospital came into view, its solid red exterior stretching toward the sky.

"Things were creepy for a while," Colin said. "Shadows in front of my apartment and cars tailing me. Everything felt like a bad omen. I was so sure they'd planted chips on me and compromised my EarLink. Messed with my GeoTrack device while I was sleeping."

"The work you're doing is meaningful. But it's also intimidating, so your imagination ran away with you," Lexi reasoned.

Colin nodded. "It did. I'm a small fish, Lexi. I contribute to DefenderTech, but I'm not the key player. I'm a sidelined character at best, a consultant who helps as needed. Nobody worth chasing after. That would be a waste of everyone's time. Plus, we were thorough and precise. We covered our tracks."

"I bet you didn't miss a thing," Lexi mused, familiar with her brother's attention to detail concerning any coding project.

"Yeah. This was my chance to make things right," Colin mused. He turned toward the window, his face hidden from Lexi. "My relationship with Marco was doomed. We were so close to getting married when things crumbled. It felt like I could never recover from that, you know? But I started rebuilding my life. I made it through the meteor shower and ContaCan. There had to be a reason for that, I figured. There was work to be done, and I was here to make sure things went off without a hitch. Collaborating with DT gave me a clear purpose. It also happens to be something I'm good at."

"You're good at lots of things, kid. This is just one example of your talents. You're unstoppable when you commit to a project."

"But this specific project was different. I didn't notice I was unraveling until it was too late."

"How was this time different from the past?"

"Before, our efforts were more grassroots. They mostly centered around people who had been failed by the system. We helped families through a series of creative hacks. Dealt with things like lottery tickets and healthcare access. We crashed the ridiculous vigilante website Texas set up to attack women, stuff like that. It was deeply satisfying work, but it wasn't exactly a revolution."

"I see. In this case, the stakes were higher?"

"The more we learned, the more we realized the government was going full-tilt. Our goal changed. In some ways, this was an effort to overthrow the system. We scrambled the national database and fried the tracking system at the state borders. The feds could've nailed us for espionage and treason, but we had no choice. We had to do something drastic. People's lives depended on it. There was zero room for effort or delay. Plus, everything had to be perfect."

"Good thing you're precise," Lexi murmured.

"Yes, I'm neurotic when it comes to this stuff. Everyone at DT is meticulous. But the pressure messes with me. I wasn't sleeping much, and I barely ate. Things spun out of control. I became frantic. Every noise felt like the end, like someone had arrived to finish me off."

Lexi bit her lip. "Given the circumstances, it's understandable that you'd grow a little paranoid."

"But it consumed my life," Colin pointed out. "In hindsight, there were signs along the way. I skipped pills. Not all the time, just when I needed to focus and stay awake. I quit sleeping. Eating, too. Shit got really distorted. It's hard to stop the spiral once it starts, which is why I need to catch myself early on and stick to a routine. Check in with a professional regularly and work things out before they become an issue."

Lexi opened her mouth, then promptly closed it. Years flashed before her like lighting bursts, scenes from different cities and bars and dorm rooms and apartments. All the heartache in the world belonged to Lexi's past, so she'd found an escape hatch. One that stripped her of the ability to think or feel.

She was no stranger to Colin's struggle for balance. Once the downward spiral began, it was nearly impossible to stop. The chaos became the baseline.

Lexi cruised to a stop in front of the hospital entrance. She leaned over the console and wrapped her brother in a tight hug. "Nobody should have to live like that, constantly fearing for their safety. I'm so glad you got help. You're making progress, and now you're in a better position to help all the folks who need you."

Colin pulled away and gripped her shoulders, looking her

square in the eye. "I'm trying, Lex. Who knows what shape I'll be in next week."

"Well, you're off to a great start. And we can cross that bridge when we come to it."

Colin opened the car door, stepping out into the sunshine. He paused for a moment. Then he poked his head through the passenger side window. "You're sharing your plan with Reggie this afternoon, right?"

"Yep."

"He'll love the idea, Lex. How could he not?"

"Thanks. Cross your fingers for me, kid." Lexi watched her brother step inside the building. Then she navigated to the highway and drove west toward San Francisco.

"Reggie should call any minute," Tamika said, pointing to her tablet. "Do you want me here for this, Lex?"

Lexi nodded. "Yes, please."

"Nervous?"

"A little."

Tamika smiled. "Don't be. I've never heard of a more timely or important class. You've designed something amazing, Lexi. I need this tutorial for my own personal sanity. The stuff happening in our country isn't okay. What they're asking us to do, it's criminal."

"We can end it. Or at least slow it down," Lexi reflected. "We have to try, right? We have to do something. This could've easily been my brother. It could've been any one of us. It *was* Jorge, except he passed before things went downhill. Think of all the flight attendants who would have been targeted if they'd lived to see the day. If they'd survived the early phase of the antidote, they would be subjected to these laws now. We'd have to report our own coworkers to the government, knowing they'd be sent away to die."

"It's fucking evil."

"No kidding." Lexi sighed. "This class requires intense prep work. I'll have to collaborate with SkyLine's lawyers. Sort through the legalities and recruit some experts with relevant testimonies. Doctors who can describe the impact of ARs and explain how low the transmission rate is for those who are antidote-compatible. Plus, I need to cover my own ass. There's a long road ahead."

"But you have the guts for it," Tamika noted. "You're unstoppable, Lex. I have zero doubt you can tackle all the logistics and bring this project to life."

"You're sure Reggie will approve the idea?"

Tamika frowned. "Reggie's a middle-aged, gay Black man. I'm going to go out on a limb and say he would *absolutely* support a comprehensive curriculum striving to attain justice. That's what you're doing, Lexi. You're reminding people how to preserve basic human rights."

Tamika hopped on a table and dangled her legs over the side.

Lexi glanced at the work they'd completed in one afternoon. The classroom was officially ready. Red lasers hovered over each wall, displaying the time and date along with the internal and external temperature. Nanoscreens embedded in the walls would reveal themselves on command, providing visual aids for future students.

"We did a good job," Tamika noted. She rocked her legs like a child on a swing, her tan boots grazing the floor.

"Everything's ready to go."

"Including your badass new proposal." Tamika's eyes twinkled. "Let me get the ball rolling. I'll hype it up."

Tamika's tablet emitted a loud buzz, indicating that Reggie had initiated contact.

Reggie materialized before them wearing a blue blazer and a patterned tie. The man looked impeccable. As always.

"Ladies, this setup is great," he said. He spun around to

evaluate the classroom. "I love the chalkboard. Old-school, huh? Nice touch. Room dividers were placed in the corner for PersonableSpin sessions, I assume."

Tamika nodded. "We wanted to offer a space with minimal distractions."

"It's perfect. Did you run through a mock class?" Reggie asked.

"We practiced most of it," Lexi informed him. "All that's left is the updated biotech portion of the manual."

"Everyone's favorite part, right?" Reggie asked with a chuckle. "Sounds like you two are in good shape. Do you feel comfortable leading your first class in a week?"

"I think we're ready. Lexi and I are a good team. And we know how to reach you if any questions pop up," Tamika said confidently. "I don't have much more to add, but Lexi wanted to talk about something. She has an amazing idea, Reggie."

Lexi smiled, feeling slightly shaky beneath her wide grin. "I have a proposal. It'll take a few minutes if that's okay."

"I've got time. Let's hear it," Reggie said.

"Well, I came up with an idea for a future SkyLine tutorial. I wasn't sure where to start, so I wanted to ask you about the protocol for something like this."

Reggie scratched his chin. "It's a simple process. First, you submit a formal letter to the head of the training department, which happens to be me. Then you request an in-person interview. Luckily for you, I'm standing right here. And I already know you, so we can skip all that."

Lexi bit her lip, running through debacles that could occur if her plan wasn't formally sanctioned. "Should I go through the usual channels? I can draft a proposal."

"Lexi's just overthinking things," Tamika said with a quick laugh. She reached across the table and squeezed Lexi's arm. "Her plan is incredible, Reggie. It's awesome."

Reggie lifted a perfectly-tailored eyebrow. "Now I'm

intrigued. Tell me more."

Lexi swallowed. "I figured flight attendants could benefit from a technology tutorial. With the government issuing new ARtrack devices and uploading a corresponding app on our tablet, it can feel overwhelming. Especially for the stews who aren't very skilled with this kind of thing."

Reggie nodded. "Those devices are absurd. SkyLine's still fighting them in court, but the justice system is basically dead in the water. It looks like the government is going to win this battle."

"Which doesn't mean the war is over," Lexi pointed out. "Reggie, I'd work closely with SkyLine's lawyers on this. I'd make sure everything was pristine. We would follow each guideline, down to the smallest detail. But if I began the class with some eye-opening material, maybe news clips or interviews with doctors who treated ARs, I could show our flight attendants why this is a crisis. I could help them see what's happening and the impact of our identification checks."

Reggie scratched his chin. "So you'd explain how the ARs have been targeted?"

"In a way, yes. I would provide info on the *dangers* ARs pose by going into a brief history of the laws implemented to control them." Lexi carefully observed Reggie's reaction. He seemed to understand. "Which would lead us to the technology portion. I'd remind folks if they charge their tablets too long, the app will fail. Direct sunlight to fuel the solar fuel cell, instead of filtered sunlight through a window or something, could fry the battery. Which would be super irresponsible."

Reggie scratched his chin. "I see. You'd show folks all the careless ways their ARtrack connections would be disabled."

"Right. Lexi would educate students on the activities to avoid so the app functions correctly," Tamika quipped.

"There are other topics we could discuss, including airplane etiquette," Lexi continued. "Clumsiness is a fatal error for the government devices. The box in the forward galley is sensitive to heat and water. Any spilled liquids would be a mechanical disaster. Even holding a coffee pot too close could cause the thing to malfunction. Also, if a flight attendant tripped and snagged the blue wire, which is exposed at the bottom, the whole box would be useless. There are so many careless mistakes that could occur. Ones we obviously need to avoid."

"Obviously," Reggie agreed.

"Obviously," Tamika echoed, her lips curving up.

"And you'd show folks how to dodge those errors," Reggie concluded.

"I'd give them the information. They'd decide how to use it," Lexi clarified. "Our flight attendants are free to act however they want, preserve the integrity of the app and physical box if they choose. At least folks would know the full story. They'd have a better view of the situation so they could make an informed decision."

"I think this will work. Just need to get the directors behind it, which shouldn't be too hard," Reggie said.

"I've been thinking about that. Maybe this will help," Lexi began. "SkyLine didn't mince words in May. The company firmly supported progress and equality. Our CEO was straightforward, and the board agreed with her. So did most employees. Passengers, too."

"It was a proud moment for us," Reggie reflected.

Lexi nodded. "Other airlines tanked after ContaCan, but SkyLine emerged stronger than ever. As far as I can tell, that's because we stood on the right side of history. When the feds doubled down on hateful policies, SkyLine advocated for fairness. I believe passengers, shareholders, and employees welcomed our perspective. There were some who disagreed, sure. But most people found SkyLine's stance refreshing. In a year characterized by death, abuse, and discrimination,

SkyLine said enough is enough."

"SkyLine spoke up," Tamika quipped. "And people listened."

"Exactly. I think this class aligns with that sentiment. The airline publicly declared its goal. This tutorial will get us one step closer to achieving it." Lexi blinked rapidly at the conclusion of her pitch.

Reggie smiled. "Your class is approved on my end, Lexi. I'll let you know about the directors. I suspect you're right. They will grasp the relevance of this material. I predict they'll give you the green light."

Tamika elbowed Lexi's side and grinned.

"We've needed this sort of program for a long time," Reggie said. "As a country and as an airline. I'm glad you took the time to conceptualize this project."

"Thanks, Reggie. I had some help along the way."

CHAPTER EIGHTEEN: OCTOBER 22, 2038

"This one's unlabeled," Lexi called from the living room. She turned the box on its side, checking for a barcode she might've missed. She summoned AutoScan to scan for a chip.

A dull thud confirmed Lexi's suspicions. The box had zero identifying marks. Lexi scratched her head, contemplating whether she had enough energy to tear open the thick water-soluble tape spanning all four sides. Her biceps ached from hauling large items around Jason's condo for the last few hours. Despite the heavy lifting, it had been a pleasant afternoon. Jason's condo, which faced the bay, had a sparkly glow.

Jason emerged from the hallway. "Tired, Lex?"

Vella trailed behind him, tail wagging eagerly. She'd swarmed Lexi earlier, sniffing furiously for probably an hour.

Lexi set the box down and scratched Vella's chin. "Huh?"

"You look like you're wiped out. And ready for a drink," Jason said.

"I'm always ready for a drink." She chuckled. "But we can finish unpacking first."

Colin strolled past, carrying a box of silverware to the kitchen. "Lexi's out of shape. Like me."

"You should be used to this, Lex. Isn't the drink cart heavy?" Jason mused. "Solid metal held together by a couple screws. I've repaired dozens of them."

Colin snorted. "Lexi flies the lead position so she can hand-deliver drinks to first class."

"Well, it's also easier to snag free minis for the layover. I brought several with me today, in fact. You're welcome." Lexi grinned. "Hey, can someone tell me where that box belongs? There's no label."

"Let's put it in the guest room. I'll sort through it later," Jason said. "I've got a few shirts to hang up, then we can get dinner."

Colin hummed while easing Jason's flatware tray into a kitchen drawer.

Lexi scooped up the cardboard box. It was heavy, packed to the brim with bulky objects. Most likely books or electronics, Lexi guessed. Her muscles tensed under the weight, yet she was overcome by serenity. Achy arms and all.

Colin's humming was a welcome respite from the lingering tension of the last few weeks, months, years, and decades. Lexi stood still, as though any form of movement might slash the jubilant noise. These tones were the soundtrack to Lexi's best and brightest moments with her brother. He used to sing show tunes and oldies while doing weekend chores. Didn't matter that he never got the lyrics right. Didn't matter that he couldn't hit the high notes.

This was the version of Colin that gave Lexi abiding hope. Even during the valleys, the terrifying low points, she couldn't deny his soul's radiance. Colin would forever remain the big-hearted, sensitive human who sang off-key and carried the weight of the world on his narrow shoulders. He would always be Lexi's big brother. Her ally. The man was gentle, wounded, and somewhat unsteady. He was also the exact sort of person this world needed. Colin was deeply attuned to others' suffering. He was determined to help ease it.

Jason reappeared from the hallway. While Lexi watched, he lifted the cumbersome box from her arms. He carried it to the guest bedroom, then declared it was time to get food and drinks. Lexi's stomach grumbled on cue, as though agreeing to Jason's dinner plans. Lexi hadn't eaten anything since she'd arrived in San Diego with Colin at noon. She was famished.

Once everyone had piled into Jason's car, he put the vehicle in self-driving mode. The sedan drifted effortlessly down streets lined with cafes and boutiques. Colin spoke up occasionally, pointing out a couple restaurants he'd visited in the past. Lexi stared through the window at the glittering storefronts. A thin strip of buildings separated their two-lane road from the shoreline.

San Diego was magnificent during the day, Lexi knew, an architectural masterpiece encompassed by a white-foam ocean. At twilight, however, the city revealed even more character. Once the sun retreated past the water, San Diego became downright ethereal.

Lexi's breath got caught in her throat. Houses stretched before her, beacons of light perched on the rolling hills of La Playa.

Jason's car cruised to a stop in front of an open-air market near the Midway District. Colin ventured off in search of a burger while Jason and Lexi ordered food at a Mediterranean booth. With their dinners in hand, they regrouped at a picnic table on the far end of the pavilion. Tiny yellow lights blanketed the space.

Lexi smeared hummus on a pita and chewed her dinner while Jason explained his schedule for the week. Colin paused between bites of a dripping burger. He hung on every word, periodically asking Jason about the condition of the planes and the specific tasks he'd perform on each one.

When they transitioned to the topic of the ARtrack box, Colin put everyone's AutoScan in auto-erase mode. After he selectively disabled the cameras hovering at the perimeter of the outdoor dining hall, he leaned forward. He spoke in hushed tones.

Lexi could picture their plan coming together. She knew it would be successful. With Colin restricting the program's connectivity and Jason disabling each device, there was no chance of failure. Those two were experts in their respective fields. And Lexi would teach flight attendants the best ways to derail the tracking device in the unlikely event that one happened to function properly.

After everyone finished eating, Colin announced he was meeting up with friends.

"You sure, kid?" Lexi asked. Colin hadn't ventured out on his own since before his most recent hospital stay.

He nodded. "I'm excited to see some old buddies. It's been too long."

"Will Marco be there?" Lexi asked gently. "Just curious."

"Nope. I thought about calling him, then decided against it. I'd prefer to make my own memories here."

"Clean slate," Jason reflected. "I get it."

"Fresh start," Colin said with a resolute nod. "I'm going to meet up with a couple buddies I've known for a million years. Since surf camp in middle school."

"Felix? Gianni?" Lexi asked.

Sadness washed over Colin's emerald eyes. "Gianni was sent back to Italy, Lex. Forcibly extracted."

"Crap. I didn't know he was an AR. Poor guy."

"Yeah, he was such a good dude. He didn't deserve that shit. But this is why we're doing what we're doing, right?" Colin lowered his voice. "No more forced deportations. Screw the system."

"Screw it," Jason said, reaching for his beer.

"It's about to get screwed," Lexi chimed in. "Hard."

"Felix lives close by," Colin continued. "He wanted me to meet his friends. I already ordered a *Swyft*. I should return to the condo by midnight."

"We'll come get you if you need a ride home," Jason offered. "Or send my car in auto-mode."

Colin waved his hand. "Don't worry about it. Just have fun tonight."

With that, he rose from the table and strolled toward the front of the market. His steps appeared purposeful. Deliberate. Lexi could tell a lot by Colin's gait. When he slipped into the dark place, he moved slowly. As though his feet couldn't locate solid ground.

At the moment, however, there was confidence in his stride. Relief surged in Lexi's chest.

"Where to next?" Jason asked, turning to face Lexi.

"Let's keep it low-key. How about a movie at your new place?"

Lexi pressed her thumb to the wall sensor. The sole source of artificial light in Jason's bedroom, a brass floor lamp, went dark. Moonlight was all that remained. It was more than sufficient. With Jason, Lexi had learned to navigate by touch rather than sight.

Her clothes lay in a messy pile in one corner of the room. Jason's shirt and pants dangled from the edge of the dresser.

"You know I care about you, right?" Jason asked as Lexi slid into bed beside him. Vella sighed dramatically from her dog bed, an oversized round pad near the closet.

"I have a pretty good idea, yes."

Jason inhaled sharply. "Well, I'm rusty. It's been four years since I started a new relationship. So I'll just come right out and say it. I want to be with you. It feels like we're already together, doesn't it?"

Lexi lifted a hand to his cheek. Her fingers traced his jaw. She'd never imagined a face would fit neatly in the palm of her hand, at once rigid and soft and familiar and sweet. "Are you asking me to be your girlfriend, Jason Bresline?"

"That's exactly what I'm asking."

"Noted. To be honest, I'm not sure how I feel about relationships," Lexi admitted. "But life makes sense with you. It feels like things will be okay even when the world is a hopeless mess. Dumpster fire on steroids."

"We're about to change that, little by little," Jason said. "Two airline employees on a mission to save humanity."

"And during the downtime, we can get it on. When we aren't busy plotting some sneaky government sabotage," Lexi mused. "Apocalypse dating is weird."

"The weirdest." Jason pulled Lexi closer to him. She nestled into the crook of his neck. "I need to tell you something, Lex. When I got to town yesterday, before I unloaded a single box from the truck, I did a Predictive PersonableSpin session with Colleen."

"You did?"

Jason cleared his throat. "Yeah. I didn't give myself time to second-guess it. I wanted her to see my new place, to be part of this new chapter of my life. I know it was just her avatar, but it was powerful. It felt so real. All the things she said, I swear those words came straight from Captain Colleen."

Lexi propped her elbows on Jason's chest, making eye contact with him. "How are you holding up? It's super emotional."

"I'm glad I did it. Turns out Colleen's brother-in-law is an AR. Colleen would have been so proud of our current project. She would've found a way to help from the flight deck, I'm sure of it. Hell, she might've purchased a turboprop to fly folks to safety herself." Jason paused. "I told her I wanted to make things official with you. Here's what she said—*do it right away, and don't fuck this up*. Direct quote."

Lexi chuckled. "She sounds fun. I like this lady. For the record, I doubt you'll fuck it up. That's typically *my* specialty."

"Try your best." Jason leaned forward to kiss Lexi's neck.

She welcomed the gesture, pulling his sculpted body toward hers. Beneath soft sheets and starlight, they embarked on a new adventure. Together.

Epilogue: January 27, 2039

As the last few students trickled out of the room, Lexi pushed in their empty chairs.

"It's funny," she told Tamika once the classroom had cleared out. "I assumed the last day of this health and safety class would be dramatic and sentimental. Right?"

"It was chill. And there's a good reason for that, girl," Tamika said, smiling from the front of the room. Her eyes flicked left to right as she entered data from their final class into her Holoscreen. "You're two steps ahead, mentally. I don't blame you."

"Can't argue with that," Lexi admitted.

"When does your course officially start?"

"Sign-ups begin at the end of February. March first is the inaugural class. It's coming together so fast, Tamika. Meredith and Kamilla message me every day. We've got a lot to accomplish in a short amount of time."

"You're gonna crush it."

"Let's hope so. The stakes are high." Lexi paused. "Tell you what, I'm going to miss teaching with you. You're a great partner."

"You, too."

Lexi made her way through vacant tables, searching for items the students had left behind. Someone had tossed a gum wrapper on the floor, and somebody else had dropped an allergy pill. Lexi threw the items in the trash unceremoniously.

In a flourish, Tamika grabbed Lexi's tablet from the podium and hoisted it above her head. "You've got a call coming in. Looks like a PersonableSpin session."

The notification flashed across Lexi's eye. "It's Jason. Should I tell him to call back later?"

"Nah," Tamika commented with a mischievous smile. "Do it now. I've got an ax to grind with your boyfriend."

Lexi accepted the session via AutoScan. Jason materialized between her and Tamika, the image choppy. Lines of static carved a path from his chin to his chest.

"Hey. I'm on break. My reception's garbage down here," Jason said. "Let me switch over to video chat."

With a flash of light, his avatar disappeared. A second later, he reappeared on Lexi's Holoscreen. A rectangle hovered above her tablet with Jason in the center. Tamika propped the device on the podium so both women had a clear view of him.

"Hey. Just checking how your final day of class went."

"Final day of class for me. But Lexi's got a whole new curriculum ahead. This is just the beginning for her," Tamika clarified. "Listen, I need you to talk some sense into your girlfriend."

Jason grinned. "Pretty sure Lexi does what she wants."

Lexi winked at him.

Tamika folded her arms across her chest. "Look, I've been trying for a week to convince her, but your woman is stubborn as hell."

Jason leaned back in his gray chair. Behind him were white walls and a marbled countertop stretching the length of the room. There was a snack basket on the counter overflowing with chips and candy. Beside the basket, a coffeemaker appeared to be brewing a fresh pot of coffee.

"Fill me in," Jason said. "What's the problem?"

"I'm moving to Seattle in March. I already closed on my condo. It's a done deal," Tamika began. "Which means I need to sublet my kickass apartment in the Mission District. It's three blocks from Dolores Park. Two blocks from the Mission BART station."

"Nice," Jason said. "Congrats on your new place."

"Thanks. You and Lexi better come visit me. But that's another topic for another time," Tamika said. "My apartment in SF is a dream come true. The bullet train is around the corner. That thing hauls ass to San Jose in twenty minutes. Lexi's commute to the SkyLine Special Projects Building would be a piece of cake, but she keeps refusing my offer."

"You know I can't leave Sacramento," Lexi reminded Jason. "Reggie already approved my plan to work remotely while creating the new curriculum. Technology is so advanced these days. It'll be like I'm right there in San Jose . . . from the comfort of my own apartment in Sac. And Cleo is happy where we are. Why move her to a whole new place? A new city?"

"Your cat will be fine, Lexi. She'll love my apartment. Picture those bay windows with a floor-to-ceiling view of Dolores Park. She can look at birds all day," Tamika said, turning toward Jason. "It's true that Lexi can plan the class from a hundred miles away. But how much more efficient would it be to have a physical office in San Jose? And make an appearance there every few days?"

Lexi remained quiet. She bit her lip.

"This new class will be detailed and complex," Tamika continued. "Lexi's got the lawyers triple-checking everything. She's collaborating with Kamilla and Meredith daily. They both work in San Jose. Since it's a sensitive training, she'll need approval from the ADA and civil liberties unions. The subject matter will have to pass a bunch of certifications. Government officials will be observing this class, Jason. Lexi is going to rock it, no doubt. But it's easier to meet all those demands if she's at the San Jose building. In person."

Lexi didn't protest. She knew Tamika was correct.

"Having a physical presence at the Special Projects Building would make life infinitely easier," Tamika concluded. She folded her arms across her chest.

"Sure sounds like it. I forget what day the class launches, Lex. March first, right?" Jason asked.

Lexi bit her lip. "Yes."

"See?" Tamika burst. She tossed her hands up in the air. "It's ideal timing. This is fate. My sublet would begin in March and last through July. Then Lexi would have the option to switch the lease to her name. The stars are aligned."

Jason scratched his chin. "When's your lease up in Sac?"

"End of February. It's too late to give my thirty-day notice."

"Is it, though?" Tamika prodded. "Last I checked, there were twenty-eight days in February. That means you've got one more day to inform your apartment complex that you're outta there."

Lexi frowned. Tamika was right. She did have another twenty-four hours before her decision was due. She'd already prepared the renewal forms, though. Lexi had planned to submit her request later that day. With a single flick of her eye, she would officially be locked into another year in her same old apartment on J Street. She would remain a resident of her hometown for another trip around the sun.

Like all the years before and all the years to come, Lexi reflected.

"Jason, I'm staying in Sac. Colin needs me." Lexi's voice was shrill, a desperate plea to remind everyone that the threads which bound her were not threads at all. They were steel bars. "I can accomplish everything important from Sacramento."

"You don't have to be a lifelong martyr," Tamika said, placing a hand on Lexi's shoulder. "You're allowed to prioritize your own happiness sometimes. Right, Jason?"

"I'm not going to persuade Lexi to make a choice based on

what I believe is best. Sorry to disappoint," Jason said, flicking his eyes briefly to Lexi's co-teacher. "Tamika, I see where you're coming from. This has to be Lexi's decision, though."

Tamika sighed. "She keeps ignoring the opportunity right in front of her. This could be life-changing, you know? Think of all the networking that happens inside that SkyLine Special Projects Building. I'm not exaggerating when I say this experience could land her a position similar to Reggie's. She might end up department head, or whatever else her heart desires. The possibilities are endless."

"I've got other responsibilities," Lexi said flatly.

"Has Colin been doing well?" Jason asked.

"Yes. The extended-release pack seems to be working. That's the cycle, though. Highs and lows. There will be another low, Jason." Lexi frowned. "Nobody knows when. I need to stay nearby in case it's tomorrow or next week or next year."

"You wouldn't be on Neptune, Lex," Tamika pointed out softly. "You'd still be in the same state as your brother. The Mission is a two-hour drive from Colin, tops. You can always go home if he needs you. But you gotta live your life, right? At some point, you need to prioritize *you*."

"Maybe you should discuss this with your brother," Jason suggested. "Wade through all the tough stuff, then reach a conclusion that works for both of you. Or . . ."

"What's that?" Lexi asked, her eyes fixed on the Holoscreen. Jason's expression radiated empathy and care.

"Or you could do a Predictive PersonableSpin session with Jorge," Jason said. "Just an idea. I consulted with Colleen before making a really important decision a few months back. I'm glad I did."

Lexi knew exactly which decision Jason was referring to. She smiled at her boyfriend, thankful for the advice of an airline pilot she'd never met. One who perished about a year before Lexi and Jason crossed paths in Orlando.

"That's not a terrible idea," Lexi mused.

"It'll help you find peace with whatever you choose," Jason insisted. "I bet Jorge can remind you what matters most, what makes the most sense with Colin. I want you to feel confident with your final decision and the logic behind it."

He meant it, Lexi knew. This wasn't a half-hearted, careless recommendation. If anyone understood how complicated and nuanced sibling relationships could be, it was certainly Jason. Lexi had watched him agonize over his own complex family dynamics.

Without any further prodding from Lexi, Jason had reached out to Jen several times in December. She didn't answer. A few weeks ago, Jason's sister finally accepted his call. The conversation went better than expected. Jen had invited him to visit Colorado Springs in February. She even asked him to bring Lexi along.

"If it's too gut-wrenching to see Jorge again, scrap the idea," Jason said, his tone soft and soothing. "I get that. I debated meeting up with Colleen for a long time. I was worried it would hurt like hell, which it did. But it was worth it. I bet Jorge will help guide you."

"Yeah. That's doable," Lexi conceded, biting her lip. "I'll consult with Jorge. He won't steer me wrong. Colin was family to him. They were like brothers."

"Then he'll know Colin wants you to chase your dreams, no matter where they lead," Tamika predicted. "But don't take my word for it. I've got ulterior motives. Go ahead and ask Jorge yourself."

Lexi lifted an eyebrow. "Are you admitting you might be a tiny bit biased?"

"Listen, I won't apologize for envisioning you as a department head and overall SkyLine superstar." Tamika broke into a sly grin. "Changing the world one cheap-ass, damaged

ARtrack box at a time."

"That reminds me, Lex, I found another loophole today," Jason said. He finished his cup of coffee and tossed the cardboard cup in the recycle bin. "Easy to tweak. I can tell you all about it this weekend."

Red lasers hovered on the wall of the breakroom, displaying the time in oversized numbers. They began to flash, which drew Jason's gaze in that direction.

"Crap," he said. "Break's over, and the plane at Gate Four is covered in guts."

"Bird strike?" Tamika guessed. "Gross."

"Poor birds. Hope it's not too bad. Talk later, Jason," Lexi said, lifting her hand to wave.

He waved back. "Congrats on completing your health and safety class, ladies. Bye, Tamika. See you in a couple days, Lex. Looking forward to it."

"Same here," Lexi said, closing out the call.

Tamika wrapped Lexi in her arms, gripping her so tight Lexi thought her ribcage might collapse.

"You'll be okay, girl. Call me if you need anything, and I'll drive straight back to the airport. Deal?"

Lexi nodded. "Thanks, Tamika. I'm just going to chat with him a few minutes. I'll lock up the room after."

"You're stronger than you know," Tamika said. She stepped through the door into the bright hallway. "Don't forget that, Lexi Brennan."

Lexi stared at her friend for a moment. She wanted to believe in her own strength the way Tamika believed in it. The way Jorge had always believed in it, too.

But she hadn't been there in the toughest moments. Colin had tried to hurt himself while Lexi smoked weed with her friends behind the high school stadium. Jorge died on a doomed plane while Lexi was hopping into bed with a stranger.

She wasn't strong—she was a flight risk. A magician who left her own body to evade reality. Lexi had lost and abused and concealed her soul, purposely, to avoid facing the difficult shit.

Maybe it's not too late to do better. She inhaled sharply.

Tamika smiled one last time. Then she was gone. Lexi was alone in the classroom, a complex and nostalgic task awaiting her.

She closed her eyes, summoning every fiber of courage she could. She assured herself it would be okay. She'd done this once before. She could do it again. Lexi opened her eyes and gulped down a few big breaths, counting to five each time. Deep breathing had helped before. At the moment, however, it didn't seem to make much difference.

Before she could second-guess the decision, she selected Predictive PersonableSpin through AutoScan.

Jorge's name flashed against her eyelid in red letters. There were no other people listed in her Predictive PersonableSpin history. Jorge's ghost was the only one she'd ever evoked. His public history, private sentiments, idiosyncrasies, quirks, and character traits were already synced with the system.

With a flick of her eye, Lexi could bring her best friend back to life. For fifteen to twenty minutes.

She blinked, and Jorge materialized before her.

Lexi spotted a few additional flecks of gray in his jet-black hair. PersonableSpin had accounted for the passing months. Jorge looked mostly the same as he had in October with a few minor differences. Or maybe Lexi was the one who had changed.

After all, she was less nervous than she'd been the first time. Her hands didn't tremble at her side, grazing her jeans uncontrollably, a visceral reminder of her shameful shortcomings as a friend and buddy bidder to Jorge.

Sorrow still crept through her veins as she observed Jorge's face, but it was balanced by affection and gratitude. She could meet her best friend's gaze without falling to pieces.

"Hey, you," Lexi said. Her mouth curved into a sad grin. "I promise this won't become a regular thing. But I need to ask you a question."

"I'm here anytime, Lexi," Jorge crooned, placing a weightless hand on top of hers.

"I can't hold you captive, though. You're not mine anymore." Lexi swallowed. "You deserve freedom. You should be living it up in Gay Heaven, not a sophisticated figment of my imagination. That's how I want to picture you . . . dancing and drinking mimosas every day. In crop tops. I need to envision you that way, J.R. You should be eternally happy."

"For the record, you made me *the most* happy," Jorge said. "And I appreciate your warm wishes. It's next-level shit in Gay Heaven. Endless euphoria with no comedown."

Lexi nodded. Jorge deserved nirvana. The guy was truly radiant. He'd been the bright spot when Lexi's outlook dimmed, which had happened repeatedly. Jorge had seen all of Lexi's shattered fragments. He'd loved her despite them, or perhaps because of them.

J.R. deserved to rest easy in whatever plane of existence his bold heart had found post-death.

Lexi resolved not to stand in the way of Jorge's utopia. Determination gripped her, wrapping its fingers around her heartstrings.

After this, you'll be liberated forever. Lexi made the promise without uttering a word. *I won't hold your memory captive, Jorge.*

Jorge's lips curled into a grin. "Glad to see you're as stubborn as ever. Listen, even if this is our last PersonableSpin session, I'll still be around. You know that. I'll help pick your outfit next time you go on a date with Jason."

"I need help with that?"

"Eh, not really. Any outfit you pick will just end up on the floor of Jason's beachfront condo."

"Damn, I see nothing's changed. You're still up in my business." Lexi chuckled.

"Am I right, though?"

Lexi shrugged. "Maybe."

"Knew it! Just calling it like it is, babe."

"Straight to the point. I always loved that about you." Lexi cleared her throat. "Listen, Jorge, I followed your advice in October. Searched the Expulsion Registry."

"So you know about my gene pool?"

"Yes. Really made me think about everything that's happened recently. I decided to protect the ARs at all costs. They're human. People just like you, J.R. I would've died to protect you. I wish I could have." Lexi paused, surprised by her own assertion. Of course, she'd been aching for that role reversal since the sky had imploded and turned her best friend to ash. But she rarely uttered it aloud. The words were too painful.

Jorge rolled his eyes. "Not this again. Look, I'm glad you didn't die in my place. You need to be here. You're doing good work, and I am proud of you. You know that, right?"

Lexi nodded. *You always made me feel so special.*

"Because you are, dummy." Jorge's smile illuminated the empty classroom. "As a reminder, I wouldn't trust anyone else with my Cleopatra."

"She's well-loved," Lexi assured him. "We miss you, of course, but your kitty is doing great. Sassy as ever. A little chubby. It's just her winter coat."

"Which reminds me! Another bonus point for Gay Heaven . . . you never gain weight. I eat fries and chocolate cake all day. Hell, I put whipped cream on my bacon burgers."

"Sounds disgusting." Lexi chuckled.

"You'd be surprised. It's my favorite afternoon snack. Now go ahead and ask what you came here to ask," Jorge prodded.

"What should I do next? Tamika wants me to take over her lease in SF. What about Colin? You're the only person who knows the full extent of my brother's situation. You were always my sounding board."

"Lots of late nights," Jorge reflected. "Wine and tears. Movies we never got around to watching."

You know it all. Every ugly detail. I can't leave him, right? Lexi asked silently. *I can't move two hours away. Things will crumble. They always do. I should be there when stuff falls apart.*

"You'll still be with him, Lex," Jorge informed her. "You care about him more than anything. Colin knows that. You're beside him through thick and thin, the same way I'm with you even though I've moved on to another dimension."

"But you're not with me physically," Lexi pointed out. "And that's a big difference. Trust me, it sucks. I miss you every single day."

"Love isn't tangible, Lexi," Jorge insisted. "Love doesn't have time constraints, and it certainly isn't limited by distance. I love you through life and death. And you love your brother so much. That means you're always there with him. Now you have to do something for yourself. Finally, after all these years, you need to choose *your* future."

"What if I fail?" Tears pooled in Lexi's eyes. She didn't fight them.

"You've already succeeded, Lex. You can't possibly fail when you choose to live with compassion. You're going to save people. All those humans have the same DNA as me. You'll protect them. You're making history, my dear."

"Not just me. Jason and Colin are part of this, too."

"Those two are combining their skills and brainpower. Meanwhile, you're influencing your own sphere. That's a beautiful partnership. The best kind of collaboration, really," Jorge said. "Lexi, your brother doesn't want to stand in the way of your dreams. You're meant to do big things, and he knows that. Colin wants you to shine, baby girl. Sparkle like the goddamn sun."

Lexi bit her lip. She wanted to hug her best friend more than anything. She needed to feel the weight of his body and soul, the one he inhabited before he exploded into the nighttime sky.

"Turn on the sensory function," Jorge suggested.

"I didn't even know that existed," Lexi admitted. She scrolled through her AutoScan settings, selecting the correct one with a flick of her eye.

Jorge immediately scooped her into a hug. Lexi's breath caught in her throat. He felt exactly like he had before, in his real and waking life. He was compact. Inviting. Safe. His arms were solid and strong.

He was her favorite companion, her one-in-a-million best pal. This was exactly how she remembered him.

Lexi had hugged him so many times before. Hundreds of hugs. Thousands, maybe. But she hadn't known those embraces had been numbered. She never imagined that one of them would be her last chance to hold her best friend.

Well, now this *can be our final hug*. Fortunately for Lexi, it was a really good one.

Lexi shifted her car into cruise control. She silently resolved to chat with Colin as soon as she got to her parents' house, and she needed to reach a decision fast. Her apartment renewal notice was due within twenty-four hours.

I'll listen to Colin this time. She leaned back as her car continued along the highway. *Really listen. No interruptions. No assumptions or projections.*

Colin would encourage her to fulfill her wildest dreams. Lexi was certain of that. Her brother was thoughtful and selfless, often too selfless for his own good. He would beg Lexi to choose the option that enhanced her career. Even if it made his life more difficult.

Emotion bubbled up in Lexi's throat as she reflected on all the ways Colin had expressed his support over the years. Memory after memory surfaced in her mind. Colin was the one who encouraged her to apply to school in San Diego when she'd been more than happy to start out at the University of Sacramento. He'd helped her prep for her initial interview at SkyLine Airways, even though it meant she'd spend fourteen to sixteen days each month flying around the country.

Lexi knew that, when it came down to it, she and Colin had always been motivated by the same thing.

Even when his vision was distorted by fear, he'd always loved Lexi. He'd wanted nothing but the best for her. When Colin was drowning in paranoia and self-doubt, that part of his heart never closed up. He felt immense guilt for her loyalty to him, she knew. He felt unworthy of her devotion over the years.

On the flip-side, Lexi viewed herself as a lifelong caretaker because she cared about Colin. For nearly two decades, she'd punished and erased herself in a misguided effort to counterbalance the ache her brother often felt. She'd made so many mistakes. Lexi knew she'd fucked up over and over. But the same driving force had been behind each misstep.

Maybe love isn't meant to be a cage. Lexi edged toward the right-hand lane. I-80 stretched on, the same highway she'd taken for four and a half years, since she signed on as a San Francisco-based SkyLine flight attendant living in Sacramento. Her hometown.

As she drove, Lexi considered all the possibilities Tamika had mentioned earlier that day. A world of opportunities awaited her in San Francisco. She'd have the whole Bay Area at her fingertips. She would meet so many people. Easily. Effortlessly. In a city marked by innovation and acceptance.

Lexi glanced up. Signs overhead indicated she was approaching Sacramento. On her windshield, a single red line began to flash. She gripped the steering wheel tighter, anticipating the exit she'd take in just a few moments.

Lexi wondered if it was possible to redefine her connection to her brother, her closest ally in this chaotic world. There had to be a healthier way she and Colin could support each other, right? Shame and self-loathing hadn't done any favors for Colin. Martyrdom and twisted logic hadn't helped Lexi.

Magical short-term escapes had led to a deeply flawed fantasy world. In the end, Lexi was forced to return to herself. Wounded parts and all.

She figured she and Colin had tried this path long enough, warping their admiration for each other into a suffocating, all-consuming type of pressure. Love had become an obligation neither of them could ever fulfill, not without losing their souls in the process.

That's not productive. It's a death sentence.

Lexi wondered if she and her brother could create a new paradigm. One based on mutual advancement instead of mutual suffering.

She had no idea what to expect. Maybe they would screw up and backslide and doubt the process. They would take baby steps, then retreat. Their progress might be dulled by frustration. It wouldn't be a straight line, nor would it be a smooth ride.

Colin might dive into the dark place again. Lexi might respond by attempting to delete herself—as she'd done for the last eighteen years.

We can still try, a tiny voice whispered in her mind. *We have to see if there's a better way.*

Maybe love ebbed and flowed, Lexi mused. Instead of a perfect crescendo, maybe it was choppy and uneven. Beautiful in its own way, but by no means expected or conventional. Just like the irreversible marking on Lexi's shoulder.

And maybe, just maybe, that was okay.

About the Author

Lisa Wilkes has flown for a major airline since 2010. In that time, she has composed 12 internal articles and revised the company's 500-page flight attendant manual.

Her romance novel, Flight Path, was published in January of 2020. That same year, Lisa published a short story, Six Hours or So, in a charitable anthology.

Mid-Flight is Lisa's first foray into the realm of science fiction. Her internship in a Behavioral Health Unit, while attaining her Master's in Social Work, shaped this futuristic thriller.

Made in the USA
Columbia, SC
31 March 2023

14559213R00157